编辑委员会

中国知网（CNKI）全文收录　维普期刊网全文收录

探索与批评

第十辑

主编／王　欣　石　坚

四川大学出版社

SICHUAN UNIVERSITY PRESS

图书在版编目（CIP）数据

探索与批评 . 第十辑 / 王欣，石坚主编 . — 成都：
四川大学出版社，2024.5
ISBN 978-7-5690-6906-8

Ⅰ．①探… Ⅱ．①王… ②石… Ⅲ．①外国文学—文
学研究—文集 Ⅳ．① I106-53

中国国家版本馆 CIP 数据核字 (2024) 第 103951 号

书　　名：探索与批评 第十辑
　　　　　Tansuo yu Piping Di-shi Ji
主　　编：王 欣 石 坚

选题策划：陈 蓉
责任编辑：陈 蓉
责任校对：刘一畅
装帧设计：墨创文化
责任印制：王 炜

出版发行：四川大学出版社有限责任公司
　　　　　地址：成都市一环路南一段 24 号（610065）
　　　　　电话：(028) 85408311（发行部）、85400276（总编室）
　　　　　电子邮箱：scupress@vip.163.com
　　　　　网址：https://press.scu.edu.cn
印前制作：四川胜翔数码印务设计有限公司
印刷装订：四川五洲彩印有限责任公司

成品尺寸：170 mm×240 mm
印　　张：10.75
插　　页：2
字　　数：223 千字

版　　次：2024 年 6 月 第 1 版
印　　次：2024 年 6 月 第 1 次印刷
定　　价：52.00 元

扫码获取数字资源

四川大学出版社
微信公众号

目　录

广义叙述学研究

文类研究

批评理论与实践

跨学科研究

书　评

Contents

General Narratology

Literary Genre Studies

Critical Theory and Practice

Interdisciplinary Studies

Book Review

广义叙述学研究　●　●　●　●　●

如何理解"非自然叙述理论"
——与江澜先生商榷①

王长才

摘　要：本文针对江澜《"非自然叙事"有多"自然"?》一文，从非自然叙述理论与自然叙述学的关系、非自然叙述理论的多元性、非自然并非不能理解、非自然心理并非人力上的不可能等方面提出商榷。非自然叙述理论不是明确统一的理论体系，不同倡导者的立场和观点存在着明显差异，要深入理解必须要明了其多元性和复杂性。

关键词：非自然叙述　非自然叙述理论　自然叙述学　多元性

How to Understand "Unnatural Narrative Theory"? A Discussion with Mr. Jiang Lan

Wang Changcai

Abstract: This article discusses the paper "How Natural Are 'Unnatural Narratives'?" by Jiang Lan, focusing on various aspects such as the relationship between unnatural narrative theory and natural narratology, the plurality of unnatural narrative theory, the understanding that the unnatural is not incomprehensible, and the recognition that unnatural mental processes are not

---

①　本文系国家社科基金项目"非自然叙述学研究"（16BZW013）研究成果。

humanly impossible. Unnatural narrative theory is not a clearly unified theoretical framework; there are significant differences in the positions and perspectives of different proponents. To gain a deeper understanding, one must grasp its plurality and complexity.

Keywords: unnatural narrative; unnatural narrative theory; natural narratology; plurality

"非自然叙述理论"① 作为后经典叙述学的重要分支，近年来成为西方叙述学界的一大热点，也得到国内学者的关注，接连有论文和相关译介成果出现，但由于其复杂性，存在颇多争议，甚至存在一些误解。江澜先生的《"非自然叙事"有多"自然"？》一文发表在权威核心期刊《外国文学》上，持激烈的质疑态度，产生了较大影响。但遗憾的是，在笔者看来，或许由于作者所见文献并不全面，对非自然叙述基本概念的理解有误，该文章更像是自己树立靶子进行批驳，而其所批驳观点和非自然叙述理论倡导者的主张有相当大的出入，似乎平添了一些混乱。本文试图澄清一些误解，以向江澜先生及其他专家学者请教。

一、"非自然叙述学"与莫尼卡·弗卢德尼克的"自然叙述学"是针锋相对的吗？

著名认知叙述学家莫妮卡·弗卢德尼克（Monika Fludernik）1996 年出版的《建构"自然"叙述学》（*Towards a "Natural" Narratology*）一书产生了深远影响。从字面上看，非自然叙述理论是自然叙述学的对立面，往往会让读者误以为非自然叙述理论是对自然叙述学的挑战，两者是对立关系。按照江澜先生的描述，布莱恩·理查森（Brian Richardson）写的《非自然声音：现当代小说的极端化叙述》（*Unnatural Voices: Extreme Narration in Modern and Contemporary Fiction*，2006，以下简称《非自然声音》）与莫妮卡·弗卢德尼克的著作观点是"针锋相对"的，由此"叙事的自然与非自然之争拉开序幕"（江澜，2018，p. 113）。但事实似乎并非如此。从表面上看，《建构"自然"叙述学》出版于 1996 年，而理查森的《非自然声音》出版于 2006 年，似乎后者是对前者的挑战。但如果对布莱恩·理查森的研究多一些了解，就会发现，他对非自然叙述理论的讨论可以追溯至更早，这部书的第二章和第四章来自他 1991

---

① 学界对 "narrative" 的翻译，有 "叙事" 和 "叙述" 两种，笔者采用 "叙述"。

和 1994 年发表的论文。而他的第一篇非自然叙述理论的论文可以上溯到 1987 年，讨论的是戏剧的叙述模式与时间（Richardson，1987），随后 1989 年的论文讨论《麦克白》中倒置的时序和因果关系，1991 年有论文讨论品特戏剧与叙述的边界，1992 年有论文讨论贝克特小说《莫洛伊》中的叙事违规和元小说悖论，这些论文都在弗卢德尼克的《建构"自然"叙述学》出版之前。理查森的第一部专著《不可能的故事：因果关系与现代叙述的本质》（*Unlikely Stories: Causality and the Nature of Modern Narrative*，1997）也已经涉及了当时理论家忽视的"不可能的虚构世界"，并讨论了"元虚构的"因果律（"metafictional" causal laws，即叙述者可以更改的因果律）（Wang，2019，p. 114）。显然，出版于 2006 年的《非自然声音》与这些研究是一脉相承的。而在《非自然声音》中理查森也没有将自己的研究视为对弗卢德尼克理论的挑战，相反，他在讨论第二人称叙述、"我们"叙述时还引用弗卢德尼克的观点，在提到"以系统方式描述非自然叙述者和极端的叙述行为"的理论家时，将弗卢德尼克作为"在当代叙述理论家中最突出的一个"（Richardson，2006，p. 134），而在该书"致谢"部分，理查森特别感谢了通读大部分章节并做出评价的三位学者，其中排在第一位的就是弗卢德尼克（p. Ⅷ）。

从"非自然叙述理论"兴起的过程来看，至少理查森最初并没有和弗卢德尼克的"自然叙述学"有直接关系。2000 年时理查森将自己讨论的文本称为"后现代的"或"反模仿的"（2000a），在作为客座编辑为《文体》（*Style*）杂志编辑的"叙述的概念"（Concepts of Narrative）特刊中，他将一批理论家对现有叙述学模式的挑战称为"后现代叙述理论"（2000b，p. 169），在 2006 年《非自然声音》中，他勾勒了一种反模仿的理论。而与此同时，扬·阿尔贝（Jan Alber）、亨里克·斯科夫·尼尔森（Henrik Skov Nielsen）等一些年轻的学者也在独立地做着类似的工作。2008 年国际叙述研究学会的年会上，理查森和扬·阿尔贝、斯特凡·伊韦尔森（Stefan Iversen）、尼尔森组成了"'非自然'叙述－'非自然'叙述学：超越模仿模式？"（"Unnatural" Narratives-"Unnatural" Narratology: Beyond Mimetic Models?）分论坛，后来将发言合写为一篇文章，2010 年发表于《叙述》上，这就是被视为建构"非自然叙述学"的宣言的《非自然叙述，非自然叙述学：超越模仿模式》。随后这场运动才轰轰烈烈地展开。理查森本人更希望用"反模仿"而不是"非自然"，甚至"一直觉得'非自然'这个词是别人强加给我们的，我们带着不同程度的犹豫或热情，最终才同意接受"（2016a，p. 498）。理查森多次强调"非自然叙述理论在意识形态上是中立的"（2015，p. xvii），也颇为无奈地澄清他们所说的"非自然"并没有文化实践、性别上的特别内涵，只是因为"非自然叙述"一词已经广泛流传开来，所以也只能接受。（p. 6）

理查森后来也将自己的工作与弗卢德尼克的"自然叙述学"关联起来："我认为我的工作是莫妮卡·弗卢德尼克在《建构〈自然〉叙述学》（1993①）所做工作的一种激进的延伸和补充，其中，她将自然叙述的范式贯彻到了它的极限。"（p. 6）但他也强调："我更可取的定义没有提及自然叙述，因为我的核心的、定义性的范畴，即模仿性和反模仿性的人物和事件，都可以在自然叙述中找到：对话性的、非虚构的自然叙述是模仿性的，而夸大的故事和更极端的那种自叙体（skaz）可以是反模仿性的。我也倾向于避免关于（自然化）的争论，因为它们对我阐明和澄清自己的立场没有那么大的帮助。"（2016b, pp. 392-393）由此可见，理查森最初的讨论并非专门针对莫妮卡·弗卢德尼克，只是由于他的工作汇聚到"非自然叙述理论"这一更广泛的运动之中，又追认了与弗卢德尼克"自然叙述学"的关联，但也强调他对非自然的界定（反模仿）与自然叙述也不是对立关系。

另一位非自然叙述理论的代表人物扬·阿尔贝，与弗卢德尼克的关系就更加密切了。阿尔贝的博士学位论文就是由弗卢德尼克指导的，他的非自然叙述理论在很大程度上与弗卢德尼克的理论一脉相承。阿尔贝在专著《非自然叙述：理论、历史与实践》（*Unnatural Narrative: Theory, History, and Practice*）中，也特别感谢弗卢德尼克"对本研究的理论和语料库都提出了宝贵的意见"（Alber, 2016, p. Ⅷ）。对阿尔贝来说，"非自然"是弗卢德尼克所说的"经验性"，"对'真实生活经验'的准模仿性唤起"的一种具体表现。（p. 61）

在阿尔贝与弗卢德尼克为共同主编的《后经典叙述学：方法与分析》（*Postclassical Narratology: Approaches and Analyses*）撰写的序言中，更是有这样的表述："从某种意义上说，非自然叙述学是后现代主义叙述学和认知叙述学的结合。"（Alber & Fludernik, 2010, p. 14）"然而，非自然叙述学（作为弗鲁德尼克的'自然'叙述学和一般认知叙述学的发展）并没有解构叙述学的构成二元论，而是试图建立一种实验文本的叙述学模式，它既是对古典叙述学的补充，又通过认知框架与之相关联。"（p. 15）在2012年四人联名回应弗卢德尼克的文章中，尽管也说明了非自然叙述理论与弗卢德尼克观点

---

① 原文如此，应为1996。——引者注

一致的地方——"非自然叙述理论部分地受到弗卢德尼克的研究方法的启发，受惠于它。我们同意她的说法，即'阿尔贝等人本着'自然'叙述学的精神进行研究'"（Alber et al.，2012，p. 371），但这些表述更多强调非自然叙述理论是对弗卢德尼克理论的发展。在扬·阿尔贝提出的非自然叙述的 9 大阐释策略中（Alber，2016，pp. 47-57），前 8 种都是将非自然叙述理解为自然叙述，明显地脱胎于弗卢德尼克从乔纳森·卡勒那里沿用的"自然化"（naturalization）的概念。

由此可见，弗卢德尼克的"自然叙述学"与"非自然叙述学"并非对立冲突的关系，甚至还有较深的渊源，其中有些部分是"你中有我，我中有你"的复杂关系。而江澜先生的描述，"……不难发现非自然叙事学之所以迅速壮大声势，只不过是因为在论辩中自然叙事学（natural narratology）的倡导者例如弗鲁德尼克等，没有抓住对方存疑的关键词和相关例证，针锋相对地提出反对意见"（2018，p. 113），似乎将弗卢德尼克的自然叙述学，与理查森等人倡导的"非自然叙述学"彻底对立起来，将两者的关系视为此消彼长的话语权争夺，非自然叙述理论此后的发展只是因为前者错失良机。这显然不太妥当。

二、"非自然叙述学"是统一的，还是多元的？

江澜先生对非自然叙述学的批评，仍然主要集中在 2010 年四位学者联名发表的《非自然叙述，非自然叙述学：超越模仿模式》一文。的确，这一篇文章因为明确地倡导"超越模仿模式"而引起了学界的极大关注，并引发了多位学者的讨论，比如江澜先生提到的弗卢德尼克的《"非自然叙述学"有多自然？或，什么是非自然叙述学的非自然？》（Fludernik，2012）。而他没有提到托比亚斯·克劳克（Tobias Klauk）、梯尔曼·科佩（Tilmann Köppe）的《重估非自然叙述学：问题与展望》（Klauk & Köppe，2013）。其实这一篇文章火力更甚，对《非自然叙述，非自然叙述学：超越模仿模式》一文进行了精确的剖析，指出了论文中的逻辑矛盾和含混之处，也对其中一些命题提出了尖锐的批评。然而，这一篇联名文章存在问题，并不意味着能够全盘否定非自然叙述理论。被批评的联名论文只突出了几位非自然叙述理论倡导者的共识，是妥协的产物，并不能反映非自然叙述学的多元、复杂的面目，因而尽管批评很有力，但因为批评对象并不能完全代表非自然叙述学，尤其是随着后来理论家们进一步明确各自的立场，有些批评已经失去了意义（比如，没有统一的非自然叙述的定义；非自然叙述学不能构成一种新的叙述学等）。其实 2012 年四位学者联名回应弗卢德尼克的文章《什么是非自然叙述学的非自然？——对莫妮卡·弗卢德尼克的回应》（Alber et al.，2012）就已经明确地承认非自然叙述理论阵营内部的分歧，之后几位代表学者又多次在论文与专著中重申彼此的差异。理查森也指出，其他批评群体也有多元性，比如认知叙述学内部在研究方法、角度、立场上也有很大差异，并不能整合为一，但没有人苛责他们。他希望对非自然叙述学家们也可以用类似的标准来衡量。（Richardson，2016a，p. 498）

非自然叙述学的倡导者都有各自的界定，这就使得非自然叙述理论并非一种统一的面貌，几乎任何对非自然叙述理论的笼统谈论都不准确。这在有些学者看来，是非自然叙述学的致命问题。不过，这在理查森和阿尔贝看来并不是问题，恰恰是这种多元和开放意味着多种可能性。他们编辑的《非自然诗学》《非自然叙述学：扩展、修正与挑战》等论文集都没有强求撰稿者的观点与自己的一致，甚至带有某种欣赏意味展示了各自的差异。而江澜先生有意无意地忽略了非自然叙述阵营内部的分歧，将不同理论家的论述当作统一的整体进行批评，而将体现了非自然叙述理论进一步深化和修正的分歧和差异，只放在论文结尾部分当作"没有足够的底气，甚至坦承其自身的不足""由于缺乏坚实的理论基础，非自然叙事学并不能自圆其说"（江澜，2018，p. 122）的证明，这似乎也不太合适。

三、"非自然"等于难以理解吗？

另一个更值得商榷之处，是江澜先生对"非自然"的认识，文中重复多次：

> 总之，所谓的"非自然"或"不可能"只是普通读者的一种主观判断。这种主观判断源于普通读者自身的认知水平不足……（2018，p. 121）
> 从创作美学的角度看，所谓的"非自然叙事"的"非自然"只不过是自然叙事中的创新元素。从接受美学的角度看，只要读者不断提高自身能力，在认知水平方面达到或超过作者，那么就能够跟得上甚或领先于作者的创作思路，也就能够准确理解作者创作出来的叙事作品，包括所谓"非自然叙事"。（p. 122）

江澜先生在此非常遗憾地将"非自然"与"读者的不理解"混为一谈了，显然这与非自然叙述理论家的主张截然不同，也有违这些理论家提倡非自然叙述理论的初衷。的确，典型的非自然叙述容易让读者产生"难以理解"这一阅读体验，但这并不是非自然叙述理论倡导者重心所在。理查森和阿尔贝主要是从文本自身来确认"非自然"，尼尔森和伊韦尔森尽管引入了读者要素，从引发读者采取不同阐释策略或"永久陌生化"方面来确认"非自然"，但都从未将"非自然叙述"与读者的"认知水平不足"联系在一起。对于理查森来说，如果要理解非自然叙述，读者需要有双重的阅读框架，即读者需要既意识到模仿性框架，还要领会作者对模仿性框架的有意颠覆。相比而言，这种阅读更复杂，对读者要求也更高。即使按照阿尔贝的观点，也不好说意识到"不可能"就是"认知水平不足"。恰恰相反，阿尔贝提出了9种针对非自然叙述的解读策略，就是致力理解种种不可能。在他看来，那些大家习以为常的童话、科幻小说文类中，也存在着不可能，只是已经规约化而人们意识不到而已。那么，能够意识到这些现象的不可能属性，且认为是被规约化的结果，比起没有意识到它的不可能，显然也不会是"认知水平不足"。

另外，江澜先生这一表述本身体现出的某种本质主义的倾向也值得探讨。比如，如何判定普通读者和专业读者呢？是否存在一种先在的、固定不变的专业读者标准，又如何确认呢？新的文学实践的出现，往往都会对原有的阅读惯例构成挑战，训练有素的批评家也有可能做出错误的判断，就如同米兰·昆德拉所说，艺术史和一般历史不同，都伴随着一种美学判断的风险，"每一个美学评判都是个人的赌博"（2006，p. 21），文学史上这样的例子屡见不鲜。我们又如何将某一种认识确立为专业标准呢？

非自然叙述与创新的关系，也似乎并非如同江澜先生所言。的确，有些非自然叙述策略相对于主流的自然叙述最初是一种创新，但并非所有创新都是非自然叙述，也不是所有的非自然叙述都属于创新。比如，按照理查森的观点，那些仅仅在文本特征、话语层面进行探索的作品，并未打破模仿框架的作品，并不是非自然叙述。而按照阿尔贝等人的观点，全知叙述这种最习以为常的手法也是一种非自然叙述的手段，只是已经常规化了。

很遗憾，江澜先生是从字面意义上理解"非自然"，而不是按照非自然叙述理论提出者原本的逻辑来理解。正因如此，江澜先生文章看似雄辩，但似乎只是自说自话，甚至有的例子恰恰佐证了非自然叙述理论家的观点。比如，江澜先生展示了自己如何阅读《变形记》《保姆》等作品，认为对于《保姆》的碎片式叙述，可以增加连接词，使之可能构成一个整体，从而得到理解，因而就不是非自然的。这种阅读明显是读者基于自己的认知框架进行补充与选择，属于阿尔贝的"自然化"式的解读策略①。

四、什么是"非自然心理"？

对于什么是"非自然心理"，江澜先生文中写道："阿尔贝所谓'人力上'的'不可能'，是指在叙述过程中出现的伊韦尔森所谓的非自然心理（unnatural minds），即叙事心理的不可能。"（2018，p. 120）这涉及阿尔贝和伊韦尔森两人的相关定义，似乎也有欠准确。

阿尔贝所说的"人力上"的"不可能"是以通常的人的能力为标准的，是以真实世界的认知参数作为依据的，超常的千里眼、顺风耳等都属于"人力上"的"不可能"。超出人类感知能力的非自然心理，像第一人称全知叙述等，只是"人力上"的"不可能"的一种。而对于伊韦尔森而言，"非自然心理是一种呈现的意识，在其功能或实现中，违反了主宰可能世界的规则，它以一种抵制自然化或常规化的方式成为其中的一部分"（Iversen，2013，p. 97）。这一定义与阿尔贝的界定在大前提上是一致的，也是物理上和逻辑上不可能，但相比之下，他更强调具体作品中对主导规则的违背，与文类和惯例有关，从而"这个定义的主要优点是它从根本上限制了非自然叙述的数量……提高了该定义的解释力和精确性"（pp. 97-98）。对于伊韦尔森来说，"不可能的心理（impossible mind）是指在生物学上或逻辑学上不可能的心理，比如读心术心理、亡灵心理、极端的跨层心理（metaleptic mind），或无容身硬件而运行的心理（a mind running without the hardware that the human mind as we know it is nested in）"（p. 104）。因而，将阿尔贝的"人力上"的"不可能"等同于伊韦尔森的"叙事心理的不可能"也是不妥的。

江澜先生文中还有这样的表述："文学虚构世界完全能够容纳逻辑上的不可能世界。从这个意义上讲，故事中根本不存在'非自然'或'不可能'的事件。"（2018，p. 122）理查森和扬·阿尔贝等人谈"非自然"并不是指文学作品中不能呈现这些"非自然"，本来非自然叙述理论的倡导者就将非自然叙述视为虚构叙述的一个子集，也正是文学中存在大量的"非自然"叙述，而这些并没有得到足够公平的对待，他们才倡导对已有叙述学理论的补充。

结语：如何理解"非自然叙述理论"？

相对于后经典叙述学的其他分支，非自然叙述理论出现的时间最短，又

---

① 在笔者看来，这样解读《保姆》未必恰当。

迅速引起了广泛关注，相关著述、讨论至今仍在不断涌现。尽管它的发展一直伴随着质疑与误解，但其贡献与价值也得到了不少理论家的肯定。比如修辞叙述学家詹姆斯·费伦对于非自然叙述理论给予了高度评价，在两次对叙述学现状的梳理及未来展望中，都对非自然叙述理论给予了特别的关注，并将非自然叙述学（反模仿叙述理论）作为主要趋势的代表（Phelan，2006，2018）。在他看来，非自然叙述理论"迄今为止的结果是有益的，因为理查森成功地引起人们对故事讲述史中非自然重要性的关注，因为他提出了很多富于洞察力的工具与概念以处理这种语料，（比如'消解叙述'的概念，对第二人称叙述与第一人称复数叙述的描述），因为他已经发展了对具体叙述的许多富于洞察力的分析"（Phelan，2016，pp. 414-415）。著名文学理论家乔纳森·卡勒（Jonathan Culler）也表示："……最吸引我的是所谓的非自然叙事学。………非自然叙事学的起点是抵制模仿还原论，抵制那种我们可以通过基于现实主义参数的各种模式来使叙事产生意义的假设，所以它在我看来是一个非常有前途的诗学分支，是对我们使各种怪异的文本产生意义的各种程序的研究，而怪异文本正与怪异行为和非自然的声音一起日益不满虚构的世界。"（2019，pp. 5-6）

在笔者看来，尽管非自然叙述理论并没有形成一个有着统一定义和框架的理论整体，但它确实已经产生了深远影响。它对非自然叙述实践进行了细致的梳理与归纳，以此作为对照，重新审视原有叙述学框架，提出了一些新的概念，对叙述学理论有所补充与修正。它并非另起炉灶，颠覆已有的叙述学体系，而是针对非主流叙述的特殊叙述实践提出一些范畴，以使这些叙述得到公正对待，也对原叙述学体系有所修正、拓展，从而使叙述学的版图更为完整和全面。因此，"非自然叙述学"不是一种针对所有叙述的"非自然"的叙述学，而是"非自然叙述"学，即对非自然叙述的理论化。尽管非自然叙述理论并非针对所有叙述，但它也引发了重新审视各种叙述要素的新视角。非自然叙述理论不是明确统一的理论体系，不同倡导者的立场和观点存在明显差异，要深入理解必须要明了其多元性和复杂性。将之简单化并予以轻松否定，似乎是欠妥的。

引用文献：

江澜（2018）."非自然叙事"有多"自然"？外国文学，4，112-123.

昆德拉，米兰（2006）. 帷幕（董强，译）. 上海：上海译文出版社.

卡勒，乔纳森（2019）. 理论中的文学（徐亮、王冠雷，等译）. 上海：华东师范大学出版社.

Alber，J.（2016）. *Unnatural Narrative: Impossible Worlds in Fiction and Drama*. Lincoln：University of Nebraska Press.

Alber，J.，Iversen，S.，Nielsen，H. S.，& Richardson，B.（2012）. What Is Unnatural about Unnatural Narratology?：A Response to Monika Fludernik. *Narrative*（3），371−382.

Alber，J.，& Fludernik，M.（2010）. *Postclassical Narratology: Approaches and Analyses*. Columbus：The Ohio State University Press.

Fludernik，M.（2012）. How Natural Is "Unnatural Narratology"；or，What Is Unnatural about Unnatural Narratology? *Narrative*（3），357−370.

Iversen，S.（2013）. Unnatural Minds. In J. Alber，H. S. Nielsen，& B. Richardson（Eds.），*A Poetics of Unnatural Narrative*（94−112）. Columbus：The Ohio State University Press.

Klauk，T.，& Köppe，T.（2013）. Reassessing Unnatural Narratology：Problems and Prospects. *Storyworlds:A Journal of Narrative Studies*，5，77−100.

Phelan，J.（2006）. Narrative Theory，1966−2006：A Narrative. In R. Scholes，J. Phelan，& R. Kellogg（Eds.），*The Nature of Narrative*（283−336）. Oxford：Oxford University Press.

Phelan，J.（2016）. Unnatural Narratives and the Task of Theory Construction. *Style*，50（4），414−419.

Phelan，J.（2018）. Contemporary Narrative Theory. In D. H. Richter（Ed.），*A Companion to Literary Theory*（72−84）. Hoboken：Wiley-Blackwell.

Richardson，B.（1987）. "Time Is Out of Joint"：Narrative Models and the Temporality of the Drama. *Poetics Today*，8（2），299−309.

Richardson，B.（1989）. "Hours Dreadful and Things Strange"：Inversions of Chronology and Causality in "Macbeth". *Philological Quarterly*，68（3），283−294.

Richardson，B.（1991）. Pinter's Landscape and the Boundaries of Narrative. *Essays in Literature*，18（1），37−45.

Richardson，B.（1992）. Causality in "Molloy"：Philosophic Theme，Narrative Transgression，and Metafictional Paradox. *Style*，26（1），66−78.

Richardson，B.（2000a）. Narrative Poetics and Postmodern Transgression：Theorizing the Collapse of Time，Voice，and Frame. *Narrative*，8（1），23−42.

Richardson，B.（2000b）. Recent Concepts of Narrative and the Narratives of Narrative Theory. *Style*，34（2），168−175.

Richardson，B.（2006）. *Unnatural Voices: Extreme Narration in Modern and Contemporary Fiction*. Columbus：The Ohio State University Press.

Richardson，B.（2015）. *Unnatural Narrative: Theory，History，and Practice*. Columbus：The Ohio State University Press.

Richardson，B. (2016a). Rejoinders to the Respondents. *Style*，50（4），492－513.

Richardson，B. (2016b). Unnatural Narrative Theory. *Style*，50（4），385－405.

Wang，C. (2019). The Unnatural and Unnatural Narrative Theory：An Interview with Professor Brian Richardson. 符号与传媒，1，112－122.

作者简介：

王长才，西南交通大学人文学院中文系教授，主要从事叙述学研究。

Author:

Wang Changcai, professor in the Department of Chinese Language and Literature, School of Humanities at Southwest Jiaotong University. He is mainly engaged in research on narratology.

Email：Wang _ changcai@163.com

互动叙述的伦理批评向度：媒介化社会的文化研究视角①

马翾昂

摘　要：叙述与伦理的高度同构决定了叙述伦理研究的必要性，然而作为叙述学研究的重要领域，叙述伦理批评对各类新兴的互动叙述形态却介入甚少。结合《王者荣耀》这一互动叙述典型案例的性别伦理分析，本文认为，互动叙述依赖于携带设计者意图的内文本与作为"类隐含读者"的参与者之间的双向激活，从而共构了叙述伦理。互动叙述文本是多层级的叙述和常态的跨层行为下形成的复杂整体，各类以内文本为核心，聚集在某种互动叙述周边的类隐含读者文化社群不断生产叙述文本，完成伦理的再生产和社会化。经由数字互联网连接的媒介化社会构成了一个巨大、开放、多层级的互动叙述系统，互动叙述已然成为媒介化社会中伦理生产的主要方式，互动叙述伦理批评必须打破文本内外的藩篱，成为面向媒介化社会的文化研究范式。

关键词：叙述伦理　互动叙述　内文本　类隐含读者　媒介化社会

The Orientation of Narrative Ethics Criticism of Interactive Narratives: A Cultural Study Perspective on Mediated Society

Ma Xuanang

Abstract: The highly homologous relationship between narrative and ethics determines the necessity of studying narrative ethics. However, as an

---

① 本文系国家社科基金重大项目"当代艺术提出的重要美学问题研究"（20&ZD049）阶段性研究成果。

important field of narrative studies, narrative ethics criticism has intervened very little in various emerging interactive narrative forms. Combining a gender ethics analysis of the interactive narrative typical case, *Honor of Kings*, this article argues that interactive narratives rely on the bidirectional activation between the inner-text carrying the designer's intent and the participants as "quasi-implied readers", thereby co-constructing narrative ethics. Interactive narrative texts are complex wholes formed under the norm of multi-level narratives and routine cross-layer behaviors. Various quasi-implied reader cultural communities, centered around the inner-text, continuously produce narrative texts, completing the reproduction and socialization of ethics. The mediated society connected by digital Internet constitutes a vast, open, multi-level interactive narrative system, and interactive narrative has become the primary means of ethical production in the media society. Ethical criticism of interactive narratives must break down the barriers between text and context, thus becoming a cultural research paradigm for the mediated society.

Keywords: narrative ethics; interactive narratives; inner-text; quasi-implied readers; mediated society

引言：互动叙述——叙述伦理研究的盲点

自 20 世纪 80 年代以来，人文研究领域经历了所谓的"伦理转向"，几乎在同一时期，席卷整个社会生活的"叙述转向"也同步到来。正如叙述学家赫尔曼指出的，"叙述研究领域里的活动出现了小规模但确凿无疑的爆炸性局面"（2002，p. 1），"'叙事学'不再专指结构主义文学理论的一个分支，它现在可以指任何根据一定原则对文学、史籍、谈话以及电影等叙事形式进行研究的方法"（p. 24）。叙述学蓬勃发展且影响力逐渐扩大，其研究成果被多个社会领域有意识地应用与研究。在此背景之下，叙述学显然也经历了一次"伦理转向"，文学批评家牛顿指出了叙述与伦理的合一，"'叙事伦理'成为热门研究话题便不难理解"（费伦、唐伟胜，2008，pp. 1—6），叙述伦理批评也成为文艺理论界非常重要的研究范式之一。费伦、唐伟胜将伦理转向后 30 年内的叙事伦理研究分为三类：人文传统的修辞伦理学、他者伦理和解构主义伦理、政治伦理（pp. 1—6）。尽管这三类研究的目标、假设和方法并不相同，但总体而言都是一种基于作者的封闭自足文本的研究路径。然而对 21 世纪以来飞速变动的媒介技术环境中涌现出的各类具有互动性的叙述形式，叙述伦理研究却基本阙如：玛丽·劳尔－瑞安是最早研究数字化时代诸种互动叙述，并试图将叙述学推向互动叙述学的学者，但她并未将互动叙述与叙述学传统中的伦理批评勾连起来；而宗争的《游戏学：符号叙述学研究》作为国内最早以互动叙述学范式研究游戏的著作，也并未论及游戏互动叙述中的伦理问题。

这是否意味着，这类文本不确定、依赖参与者互动生成的叙述并无伦理性？答案显然是否定的。利科认为，叙述绝非价值中立，而是首要的"道德判断的实验室"（2013，p. 207）。而布斯曾断言，"所有叙事作品都是'道德说教的（didactic）'"（Booth，1988，p. 151）。这些判断不是仅适用于文学叙述，而是适用于任何情节性文本，因为叙述化不仅是情节的构筑，更是借叙述的情节化彰显伦理目的。情节化就意味着主体意识必须在生活经验细节中进行挑选和重组，构筑成具有意义的叙述文本以理解自我与世界的关系，而这种意义首先就是道德伦理意义（赵毅衡，2013a，p. 15）。正如费伦将叙述看作一种修辞，认为其本质是作者"通过叙事文本，要求读者进行多维度的（审美的、情感的、观念的、伦理的、政治的）阅读"（2002，p. 5）。作为一种情节性的人类社会关系经验，伦理与叙述高度同构——一切叙述必有伦理，而伦理必须借由叙述形成和表达，这也是伦理转向与叙述转向几近重合的内在原因。

因此，互动叙述必有伦理。对于叙述伦理研究缺失，本文认为主要有两个原因。首先是因为传统叙述学理论和文本观无法处理当下的各类问题：经典叙述学的伦理批评只探讨文学文本内部世界的虚构伦理，后经典叙述学虽然将文本向外开放，但仍然有一个确定的静态文本存在。然而如今我们生活在"一个以互动行为为中心的后现代传媒时代，后现代信息传播之意义的多样性、片段化与不稳定性超越了传统审美的'不确定'或'相对空白'，而是受众对文本的多项选择和能动介入"（关萍萍，2012，p. 3）。当下涌现的各种以体育比赛、电子游戏乃至网络事件为代表的互动叙述类型，需要参与者的介入才能形成叙述文本，不确定性、动态性成为互动叙述文本的基本特征。因此，互动叙述的伦理批评无法采取布斯在封闭文本内推导隐含作者的办法，也不能像修辞叙述学将伦理实现看作一种经验贯彻模型的单向过程。

其次，互动叙述的"自主性"迷思，造成了对其叙述伦理的自然忽略。在劳尔－瑞安看来，"叙事意义还是故事讲述者或设计者自上而下规划的产物，而互动性则要求用户自下而上的输入"，因而理想的互动叙述"应该伪装成一个自生的故事：既要让用户相信，他们的努力将得到一个连贯的叙事作为回报；又要让他们感觉到，他们在行使自由意志，而非设计师的傀儡"（2014，p. 95）。相比于意义，互动叙述的参与者更在意的是互动过程带来的愉悦性，"甚至过程本身成为交流叙述的全部价值"（王委艳，2022b，p. 250）。游戏作为互动叙述中最为典型的代表，其自愿性、愉悦性和主观体验性尤为显著。英国学者史蒂芬森认为"大众传播最好的一点是允许人们沉浸于主动的游戏之中，也就是说它让人快乐"（Stephenson，1988，p. 1）。他正是以传播的"游戏观"反驳经验学派只关注媒介外在的功能和效果，而不关注传播参与者主观感受和情感体验的研究范式。

综上所述，对于当今媒介环境中涌现的各类互动叙述类型，叙述伦理批评作为叙述学的重要分支不但需要予以回应，还应在研究向度上进一步敞开，与更广泛、深刻的社会文化现实相勾连。本文主要结合《王者荣耀》这一当下最具影响力的多人在线战术竞技游戏中的性别伦理分析，试图探究互动叙述的伦理实现机制，从而论述互动叙述的伦理批评向度。

一、内文本的伦理倾向与"类隐含读者"

互动叙述的首要特征是文本的不确定性，即依赖参与者的互动行为而即时生成，但这种生成并不是全然无序的。宗争借鉴游戏设计师克里斯·克劳福德对互动的定义，认为"'互动'是信息的发送者和接收者同时兼具两个身份，互为对方的发送者（接收者），不断进行相互间信息传递的过程。并借此形成复杂的符号文本"（2013，p. 171）。在这样的互动观下，他进一步描述了"游戏文本的双重互动结构"（如图1），并引入游戏"内文本"（inner-text）这一新概念，即"游戏设计者提供给玩者的符号文本，主要包括了游戏规则和游戏框架两部分"；"游戏内文本包含了游戏文本所形成的核心机制，游戏文本是游戏内文本的具体衍化"。（2016，p. 106）实际上，"内文本"（inner-text）可以延伸为一个适用于所有互动叙述的概念，因为互动叙述文本的生成须依赖先在的某种规则与框架。因此，在内文本的限制下，叙述文本虽然不确定，但仍然有其可预测的方向性。

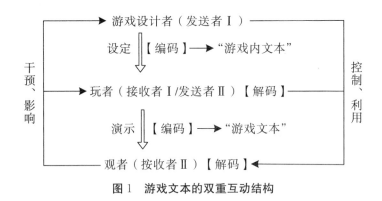

图1　游戏文本的双重互动结构

对叙述伦理而言，"内文本"作为规则和框架本身不是叙述，不具备直接的伦理性，但具有某种伦理倾向。从根本上说，所有符号都无法脱离伦理判断。"通过阐释操作，主体完满组织并关联起各种材料，而若非如此，这些材料会是碎片式的、零散的。"（佩特丽莉，庞奇奥，2012，p.185）。因此，任何符号网络的存在都建立在对其他可能世界中符号网络的否定之上，而内文本作为互动叙述文本的元语言，其伦理潜力则通过引导参与者生成限定性的互动叙述文本而实现。

从静态的内文本到动态的具备伦理性的互动叙述文本，是一个复杂的社会文化过程。宗争认为，游戏互动叙述的第一步在于"玩家通过参与游戏激活'游戏内文本'中潜藏的叙述性因素或片段，为真正的游戏叙述做准备"（2016，p.107）。在此基础上需要指出的是，互动叙述作为一种自愿性活动，吸引参与者是基本前提。参与者不会无缘由地激活内文本，二者至少需要产生某种共鸣——这是一个双向激活的过程。例如在《王者荣耀》中，游戏策划方采取的"她经济"内文本设定，成为其互动叙述中性别伦理的生成前提。据2020年11月1日《王者荣耀》官方数据统计，其日均活跃用户已达一亿，其中女性玩家比例达到54%。在长期处于男性主导下的电子竞技领域，这无疑是一个现象级的结果，而原因正是游戏内文本的属性对女性玩家文化和心理等层面的"激活"。"企鹅智酷"的深度调查报告显示[①]，女性玩家"因为周围朋友玩而好奇""被朋友推荐进来"从而开始玩的比例显著高于男性，社交成为女性玩家加入游戏的主要动机；而在内文本的设定中，《王者荣耀》本身就是一种多人在线战术竞技游戏，而游戏账户又与玩家的微信、QQ账户

---

① 参见企鹅智酷《王者荣耀深度调研报告》，https://lmtw.com/mzw/content/detail/id/147751/keyword_id/-1. 检索于2023年11月10日。

捆绑起来，并且设置了可与朋友、网友充分互动的界面。此外，《王者荣耀》的女性玩家挑选英雄时非常看重"技能适合自己操作"这一属性，相比男性玩家更看重人物的外形，而不看重团队组合的需要。内文本正好契合了这些特质：相比同类多人在线战术竞技游戏，作为手游的《王者荣耀》的上手难度对于女性玩家来说更为"友好"；在游戏设计的100多个英雄人物中，女性英雄占比超过30％，同时还有如"诸葛亮""奕星""张良"等具备温和特质的男性英雄，他们均拥有好看①的形象。内文本吸引了有特定文化身份与心理特质的参与者加入互动，为叙述文本生成某种社会性伦理奠定了基础。

在这种双向激活之下，参与者开始依照规则与框架等内文本指令展开互动，而这一过程同样受制于其自身的文化与心理特质。在《王者荣耀》游戏中，女性玩家更容易将自我投射到游戏中去，让英雄更好看是她们的第一付费动力，她们往往选择符合自我形象或理想形象的英雄角色。然而内文本的设计却存在偏向性：游戏中分别有坦克、战士、法师、辅助、射手五个职业，一般坦克、战士和辅助生存能力较强，具有保护队友的能力，法师和射手生存能力较弱，但因承担团战中的输出责任而十分重要。而女性英雄角色（及具备"阴柔气质"的英雄角色）主要集中在中路、辅助和射手三个位置（占比超过80％），与此同时，以坦克和战士为主职业的女性英雄均具有较高的操作难度，而法师、辅助和射手中的女英雄大多操作难度较低、好上手。这使得女性玩家最常用法师（65.7％），而不爱用刺客（10.8％）和战士（13.3％）——与游戏内文本的设定高度重合。与此不同，男性玩家的付费动力更多体现在对英雄的体验上，更适合操作的、符合团队组合需要的英雄更容易被他们选择，相对女性玩家而言，他们对游戏的参与更偏向以获胜为目的的"竞技"。

在此基础上，"玩者之间相互读取对方制造出的叙述文本，通过互动，形成更为庞大、丰富的互动叙述文本"（宗争，2016，p.109）。如前文所述，《王者荣耀》是社交性极为显著的多人在线战术竞技游戏，人数众多的

———————

① 这种"好看"实际上已经内蕴了伦理倾向。如《王者荣耀》的游戏内文本对社会文化中的"男性凝视"进行了再现——女性英雄几乎都拥有苗条的身材、丰满的胸部、纤细的腰身这些满足男性性幻想的特质，同时衣着也较为暴露，但这一再现并不只对男性玩家具有吸引力，更大程度上是一种"她经济"的目的实现。福柯认为，"凝视"是一种权力机制，它赋予凝视者自我认同的主体性，监督、规训被凝视者的思想、言行（2003，p.56）。生活在既有社会性别文化结构中的大多女性玩家对"好看"的认知已部分如福柯所言被规训，往往非自觉地迎合内文本并被"激活"。

女性玩家在一开始更多是受到异性朋友的影响而参与到游戏中（53.3％），许多女性玩家常常与异性一同"开黑"而非"单排"，而多数游戏场次中男性玩家和女性玩家都同时在场，因而整个游戏便成为一个两性互动的场域。两性间的伦理关系便在互动叙述中产生——由于女性玩家多选择法师、射手和辅助位置的英雄，在与男性玩家的游戏互动中往往呈现出两种故事类型：当她们选择法师、射手英雄进入比赛时，并不因为角色是关乎游戏胜利的关键位置而成为"战场"主导，而是作为以坦克、战士、辅助为职业的男性保护的对象；而当她们选择辅助英雄进入比赛时，在某种意义上则充当一种次要的、功能性的角色，辅助男性玩家"carry 全局"取得胜利。尤其以"瑶"为典型，该英雄需附体其他玩家操控的英雄，为其提供护盾加成和控制。在这两种主要的叙述趋向中，女性具备了相对于男性的从属性和脆弱性，这种伦理关系在玩者不断参与、游戏文化不断积累过程中趋于合一，形成整体的游戏互动叙述伦理。正如刘亭亭、赖子珊研究发现，源于《王者荣耀》的侮辱性流行语"躺婊"强调了女性次等于、从属于男性的地位；而同样流行的"带妹文化"则是裹挟在了女性需要被男性呵护、照顾和带领的话语之中（2022）。此外，源自《王者荣耀》的"野王哥哥""夹子"（指故意将声音变娇柔从而讨好男性的女性）等网络语言也是这种叙述伦理的有力例证。

综上，互动叙述的伦理实现并不是一种单向的故事性修辞劝服，而是携带设计者意图的内文本与有特定文化和心理的参与者群体共构的结果。实际上修辞学也已开始探讨数字时代新兴的修辞范式，美国学者博格斯特便提出，需要一种"程序修辞"理论来对我们每天遇见的软件系统做出相应的判断，并允许一个更复杂的、以说服与表达为目标的程序创作（Bogost，2007，p. 29）。刘涛、曹锐认为，程序修辞超越了古典修辞学的"劝服"和新修辞学的"同一"认识框架，而是呼唤一种"协谋"的新观念话语（2022，pp. 46－56）。当下有学者进一步认为，"在人机互动或者人机交融的趋势下，修辞不再是一种以往修辞者与修辞受众主客二元对立明显的活动，而更像是一种'共构'"（徐生权等，2023，p. 62）。诚然，"程序修辞"理论指出了电子游戏等互动性数字程序的伦理实现是传受双方共构的结果，但过于简单化了。程序修辞强调人机互动而忽略了人与人之间的互动，而这恰恰是当今亟待处理的复杂但又重要的问题，也是本文论述的重点。正因如此，该理论仍然将玩家的互动看作实现隐藏于既定程序中的主张的过程，"用户看似愉悦地'play'，实际上也是在填补程序系统中确实的逻辑闭环"（p. 61），这恐怕也将人与人、人与内文本（可以说就是程序要素）的复杂互动过程简化了。诚如《王者荣耀》案例所示，内文本设计者或许并没有明确的伦理劝服意图，而是在既有社会文化语境中与参与者达成了某种复杂而无意识的伦理再生产。据此，本文试以"类隐含读者"概念描述参与者在叙述活动中的身份。

在传统叙述理论中，"隐含读者"概念用以描述"从叙述作品的内容形式分析批评中归纳推论出来的价值观集合的接受者、呼应者，是推定作者假定会对他的意见产生呼应的对象"（赵毅衡，2013b，p. 20）。对封闭自足的小说文本而言，隐含读者与现实读者并无直接联系，二者存在一定距离。但对于开放且不确定的互动叙述文本而言，所谓"隐含读者"与现实读者之间有着十分暧昧的关系。面对并不确定的互动叙述文本，"隐含读者"只能是大量同类文本的综合文化假定，而这本身与现实的参与者同构——诚如上述，自愿性是互动叙述的首要特征，对参与者而言，内文本对其文化与心理特质的激活是互动叙述得以展开的前提，而参与者依循内文本展开的叙述也在某种程度上以其自身文化与心理预设为框架，因为参与者一旦在互动叙述过程中感受到无法调和的文化冲击，便随时可以退出。于是，本应在文本世界中的隐含读者与经验世界中的现实读者，在文本边界模糊的互动叙述中达成某种合一，可称为"类隐含读者"（quasi-implied readers）。类隐含读者不再是假定的同质化集合，而是往往以文化社群的形式存在，真切地发生互动并创制了某类互动叙述的社会文化，伦理性则深嵌其中。因此，对叙述伦理和类隐含读者的分析便成为种综合性的文化研究。

总之，内文本是互动叙述伦理分析的核心，作为叙述的规则、框架和材料，它携带了设计者的某种意图，虽然不能形成叙述，但能在与作为"类隐含读者"的参与者的双向激活中使叙述沿着某一方向展开，在一定程度上决定叙述伦理的实现。正因如此，互动叙述更偏向对整体社会文化场域中部分既存伦理的巩固与再生产，而非重构。正如在《王者荣耀》互动叙述中，女性相对于男性的从属性和脆弱性，其实都是当下社会文化中业已存在且具备影响力的性别伦理。这种传统的性别伦理在某种意义上已成为社会的集体无意识，设计者将其诉诸内文本，特定组成的参与者受到内文本吸引从而加入互动，在看似自由和愉悦的互动叙述过程中"重演"既有的社会文化戏码，完成了这一伦理的巩固与再生产。从这一角度来看，互动叙述的伦理批评的一大目标，也许就在于揭示这种无意识的伦理文化再生产。

二、互动叙述的常态跨层与伦理社会化

互动叙述的伦理不是传统叙述伦理学中封闭文本世界内的伦理，而是从

本体论上便作为一种社会化伦理存在。这并不意味着互动叙述没有文本边界，"只有边界清晰的叙述世界才能'映照'（mapping）经验世界"（赵毅衡，2013a，p. 276），倘若没有边界的区隔，那么叙述文本便无法与细节无限的经验世界区分开来从而成其为叙述。而"跨层"则是不同框架区隔的叙述层之间的相互跨越，是对叙述世界边界的破坏。从结构来说，互动叙述仍然具有不同层次的文本边界，而其伦理的社会化，便是在常态的跨层行为中自然实现的。

在宗争所提出的游戏文本双重互动结构中，第一重结构也构成了互动叙述的主叙述层，即互动的直接参与者——玩家互为发送者与接收者，生成互动性叙述文本。由于玩家本身来自现实世界，带有其自身的社会文化与心理特质，主叙述层本身因此是非封闭自足的。而次叙述层则是新增了"观者"的一种反馈层，"观者读取玩者形成的叙述文本，在叙述完结之前，观者的行为可以对叙述文本施加影响，甚至改变叙述进程"（宗争，2016，p. 109）。当下极为流行的、人人皆可开展的直播活动，使得互动叙述的反馈层越来越重要。作为玩家的游戏主播通过对次叙述层文本的媒介化，将其呈现在粉丝面前，而粉丝则通过弹幕和礼物与作为次叙述者的主播进行实时互动，干预叙述活动的进行，这一过程同样构筑了伦理意义。例如在《王者荣耀》的游戏直播过程中，主播与异性玩家的互动叙述会时刻接受粉丝的观看和评价。而粉丝作为熟知游戏文化的社群，往往代表着与游戏中的叙述伦理同构的社会文化元语言。因此，粉丝常常会在弹幕中鼓动男性主播"带妹"，或是为异性玩家"报仇"等。这种来自叙述的文化元语言的评论和干预，进一步加深和巩固了互动叙述文本的伦理实现。此外，次叙述层可以"通过自己的方式添加更多的叙述层次"（宗争，2013，p. 193），如将主叙述层或次叙述层的文本进一步媒介化、叙述化，以新的文本形式予以呈现。在数字网络化时代的媒介可供性下，这种叙述层次的添加可谓"唾手可得"，而"跨层已经成为一种常态化存在"（王委艳，2022a，p. 27），新媒体用户以各类主、次叙述层文本为素材生产的大量短视频创作便是典型。这种实践大大增加了叙述的互动交流性，"由此生成的众多文本构成了一个庞大的互文矩阵"（王强，2017，p. 48）。例如抖音短视频中八姐妹依次报数，网友将其与葫芦娃联系起来。其中"我是老六"的表现夸张而有趣，于是网友开始在游戏互动中以"老六"来称呼喜爱偷袭、暗算的玩家（因为在葫芦娃中"老六"是隐身娃）。在游戏文本不断媒介化的过程中，"老六"的语用迅速流变，最后成为整个网络文化中泛指一切带来不好事情的人的流行用语。在这一过程中，叙述伦理从始至终都诞生并发展于一个多层次而又相互影响的开放文本结构之中，它本身在与社会文化的交互中形成，又在多层级的叙述文本和跨层行为中再社会化。

学者伍茂国认为叙述伦理是一种书本世界中的虚构伦理，应该与现实伦理区分开来。（2014，pp. 101－107）但互动叙述的常态跨层，决定了过往这种简单二分的失效。劳尔－瑞安曾用"越界"来描述数字时代不同层次的叙述相互"污染"的跨层现象，但她最后也仍然坚定地认为互动叙述文本是一个虚构世界：

> 越界文本让我们摆弄我们是虚构的这一思想，我们思维的产品，产品栖居于比我们更接近地面层次的一个世界，但这些文本并不能将自身变成书写我们生活的命令语言，不能变成笼罩我们存在的非现实矩阵。最终，它们无法动摇我们的信念，即我们栖居在一个唯一"真实"存在的世界里，因为这个世界是我们肉身栖居的世界。我们可以在想象中拜访其他世界，但我们的身体将我们系在堆栈的基座上。（2014，p. 222）

劳尔－瑞安所探讨的更多是"人机互动"，因此这样的结论并不难理解。例如，单机的电子游戏本身是一个自足的世界，虽然也需要经验世界中的玩家参与才能形成叙述文本，但它仍然会被我们认为是一个非现实的虚构世界。但如果是依赖人与人之间的互动和经验共享形成的叙述文本，其虚构性质便出现了值得商榷的含混性。例如，篮球比赛作为一种游戏同样是多层级的互动叙述活动，但我们往往不会认为篮球比赛是虚构的，这是因为篮球比赛已然被实践化，成为我们共同的生活世界的一部分。同理，多人在线战术竞技游戏或许依然有其虚构性——因为内文本常试图打造一个充满细节的"可能世界"供玩家进入，但它也同时被实践化为"游戏文化产品"（赵毅衡，2017，p. 39），具备了社会实在性。其中的区别在于，后者的互动叙述依赖的不是"本真"的身体媒介，而是数字媒介，其"虚拟"特质混杂了这一问题的讨论。唐小林对此有较为清晰的探讨，他从符号学的角度将虚拟世界看作移动互联网所构成的网络世界，其"虚拟性"在于"完全用'符号物'代替或者重构了由'物符号'组成的实在世界"，但虚拟世界并不是虚构世界，"它是'实在世界'以虚拟的方式存在和运作的，具有'实在世界'的某些实在性"。（唐小林，2022，p. 10）可以极限式地预想，当虚拟现实技术在未来能够极大程度地"以假乱真"，甚至"脑机接口"成为最为平常的媒介时，一个供人们互动的"元宇宙"或许就不再会被是否"虚拟"的问题干扰。互动叙述依赖于真实参与者的即兴演示，且多级叙述层次之间不断相互影响，其文本不再是封闭自足的、对经验世界进行"映照"的虚构世界，而是直接在与既有经验世界的双向互动之中构成并成为经验世界的一部分。因此互动叙述的伦理也不是虚构伦理，而是社会化伦理。

综上所述，本文认为，在数字互联网环境下诞生的各类典型的互动叙述文本，是多层级的叙述和常态的跨层行为下形成的复杂整体，这使得互动叙述能够将不同层级的"类隐含读者"聚合为文化社群，达成对现实社会文化伦理一定程度的再生产与再社会化。《王者荣耀》游戏玩家的巨大规模参与真切地构成了大众的真实生活，而游戏的主叙述层、次叙述层以及更多再度媒介化、叙述化（如关于游戏的剪辑短视频）的多级叙述层之间的常态跨层，共同形成了关于游戏的复杂互动叙述文本，最终构成包含伦理在内的《王者荣耀》游戏文化。再如当下媒介环境中的美国职业篮球联赛（NBA）。真实的篮球运动员在球场上形成的互动演示叙述文本是整个叙述文本的重要组成部分，而球场作为主叙述层的文本边界首先就非自足，而是与现场观众相互影响。现场视频转播将观众与球场同时媒介化，形成次叙述层。次叙述层被不断再度媒介化与叙述化后产生的多层级叙述和叙述层之间的常态跨层行为，共同形成了复杂而丰富的互动叙述文本，最终构成社会生活中现实存在的、具有深刻伦理意涵的 NBA 文化及球迷圈。需要指出的是，正因为互动叙述文本是一个复杂整体，其伦理也不会是铁板一块。随着叙述层次的增加，叙述文本与主叙述层的距离愈发疏远，这常常带来互动叙述伦理的分化，该文化圈内部便可能分化为具有不同价值立场的部分。形象地说，社会中的个体就"攀附"在互动叙述的某个层级之中，以内文本和主叙述层为核心，越靠近中心，其与"类隐含读者"的重合程度便越高。

此外还应当承认，互动叙述确实可能有某种相对封闭的内在伦理，这往往与其内文本设定高度相关，诉诸的是互动规则本身的要求，不论是《王者荣耀》还是篮球比赛，都强调团队的协作共赢。但正如前文所述，内文本提供的是一种伦理潜能，需要经验世界中的参与者予以叙述激活；此外内文本设计者同样是经验世界中的人，他们并不自外于整个互动叙述过程，因此外层级叙述的反馈也常常使得内文本能够相应调整。所以并不能简单将这种看似相对封闭的叙述伦理看作虚构伦理，它同样应是互动性的社会化伦理。

三、互动叙述：媒介化社会的伦理生产方式

有论者把程序修辞看作数字时代的后人类修辞想象，那么与之相应的互

动叙述又何尝不具备这样的社会历史变革性？这不仅是因为互动叙述伦理具有社会化特性，更为深刻且真实的是，互动叙述正成为当下这个深度媒介化社会主要的伦理生产方式。

从传播学视野来看，传统叙述伦理研究无法处理互动叙述的伦理问题，根本原因在于数字互联网时代新兴媒介的发展颠覆性地重构了媒介与人的关系，导致了文本世界（媒介世界）与经验世界边界的彻底崩塌。百年前先驱李普曼从柏拉图洞穴之喻获得启发，指出我们生活在一个由信息符号组成的、区别于真实环境的"拟态环境"（pseudo-environment）中。但随着媒介技术的发展，日本学者藤竹晓意识到，真实环境与拟态环境并非界限分明，提出"拟态环境的环境化"概念，揭示拟态环境对真实环境的切实影响。正如鲍德里亚早已指出的，大众传媒的发展导致信息符号环境进一步"真实化"，从而形成了无法用"真假"进行二元区分的"超真实"世界。而今天蔚为壮观的媒介化社会理论，成为我们把握当下世界的有效思想。学者库尔德里和赫普用"媒介化"来"作为交往和社会发展过程中的所有转型，以及由此产生的社会和实践形式的简称"，它是"通过不断的循环反馈来进一步改变和稳定媒介可能使社会秩序化的各种方式"（2023，p.5）。而随着数字互联网时代的到来，"生产中的各种交往实践关系转化为信息流和信息网络；而人们在亲历空间中的互动模式则塑造了信息流动的交换和交往。网络媒介化社会中的社会关系与网络空间中的互动关系已经不分彼此"（周翔、李镓，2017）。

在这样传播生态中，无处不互联的数字媒介成为人类社会的基础设施，社会生活本身被媒介化，尼葛洛庞帝"数字化生存"的判断已经大部分成为现实。因而本文试将互动叙述进一步指认为当下媒介化社会主要的伦理生产方式——这不仅在于互动叙述的文化重要性日益凸显，更在于以互联网联结而成的媒介化社会本身构成了一个巨型互动叙述系统。唐小林认为，人类的主要叙述类型从口语-身体媒介社会的演示发展至文字-书写媒介社会的记录，又发展为数字-网络媒介社会中的拟演示，社会形态也经历了部落化、非部落化到再部落化的变迁（2022，p.83）。一方面，数字-网络媒介社会中的人们生活在一个"屏幕时代"，更准确地说是一个界面时代。无处不在的数字智能媒介界面提供了一种"区隔式"的生活，随之而来的是文学文本的彻底广义化和叙述活动的无处不在。另一方面，数字-网络媒介社会将人们接入互联网，让大量叙述活动成为一种互动性存在。在这两种动因下，社会生活本身已然成为一种具有互动性的拟演示叙述。社会学家戈夫曼曾基于对日常生活中印象管理现象的阐释而提出"拟剧论"，强调"人生如戏"，社会互动作为"前台"是被区隔的存在，"后台"则是本真的、平常的存在。数字时代愈发将这种情形改写为"人生是戏"——当媒介化导致的区隔成为社会生活的常态，所谓"前台"便逐渐统摄了"后台"，"戏剧化"反而已经在今天成为某种意义上真切的现实。正如赵毅衡的评价，"戈夫曼应未曾想到数字时代的今日，短视频这样一个互演互观的场合，几乎让人人拥有实践人生戏剧化的机会"（2023，p. 232）。实际上不仅是短视频平台，当下的媒介化社会已成为一个巨型互动叙述系统。媒介化社会中的大多数人都兼具作者、叙述者和人物的三重身份（从接受的角度而言同时也是读者和受述者），作者会尽可能在所有叙述活动中让人物形象具有统一性，也就是维护所谓的"人设"。而一旦该叙述者或其他叙述者发出了与人物形象不符的叙述文本，便有可能导致所谓的"人设崩塌"，对作者造成切身的利害影响。既然社会生活本身成了互动叙述，那么伦理作为一种社会文化，在当下正是主要以互动叙述的方式生产和运作。

有论者指出，符号学中以单个文本为中心的"全文本"概念应拓展至作为动态文本复合体的"宏文本"（macro-text），以处理海量信息时代文本跨层联合等意义问题（胡易容，2016，pp. 19—26）。至少就伦理文化而言，"宏文本"这一文本复合系统正应该拓展为互动叙述文本系统，因为在开放、可即时反馈的媒介环境中，文本意义跨层联合很大程度上是按照互动叙述的方式进行的。经由数字互联网连接而成的媒介化社会构成的是一个巨型、开放、多层级的互动叙述系统，它为社会生活的拟演示提供了总体的叙述空间（舞台）。而这一巨型互动叙述系统，又由海量的互动叙述子系统构成，子系统间并不独立，而是不同程度地相互嵌入。各类以内文本为核心，聚集在某种互动叙述周边的类隐含读者文化社群不断生产叙述文本，完成伦理的再生产和社会化。流行语"破圈"就在某种意义上描述了这些互动叙述子系统相互影响交融，共同构成媒介化社会这个巨型互动叙述系统的过程。近年来异常火爆的"村BA"文化正是一个典型的案例，而叙述伦理恰恰又是其"出圈"的关键点。"村BA"的互动叙述内文本设计非常独特——参赛者必须是农村户籍，比赛举办场地是乡村球场，不售卖门票，奖品是大鹅、香米等"接地气"的实物……这些都显著地区别于职业篮球联赛，暗含着"纯粹""去资本化"的伦理倾向。在此基础上，作为参与者的球员展开了叙述，最为经典的叙述文本是雨天他们用毛巾裹住球鞋坚持完成比赛，几万人的球场仍然座无虚席。相关新闻报道作为再度媒介化的叙述文本，迅速获得了广大网友的关注，其中不乏大量"非球迷"。不论是视频还是帖子，评论区的赞美也成为叙述文本的一部分，共构了"村 BA"的叙述伦理，俨然形成了一个多层级的，追求纯粹、反资本的"村 BA"网络文化社群。

此外，媒介化社会的互动叙述并不仅限于多人战术竞技游戏、体育比赛这些典型，而是几乎覆盖整个社会文化生活。王委艳在《交流叙述学》一书中便提出了"网络活态叙述"概念，即"存在于网络空间，以真实事件为基础形成的动态化的、处于进行时的叙述，其具有动态性、不确定性和现实针对性等特征"（王委艳，2022b，p.269）。网络活态叙述正是媒介化社会中的行动者互动生成的，它的外延可以相当广阔，各类网络舆论事件都可涵纳。此时舆论显现的"前文本"构成了互动叙述的内文本，具有引发舆论的潜能，其设计者或隐或显，内生于既存社会文化中，吸引大量参与者加入互动，生成"全民化叙述文本"，"文本构成包括事件本身、弹幕、评论、跟帖、动态进展等"（p.269）。社会伦理在这一过程中自然生成并得到彰显，"那些带有道德、法律等价值倾向的网络活态叙述事件，往往具有非常大的社会影响，其在现实中被干预并形成规范化结果"（p.268）。现实中，不论是"唐山打人事件"这类有明确事件文本的舆情案例，还是"淄博烧烤走红"这样直接派生于网络的热点现象，都是在参与者的互动过程中生成叙述，且具有明显的伦理意涵。当然，诚如前文所述，并非所有互动叙述单元都能形成"规范化结果"而实现伦理的统一。更可能的情况是，人们在不同的叙述层次中区隔为不同的文化圈层，凝聚于某个内文本的互动叙述文化社群虽然共同处于一个大的叙述边界内，却也有普遍的内部分化，这是媒介化社会命定的文化复杂性所决定的。

如果说文化是"一个社会相关意义活动的总集合"（赵毅衡，2013c，p.8），那么当下媒介化社会中时刻生成的文化，在某种意义上越来越成为相关互动叙述文本的总集合。在此社会中，伦理生产与运作的方式发生了重要变革，为叙述伦理研究提出了许多亟待解决的新问题，迫使这一领域直面发展的全新阶段。

结语：面向媒介化社会的文化研究

伍茂国虽然在《伦理转向语境中的叙事伦理》一文中指出必须将叙述伦理作为一种虚构伦理与日常伦理区分开来，认为叙述伦理存在于"书本世界"而非"现实世界"，但也同时在文中留下了推翻这一观点的伏笔——在他看来，要系统地建构叙事伦理的框架，"在理论规划的前提下，尚需通过具体的文本分析积累现代性叙事伦理研究的经验，探索新的研究视角，并测试叙事伦理研究框架在作品分析中的有效性"（2014，p.105）。从本文的分析中不难发现，限制在所谓"书本世界"中的叙述伦理批评范式已经无法经受当下各类互动叙述文本的检验。正因为互动叙述需要在内文本、参与者、观者（也是层次的参与者）的多层次复杂互动中形成文本，对互动叙述的伦理研究就必须跳出"书本世界"，将叙述伦理看作媒介化社会中借由互动叙述生成的社会性伦理，从文本研究走向一种文化研究的范式。本文试抛砖引玉，以期引发更多关于互动叙述伦理批评的讨论，进一步敞开这一研究分支的当下向度。

实际上，对互动叙述伦理批评向度的论证无疑也在方法论的层面叩问了叙述学的未来面向，正如从经典叙述学到后经典叙述学再到广义叙述学，内中是符号从封闭的结构主义到开放的后结构主义，再到皮尔斯传播符号观的逻辑演进，是对符号文本、媒介与人、世界关系的理解的不断重构。

引用文献：

费伦，詹姆斯（2002）．作为修辞的叙事：技巧、读者、伦理、意识形态（陈永国，译）．北京：北京大学出版社．

福柯，米歇尔（2003）．规训与惩罚（刘北成，等译）．上海：生活·读书·新知三联书店．

关萍萍（2012）．互动媒介论：电子游戏多重互动叙事模式．杭州：浙江大学出版社．

赫尔曼，戴卫（2002）．新叙事学（马海良，译）．北京：北京大学出版社．

胡易容（2016）．宏文本：数字时代碎片化传播的意义整合．西北师大学报（社会科学版），5，133−139．

库尔德利，尼克；赫普，安德烈亚斯（2023）．现实的中介化建构（刘泱育，译）．上海：复旦大学出版社．

劳尔−瑞安，玛丽（2014）．故事的变身（张新军，译）．南京：译林出版社．

利科，保罗（2013）．作为一个他者的自身（余碧平，译）．北京：商务印书馆．

刘涛，曹锐（2022）．程序修辞的概念缘起、学术身份与运作机制．新闻与写作，4，46−56．

刘亭亭，赖子珊（2022）．社会性别作为本土电子游戏的重要分析范畴，澎湃新闻·思想市场，https://www.thepaper.cn/newsDetail_forward_17706254，4月23日．

佩特丽莉，苏珊；庞奇奥，奥古斯都（2012）．伦理符号学（周劲松，译）．符号与传媒，2，181−194．

唐小林（2022）．信息社会符号学．北京：科学出版社．

王强（2016）．"数码受众"与"数字叙述"：新媒体叙述范式的建构．当代文坛，5，47−51．

王委艳（2022a）．数字化时代的交流叙述：当前与未来．探索与批评，2，21−32．

王委艳（2022b）. 交流叙述学. 北京：九州出版社.

伍茂国（2014）. 伦理转向语境中的叙事伦理. 河南大学学报（社会科学版），1，101－107.

徐生权，夏春祥，孙希洋（2023）. 数字时代的修辞术：程序修辞以及后人类修辞的想象. 新闻与写作，1，57－66.

赵毅衡（2013a）. 广义叙述学. 成都：四川大学出版社.

赵毅衡（2013b）. 当说者被说的时候：比较叙述学导论. 成都：四川文艺出版社.

赵毅衡（2013c）. 重新定义符号与符号学. 国际新闻界，6，6－14.

赵毅衡（2017）. 哲学符号学：意义世界的形成. 成都：四川大学出版社.

赵毅衡（2023）. 符号美学与艺术产业. 成都：四川大学出版社.

周翔，李镓（2017）. 网络社会中的"媒介化"问题：理论、实践与展望. 国际新闻界，4，137－154.

宗争（2013）. 游戏学：符号叙述学研究. 成都：四川大学出版社.

宗争（2016）. 游戏叙述原理研究——以体育竞赛与电子游戏的叙述形态为例. 四川大学学报（哲学社会科学版），1，105－111.

Bogost, I. (2007). *Persuasive Games: The Expressive Power of Videogames*. Cambridge, MA：The MIT Press.

Booth，W. C. (1988). *The Company We Keep: A Ethics of Fiction*. Berkeley and Los Angles：University of California Press.

Phelan，J. & 唐伟胜（2008）. "伦理转向"与修辞叙事伦理. 四川外语学院学报，5，1－6.

Stephenson，W. (1988). *The Play Theory of Mass Communication*. New Jersey：Transaction Books.

作者简介：

马翾昂，四川大学文学与新闻学院博士研究生，四川大学符号学－传媒学研究所成员，研究方向为传播符号学。

Author:

Ma Xuanang, Ph. D. candidate of College of Literature and Journalism, Sichuan University. His academic interest covers the fields of communication semiotics.

Email：1060801783@qq.com

文类研究 ●●●●●

奇幻文学：超自然叙述批判张力①

孙金燕

摘　要：对待超自然的态度，是奇幻文学概念界定的核心。托多罗夫"犹疑说"式的文本"内部风暴"，与托尔金对现实"第二世界"式的寓言批判，是西方奇幻文学概念界定的两种代表观念，涉及对现实与想象的区隔与缝合，也呈现出对奇幻文学"复魅"人与超自然世界的不同功能期待。中国奇幻文学概念在不同时期对现实与想象的不同倾向，同样折射出它对自身价值立场的确立，既是一种显而易见的建构，也是一种意味深长的选择。

关键词：奇幻文学　超自然叙述　现实　想象　批判

Fantasy Literature: Tension of Supernatural Narration Critique

Sun Jinyan

Abstract: The attitude towards the supernatural is at the core of defining the concept of fantasy literature. Todorov's "hesitation" in textual "inner storm" and Tolkien's allegorical critique of reality in "the secondary world" represent two representative Western views defining the concept of fantasy literature, involving the division and fusion of reality and imagination. It also presents different functional expectations for the "re-

---

① 本文为 2020 年度教育部人文社会科学研究一般项目"中国当代奇幻小说叙事研究"（20YJC751023）中期成果。

enchantment" of humans and the supernatural world in fantasy literature. The conception of Chinese fantasy literature has different tendencies towards reality and imagination in different periods. This also reflects its establishment of its own value and standpoint, which is not only an obvious construction but also a significant choice.

Keywords: fantasy literature; supernatural narration; reality; imagination; critique

奇幻元素在中国文学中古已有之，但直到 20 世纪 90 年代，随着数字媒介的勃兴才发展为一种奇幻类型文学。目前，关于其类型界定已有较丰富的成果，且在不同时段呈现出不同的认知倾向：从其早期与儿童文学的缩结，到后来"模糊地指称那些类似于《魔戒》的小说文体"（周淑兰，2008，p. 38），中国奇幻文学类型界定的变动，一方面与奇幻文学自身的形式特点有关，另一方面与奇幻文学概念中西对接时的现实语境有关。本文拟从奇幻文学概念辨义出发，抉发意旨，探讨中国奇幻文学类型界定的特点、意义，及其对当代奇幻小说发展的影响。

一、"犹疑说"与"架空说"：西方奇幻文学概念界定的两种代表性观念

西方奇幻文学研究在 20 世纪前虽有若干零星见解，涉及奇幻小说的主题、功能等，但深入的概念界定与文类探讨到了 20 世纪才正式拉开帷幕。其中，对奇幻文学的类型讨论，一直与其形式中所呈现的"现实世界与想象世界"即"自然法则与超自然法则"的关系相关，并形成以下两种代表性观念。

其一，是公认的奇幻文学现代理论奠基者托尔金（J. R. R. Tolkien）在 1943 年提出的"第二世界"（Secondary World）观点，国内最早译介《魔戒》的学者朱学恒称其为"架空"，此观点强调奇幻文学需搁置现实世界的自然法则，信奉超自然法则。

托尔金最早在《论仙境故事》（"On Fairy Story"）一文中阐述奇幻文学类型特点、产生原因、理想受众、功能诸方面，提供的系列术语中包括"原初世界"（Primary World）与"第二世界"这一对重要概念。他认为，"原初世界"是由上帝所创造的真实存在，而"第二世界"是上帝的造物即人利用上帝赋予的准创造权来打造的一个想象性存在，它以一种"内在一致性"（the inner consistency of reality）使读者信其为真："故事创作者是成功的'次创造者'。他造出了一个可供你的心智进入的'第二世界'。他在里面所讲

述的是遵循那个世界法则的，是'真实的'（true）。因此，当你仿佛置身其中时，你会相信它。而当你开始怀疑时，咒语即被打破，它所创造的魔法或艺术即宣告失败，你便被抛置于'原初世界'。"（Tolkien，1966，p.67）

其表述重在强调"第二世界"与遵循现实世界自然法则的"原初世界"不同，它创造出属于自身的另一套超自然法则，读者需要消除对"第二世界"、超自然法则的怀疑，信超自然法则为真，沉浸其中以获得与其的内在一致性。这也就意味着对现实世界自然法则的搁置。

托尔金的"第二世界"观点在若干奇幻理论中得到回应，如萨哈罗斯基（Zahorski）和波亚（Boyer）将"第二世界"细分为三种：一为"遥远的第二世界"（Remote Secondary Worlds），在时空上呈现为独立的封闭状态，如托尔金《魔戒》中的中土世界；二为"并置的第二世界"，呈现为现实世界与"第二世界"并置的状态，二者以某种通道（magical portal）为出入口，如C. S. 刘易斯在"纳尼亚传奇"系列奇幻儿童文学小说之《狮子、女巫和魔衣橱》中，设定魔衣橱为纳尼亚王国与英伦两个世界的通路；三为"裹挟的第二世界"（Worlds-within-worlds），如在"哈利·波特"系列中，即使没有国王十字火车站的九又四分之三站台，巫师们也总是自由穿梭于现实世界（麻瓜世界）与魔法巫师世界（Zahorski & Boyer，1982，pp.58—64）。在后两种类型中，"第二世界"虽与现实世界同时出现，但只是奇幻叙事所多设置的一层"框架"（方小莉，2018），改变的是进入"第二世界"的路径，其主导精神依然是对超自然的信任，而非怀疑。此外，艾布拉姆斯（Meyer Howard Abrams）在《文学术语汇编》一书中将"奇幻"解释为："描绘了一种其本质以及运作形式与我们普通的经验世界极不相同的想象的真实。"（2004，p.278）诸此种种，皆在说明奇幻文学是建立在超自然法则上的一种文类。

其二，与托尔金的观点相对，是由结构主义理论家茨维坦·托多罗夫（Tzvetan Todorov）在1970年提出的"犹疑（hesitation）说"。此种观点被认为在西方奇幻文体研究方面引起过话语通胀（inflation of discourse）（Cornwell，1990），主张奇幻文学需兼顾自然法则与超自然法则，超自然法则并不具有取代自然法则的优势。

托多罗夫的"犹疑说"，以广义的西方文学为背景，使奇幻文学类型在与其相邻的类型即"怪诞（uncanny）类"和"奇迹（marvelous）类"的关系中被推定："奇幻会贯穿这种不确定性的始终。一旦选择了这种或者那种回答，我们将使奇幻变成与之相邻的类型，即怪诞或者奇迹。奇幻就是一个只了解

自然法则的人在面对明显的超自然事件时所经历的犹疑。"（托多罗夫，2015，p. 17）

他提出奇幻文学必须满足三个条件："首先，这个文本必须迫使读者将人物的世界视作真人生活的世界，并且在对被描述事件的自然和超自然解释之间犹疑。其次，某个人物或许也会体验这种犹疑，这样，读者的角色就被委托于人物，而同时，犹疑被文本表现出来，并成为作品的主题之一。最后，读者必须采用特定的阅读态度来对待文本。"（p. 23）也就是说，推定奇幻文学类型的关键点，是读者将被描述事件解释为自然或超自然的"犹疑"，一旦确认其为自然或超自然，作品即会归入"怪诞"或"奇迹"文学类型。如此，"奇幻"更像是一个滑动的文类，它处于"怪诞"与"奇迹"两种文类的临界，由"奇幻－怪诞类"与"奇幻－奇迹类"（p. 32）共同构成。

从表面看，这似乎说明纯粹的奇幻文学类型是不存在的，其文类的确定随着读者的阅读感受而随时形成或消逝。实质上，这个定义是以读者在自然与超自然之间的"犹疑"，表明奇幻文学类型的核心在于兼顾自然与超自然，意在缝合现实与想象，而非将二者对立，更非以其中一维取代另一维。

托多罗夫的"犹疑说"，同样能在西方奇幻文学研究中寻迹到若干相类观点。除其在《奇幻文学导论》一书中所援引以证明其观点的英国作家 M. R. 詹姆士（M. R. James）、德国学者奥嘉·黎曼（Olga Riemann）、法国学者卡斯特（Castex）、路易·瓦克斯（Louis Vax）、罗杰·卡约瓦（Roger Caillois）等（pp. 17－18），即使被认为是现实主义作家代表的陀思妥耶夫斯基，也自认为其作品具有奇幻性，他将"奇幻"理解为十分贴近现实的东西，应该能使人几乎相信它是真的（陀思妥耶夫斯基，2010b，p. 1205）；他在《刊出〈爱伦·坡的三篇小说〉的前言》中也曾明确指出奇幻有其限度与规则，如爱伦·坡的创作不以现实法则为基础，其奇幻性是相当外在的，是无法与霍夫曼这样的奇幻大家相提并论的，只能称作"想入非非的作家"（2010a，p. 281）。

综合而论，两种观点的核心区别在于对待超自然的态度，涉及的是究竟应该区隔还是缝合现实与想象的问题，更深层的则是对奇幻文类的功能期待问题。

二、对现实与想象的区隔抑或缝合：奇幻文学的超自然叙述批判功能

奇幻文学的兴起，总体上与对理性主义的反叛有关。如托多罗夫所确认

的奇幻文学类型历史较短，大致囊括 18 世纪末至 20 世纪初这一时段，到莫泊桑则基本收束了这一类型。"奇幻是相对短命的。奇幻以一种成体系的方式出现于 18 世纪末期的卡佐特的作品中，一个世纪之后，莫泊桑的小说是这一类型中最后仍具有相当艺术价值的作品。"（托多罗夫，2015，p. 124）从 18 世纪末到 20 世纪初，大致是欧洲自然科学有重大发展，理性主义在思想领域占统治地位的时期。人们认知世界的方式深受其影响，反映在文学领域即是自然主义、现实主义文学的兴盛。奇幻文学在此一时段作为现实主义的对立面渐渐形成，它专注于展示人在超自然与自然法则、现实与虚幻之间的心理体验，意图是显然的：其一，承认现实与想象是可以共存的，坚信现实"真实性"的观点会带来"不安"；其二，挑战真实与想象的二元对立观念，可以复原现实中存在的"梦境"与想象；其三，在现实与想象的二维张力与彼此观照下，迫使读者重塑对现实的批判认识。

托多罗夫的"犹疑说"，强调故事本身同时提供现实/想象与自然/超自然两种事实，主人公与读者的"犹疑"，意味着需在自然与超自然两者之间不断过渡与抉择，对自然法则的违背，将使主人公与读者愈发意识到自然法则的存在。

这也就意味着，奇幻文学所能实现的上述现实－想象之间的超自然批判张力，在作品内部即可完成。当作品主人公将所有超自然叙述当作"正常"，读者需从自身所处的现实世界解读出它的"不正常"，则作品超越"奇幻"而进入了"寓言"体裁。卡夫卡式现代寓言作品便是其中的代表。卡夫卡的现代主义小说所建构的"世界"，都遵循一种与现实无关的、梦境般的逻辑，其中的超自然事件不再引发犹疑，这与传统的奇幻文学一开始假定存在真实的、自然的、正常的世界，随后再推翻它，完全不同。小说《变形记》，以一个男人格雷戈尔变成甲虫的超自然事件开始，但随着叙述的推进，作品人物中没有一人对这个超自然事件感到吃惊，"吃惊"的缺席意味着人物将超自然事件视为符合自然法则的；超自然变成世界运行法则，荒谬成为正常，带来的结果是：读者如果认同作品人物的感知，承认超自然事件是一件再自然不过的事，就会将自己排除在现实之外；读者如果以理性来纠正这个颠倒而混乱的世界，理性就会被卷入这个梦魇世界。（托多罗夫，2015，p. 130）

托尔金的"第二世界"观念正与之相反：奇幻所构建的整个世界以超自然法则为主导，故事中的人物丝毫不怀疑超自然事件的真实性，读者即使心存疑惑，明知它是想象/超自然事件，也要跟随故事中的人物将其视为真实的、自然的。奇幻是"适应"（adaptation）超自然，而非怀疑它。

这与托尔金对科学的态度有关。他虽同样强调奇幻不会模糊现实的轮廓，恰恰需要依赖现实，但他着意于恢复人与万物交融的古老的想象传统。在托尔金看来，一种古老的"思想"已然消逝，这种思想原能使人与万物平等地分担生老病死与喜怒哀乐，情感交融却并不混淆。而科学的高速发展改变了这一切，"在现代，不是奇幻，而是科学理论，使西方、欧洲乃至世界的人类与动植物的分离感被攻击与被削弱"（Tolkien，1966，p. 79），科学将人类定性为"仅仅是动物的一种"（only an animal），不仅激起人类"进入"生物体的兴趣，也引发情感的混淆，人爱动物甚于爱人，同情羊群而诅咒牧羊人，为战马哭泣却诋毁死去的士兵，如此种种对"他者"的过度关注而引起的情感混淆，反而加速了人类想象力的耗散。

所以，托尔金比托多罗夫走得更远。他所界定的"奇幻"，是要另造一个想象世界：一方面，这个想象世界以一种罗斯玛丽·杰克逊（Rosemary Jackson）对奇幻文学所总结的"虚构的自律"（fictional autonomy）（Rosemary Jackson，1981，p. 36），向着在现实世界中不可证明的方向推进，却有可能是"遥远的传统"，如同小说《魔戒》创造的"中土世界"，细节饱满且逻辑自洽，它有着自身独特的历史、地理、种族乃至语言，是一个有别于现实世界的封闭的、自给自足的系统；另一方面，它并非不再反映现实，只是不承担现实批判功能，如研究者谈方认为西方奇幻小说"与拉美魔幻现实主义小说不同，在于前者（即奇幻小说）属于一种通俗文学的范畴，并且不承担社会政治批判的使命，所展现的生活面也要狭窄得多"（2014，p. 202）。事实上，奇幻文学的超自然叙述恰恰是要与"真实"世界对话，并将这种对话吸纳为其根本结构的一部分，以不可知、不可见来烛照科学主导的现实世界的所谓已知与已见，发掘其洞见（或许未必），甚而可能是偏见，以此形成罗斯玛丽·杰克逊（Rosemary Jackson）所总结的"颠覆被认为是范式的某些原则和习俗"，乃至质疑"社会秩序、形而上学之谜和生活的目的"。（Jackson，1981，p. 15）

从这个角度来看，无论是《魔戒》中的中土世界，《狮子、女巫和魔衣橱》里的纳尼亚世界，还是《哈利·波特》中的魔法世界，这些为托尔金、朱学恒所界定的"主流奇幻"（High Fantasy）所建构的架空、超自然世界，虽与托多罗夫等认定的"经典奇幻"（Classic Fantasy）（Todorov，1973，p. 174）的形态相去甚远，却以其"非真实性"（unreality）揭示"真实"的悬搁乃至缺场，意图使现代读者重返启蒙前对超自然世界的"蒙昧"体验。它们依然在传达想象世界与现实世界在现代的复杂关联，只不过其现实批判更具有"寓言"的性质。

可以说，对奇幻文学类型的界定，是选择托多罗夫"犹疑说"式的文本"内部风暴"，还是托尔金"第二世界"式的对现实的寓言批判，事实上取决于对奇幻文学如何"复魅"人与超自然世界联系的功能期待。

三、奇幻文学概念的中西对接及对超自然叙述的倾向性选择

"奇幻文学"作为一个文类概念，在中国近三十年的译介与发展中，历经与其他文类纠葛及至逐渐被认可为一种文类的过程，其中同样隐含着对超自然叙述的不同功能期待。

西方奇幻文学在被引入国内之初，常与童话文体相缠杂，主要源于对奇幻文学现实主义层面的关注。不可否认，奇幻文学与童话有着某些形式上的相似，尤其表现在对"魔法"的共同强调方面。如儿童文学家约翰·洛威·汤森（John Rowe Townsend）认为，"童话故事无论古今，都是魔法的故事"（朱自强，2009，p. 209），而奇幻小说家托尔金以"仙境故事"（fairy story）来解说"奇幻"（fantasy）时也认为："矮人、女巫、龙、自然万物等的故事，都属于奇幻文学。仙境故事有几个要素，其中最重要的是奇幻的土魔法。"（Tolkien，1966，p. 39）此后的奇幻小说家林·卡特（Lynn Carter）以及文学与宗教学者普提尔（Richard L. Purtill）也持类似观点。林·卡特认为，"幻想小说（fantasy）所描述的，据我看，是一种既非科学小说又非恐怖小说的奇迹，这类小说的本质可以用一个词来概括：魔法（magic）"（黄禄善，2003，p. 235）。普提尔在《神话与故事》（"Myth and Story"）一文中总结奇幻的四点要素，其中之一即为技术上涉及以符号等方法操纵自然力量的魔法。（Purtill，1984，p. 33）

所以，即使较早就意识到奇幻文学与传统意义上的童话之间的区别，研究者也常常难以对二者进行严格的区分。在儿童文学研究方面颇有建树的学者朱自强，在其1992年写作的《小说童话：一种新的文学体裁》一文中，依然将"Fantasy"译为"小说童话"。他认为"将Literary fairy tales与Fantasy暧昧地用'童话'来囊括，就……不可避免地造成幻想故事型作品系列的评论中的概念混乱……我将Fantasy称为'小说童话'主要是因为，Fantasy是一种以小说式的表现方法创作的幻想故事（这里的'故事'，指叙事性作品），其母体是童话，但又吸收了现实主义小说的遗传基因"（朱自强，1992）。从其论述中可以大致梳理出以下几层意思：其一，奇幻文学与童话的区别在于其叙述形式为小说；其二，奇幻类型文学是幻想性的；其三，奇幻文学内含现实主义基因。

朱自强的上述观点，有着将强调虚构性的"小说"（fiction）等同于强调叙事性的"小说"（novel）的倾向，依循的是弗莱所指认的将"小说"概念普泛性地等同于 18 世纪现实主义小说与 20 世纪现代主义小说和后现代主义小说的主流文学观念（弗莱，2006，pp.450-469），忽略了"小说"原本为"散文体虚构"（prose fiction），同样有着非现实主义的遗传基因。直至 2008 年，他虽将"fantasy"改译为"现代幻想小说"，但所持观点仍是"运用小说的写实手法，创作一个现实世界所不存在的长篇幻想故事"（梅子涵等，2008，p.94），坚持认为奇幻文学与现实主义有着深入的关联。

与此相类的还有与魔幻小说的缠杂，如海内外研究者均指出："甚至许多在台湾被称作魔幻写实风格的作品也都可以列入奇幻文学的类别中"（朱学恒，2007）；"在中国的话语中，原本属于奇幻文学类型的作品，诸如《魔戒》，常常被称之为'魔幻文学'"（陈晓明、彭超，2017，p.35）等。究其原因，表面上是基于中文译名同有"幻"字，而对两种文体的混淆："许多时候，奇幻、魔幻、科幻、玄幻、惊幻、异幻、灵幻、神幻、大幻想等与'幻'字有关的词语是混着用的"（杨鹏，2006，p.11）；事实上，魔幻现实主义文学中的"神奇的现实仍是以现实为基石。换言之，神奇是事物的自然属性"（陈晓明、彭超，2007，p.33），将奇幻文学中的超自然视同魔幻文学中非同寻常的"现实"，依然蕴含着对奇幻文学所述"神奇"事物的"现实"属性的信任。

20 世纪 90 年代末，随着国内网络奇幻小说的发展与研究的深入，"fantasy"在学界逐渐出现更为宽泛的译名"幻想文学"，以及"奇幻文学""玄幻文学"等，学界越来越着重关注奇幻文学的超自然叙述。

早在 1997 年，研究者彭懿即在其《西方现代幻想文学论》中明确地将"fantasy"译为"幻想文学"，认为其"为我们提供了一个随心所欲的艺术空间，它催生了一大批……新神话。人们看重的是第二世界的魔法，第一世界中一切不可能的东西在那里都成为了令人信服的可能"（1997，p.329）。彭懿的译法，虽与朱学恒将"fantasy"译为"奇幻文学"不同，但二者的核心思想却趋于一致。作为台湾地区奇幻小说的重要推手，最早将《魔戒》译介到国内的朱学恒曾尝试给"奇幻文学"下一个定义，并自认为"这样的定义看来模糊，却已经是最能掌握精髓的说法了"："这类的作品多半发生在另一个架空世界中（或者是经过巧妙改变的一个现实世界），许多超自然的事情（我们这个世界中违背物理定律、常识的事件），依据该世界的规范是可能发生的，甚至是被视作理所当然的。"（朱学恒，2007）

不难看出，他们都主张奇幻文学（fantasy）所构建的世界，遵循不同于现实世界的逻辑与规则，超出现实世界常理与经验逻辑的"不可能"事件，在奇幻文学世界中都是可以"信服"且"理所当然的"。

这种主张明显与前述托尔金的"第二世界"观念相符，且类似的观点在国内学界并不鲜见。21世纪，中国奇幻文学对超自然叙述的偏好愈发明显，《2003年中国奇幻文学年度精选》的编者，将奇幻文学释义为："凡是拥有超越现实的想象力，建筑在一个与现实有区别或者完全创造出来的独特世界观之上，并且拥有严谨的创作精神的作品，就可以归类为奇幻文学之中。"（胡晓辉等，2004，p.499）2004年，叶祝弟在《奇幻小说的诞生及创作进展》一文中将"奇幻文学"定义为："广义地说，那些以通过非现实虚构描摹奇崛的幻想世界，展示心灵的想象力，表达生命理想的文学作品，都可以称之为奇幻文学。"（2004）研究者姜淑芹梳理了2008—2017十年间的中国知网学术论文，针对篇名的使用统计出"幻想小说""奇幻小说"在学界的认可度明显高于前述的"童话小说"等（2021，p.206），由此也可看出，国内学界对奇幻文学非现实主义因素的愈趋认同。

四、"重塑世界"的价值与局限：超越经验现实的自由与读者认知限度

中国当代奇幻文学越发以超自然的非真实叙述为文类区分的关键，可以说与其所处的现实语境有关，既是对科学主导的经验世界认知的超越，也是对媒介技术高速发展带来的"仿真化"（simulation）现实的回应。

随着理性和科学的推进，经验可感的现实世界取代理念世界而具有了合法性，人们越发接受经验世界作为唯一的真实的存在，超自然被放逐到"真实"之外，被先在地认为是不可能的，进而超验的理念世界只能通过想象而存在。正如文学史家评论家曼勒（C. N. Manlove）所言："现实与想象两个世界之间的缝隙已经太大了，这是当代奇幻作家所面临的首要困境。"（Manlove，1975，p.259）出于对科学主导的"真实"的质疑，基于张扬超自然叙述的奇幻文学建立起一个遥远的世界，呈现出现实世界中不可能存在的事物。它借助人的想象超越经验认识的局限，以一个全新的视野和深刻的洞察力，获取精神性的价值。从一定程度上来说，经由描述那些"不可能、不真实、不可名状、无可定形、未知、隐匿"（the im-possible, the un-real, the nameless, formless, shapeless, unknown, invisible）之物（Jackson，1981，p.26），它企图唤起人的精神力量，超越感官所限与认知的局限。

此外，奇幻文学在中国快速发展的三十年，也是媒介技术高速发展的时期，世界愈发趋向鲍德里亚（Jean Baudrillard）所指认的"超真实"："真实……已经不再必须是理性的，因为它不根据某种理想的或否定的例子来衡量。它只不过是操作的。实际上，因为它不再被包裹在想象之中，它也不再是现实的。"（Baudrillard，1983，p. 3）受欲望驱使，空洞的形象被注入意义，现实成为某种"形象"或纯粹的表征，消失在符号所编织的迷雾之中。奇幻文学对媒介的充分利用，曾被文化学者陶东风评价为"一种完全魔术化、非道德化了、技术化了的想象世界的方式"（2006，p. 11）。当现实世界趋于"仿真化"，奇幻文学以其"想象"为路径，另辟一个"世界"来参与"世界重塑"，其目的正如理论家费斯克（J. Fiske）对通俗文化所总结的："想象不是对社会现实的逃避，而是对主导意识形态及其在社会关系中具体体现的直接回复"（1987，p. 318），据此，中国当代奇幻文学对超自然叙述越来越明显的倾向性选择，既是对现实的隐喻映射与寓言，也意在从中获得自由。

而限度也由此产生。奇幻文学的批判功能，来自它所叙述的超自然事件本身，更来自超自然事件引发的反应，曼勒（Manlove）即直接将"奇幻"定义为"能够以不可化约的超自然唤起惊奇（wonder）的虚构作品"（1975，p. 1），并且，"惊奇并不是奇幻作品的副产品，而是其核心要素"（p. 7）。"唤起惊奇"是符号接受层面的，这种"惊奇"既由所描述的事件提供，也由作品中的人物及读者参与共同完成：人物确定某个事件或现象是合乎自然法则的现实，还是遵循超自然的想象，读者则选择是否认同人物的判断。也可以说，是人物/读者对什么是"真实"的界定，构成了奇幻。

但是，"真实"是一个观念问题。对所描述事件是否"真实"的判定并无客观标准，主要源于人物或读者的经验与认知能力：一方面，如托多罗夫指出，将所描述事件归为超自然的"神异"类型，源于超自然叙述"超出了我们熟悉的范围"，"在被描述的时代科技并没有发展到那种程度，但最终是可能实现的"，"在这种类别中，超自然由理性的方式来解释，但所遵循的规律是同时代的科学尚未企及的"（2015，pp. 39－40）等，是文化、智识、科技等条件限制，导致人物/读者与所述事件的距离太远，失去判断其为符合自然法则的"真实"的能力；另一方面，即使不以现实世界自然法则为判定是否"真实"的标准，单纯以架空世界的超自然叙述来观照，奇幻文学也将随着对读者"求奇追新"阅读期待的不断应和，而不断走向新奇怪异，固然能"无拘无束地宣泄个人的欲望"（张赟，2009，p. 32），但同时也失去"具体的、针对当下中国现实的特殊阐释力"，甚至被称为装神弄鬼的犬儒主义（陶东风，2006，p. 8）。

事实上，中国当代奇幻文学依然潜藏着在现实与想象的罅隙中寻求弥合的意图，即使是在"九州"系列这类被视为架空奇幻的小说中，也可看出此种努力。

"九州"系列属于多作者参与的设定型奇幻文学作品，据不完全统计，目前参与创作者已超百人，作品近千部。就255页的《九州·创造古卷》设定的大体框架及目前创作而言，"九州世界"涉及从多部落联盟的燹朝到一统东陆的徽朝近四千年历史，它架构一个世界体系，囊括了传说、天文、地理、种族、历史、军事、组织、生物诸方面。与此同时，它不断提示所建构的"九州世界"是真实的"一种可能"：细节上，如以"九州"之名召唤中国历史、文化记忆，以及不断在行文中提供参考文献、注释，解说虚构的英雄原型为现实历史人物赵匡胤、成吉思汗、托雷等，故事有据可考，使"九州世界"以宏大线索延伸向"真实世界"。除此之外，"九州"系列在设定上对古今中外诸多思想进行碎片化杂糅，如"荒"与"墟"二神构成了世界的"混沌"，源自老子"有物混成，先天地生"的道家思想；在不同创作者的笔下，"天驱"与"辰月"两大组织的分分合合以及斗争中的平衡世界秩序，暗含中国儒家、墨家和西方社会有机体思想以及社会达尔文主义等，这种"不中不西、亦中亦西"的多元思想混杂，虽折射出创作群体因创作理念"不断调整所映现的不稳定心态和自信力的缺失"（韩云波，2007，p. 131），以及关于"理想世界"建构的不确定与某种乌托邦危机，但也显示出他们对现实世界诸种生存规则的思考，以及对于世界未来的参与者、承担者而非旁观者的立场。

目前，尽管此类奇幻文学作品对世界完整体验的获得方式仍显不成熟，但它们对现实世界的关注，超越了奇幻文学一度呈现出的个人的私人欲望的符号化表达，蕴含着对现代社会变迁的症候与隐喻。

结　语

整体而言，文本的多义性往往与社会的多样性平行。奇幻文学概念对自然与超自然的不同态度，隐含着区隔与缝合现实和想象的不同意图，以及对"复魅"人与超自然世界的不同功能期待。中国奇幻文学在不同时期对现实与想象的不同倾向，同样折射出它对自身价值立场的确立，是一种显而易见的建构，也是一种意味深长的选择。

引用文献：

艾布拉姆斯（2004）．文学术语汇编．北京：外语教学与研究出版社．

陈晓明，彭超（2017）．想象的变异与解放——奇幻、玄幻与魔幻之辨．探索与争鸣，3，29－36．

方小莉（2018）．奇幻文学的"三度区隔"问题研究——兼与赵毅衡先生商榷．中国比较文学，3，17－29．

弗莱，诺思罗普（2006）．批评的解剖（陈慧、袁宪军、吴伟仁，译）．天津：百花文艺出版社．

韩云波（2007）．中国当下武侠、奇幻文学二题．现代中国文化与文学，1，123－131．

胡晓辉，陈晓杰，胡雨瑾（2004）．2003 中国奇幻文学年度精选．武汉：长江文艺出版社．

黄禄善（2003）．美国通俗小说史．南京：译林出版社．

姜淑芹（2021）．奇幻小说文类探源与中国玄幻武侠小说定位问题．西南大学学报（社会科学版），4，198－230．

梅子涵等（2008）．中国儿童文学五人谈．天津：新蕾出版社．

彭懿（1997）．西方现代幻想文学论．上海：少年儿童出版社．

谈方（2014）．奇幻文学研究的一部理论经典——评茨维坦·托多罗夫的《奇幻文学导论》．文艺理论研究，6，201－207．

陶东风（2006）．中国文学已经进入装神弄鬼时代？——由"玄幻小说"引发的一点联想．当代文坛，5，8－11．

托多罗夫，兹维坦（2015）．奇幻文学导论（方芳，译）．成都：四川大学出版社．

陀思妥耶夫斯基，费（2010a）．费·陀思妥耶夫斯基全集：第 17 卷文论（上）（白春仁，译）．石家庄：河北教育出版社．

陀思妥耶夫斯基，费（2010b）．费·陀思妥耶夫斯基全集：第 22 卷书信集（下）（郑文樾、朱逸森，译）．石家庄：河北教育出版社．

杨鹏（2006）．奇幻文学的源流．出版广角，3，11－13．

叶祝弟（2004）．奇幻小说的诞生及创作进展．小说评论，441－443．

张赟（2009）．无意义的意义之躯——对中国当代玄幻小说审美无意义的刍思．重庆三峡学院学报，5，29－35．

周淑兰（2008）．当代奇幻小说研究现状与前沿．忻州师范学院学报，3，38－41．

朱学恒（2007）．奇幻文学简介．http://bbs.tianya.cn/post-no124-114-1.shtml，03－02．

朱自强（1992）．小说童话：一种新的文学体裁．东北师大学报（哲学社会科学版），4，63－67，78．

朱自强（2009）．儿童文学概论．北京：高等教育出版社．

Baudrillard，J.（1983）．*Simulations*．New York：Semiotext(e)．

Cornwell，N.（1990）．*The Literary Fantastic: From Gothic to Postmodernism*．New York：

Harvester Wheatsheaf.

Fiske，J.(1987). *Television Culture*. London：Methuen.

Jackson,. R. (1981). *Fantasy: The Literature of Subversion*. New York：Methuen & Co. Ltd.

Manlove, C. N. (1975). *Modern Fantasy: Five Studies*. Cambridge：Cambridge University Press.

Purtill，L. (1984). Myth and Story. *J. R. R. Tolkien: Myth，Morality，and Religion*，San Francisco：Harper & Row.

Todorov，T. (1973). *The Fantastic：A Structural Approach to a Literary Genre*. Cleveland：Press of Case Western Reserve University.

Tolkien，J. R. R. (1966). *The Tolkien Reader*. New York：Ballantine.

Zahorski, K. J. & Boyer, R. H. (1982). *The Secondary Worlds of High Fantasy*. Boston：The Harvester Press Ltd.

作者简介：

孙金燕，博士，云南民族大学文学与传媒学院教授，主要研究领域为符号学、数字文化、中国现当代小说。

Author:

Sun Jinyan, Ph. D., professor of School of Literature and Media, Yunnan Minzu University. Her research mainly focuses on semiotics, digital culture, modern and contemporary Chinese literature.

Email：08yan08@163.com.

The Advocate of the "Sense of Wander": An Interview with Italian SF Writer Francesco Verso

Li Yating, Francesco Verso

Abstract: Francesco Verso is an Italian science fiction writer and publisher, devoted to enhancing the diversity of science fiction by giving voice to the underrepresented works from non-English-speaking countries. He has thereby invented the concept, Sense of Wander, which indicates that "Sense of Wonder" in SF is traveling around the world in different forms. This interview took place to shed light on his cutting-edge views through discussions about SF writers' impact on the future, contributions of non-English SF, native innovation, story selection, transmedia storytelling, and diverse worldbuilding.

Key Words: world science fiction; Francesco Verso; "Sense of Wander"; non-English SF

漫游感的倡导者：意大利科幻作家弗朗西斯科·沃尔索专访

李雅婷，弗朗西斯科·沃尔索

摘　要：意大利科幻作家与出版人弗朗西斯科·沃尔索致力传播未得到充分认识的非英语国家科幻作品，推动科幻文学的多元化发展。为此，他首次提出了科幻"漫游感"这一概念，意指科幻的"惊奇感"正以多样化的表现方式在世界各地传播。本次访谈通过讨论科幻作家对未来的影响、非英语科幻小说的贡献、各文化的本土创新、科幻故事筛选、跨媒体叙事和多元世界构建等话题，进一步探索这位"漫游感"倡导者的前沿观念。

关键词：世界科幻小说；弗朗西斯科·沃尔索；"漫游感"；非英语科幻小说

Francesco Verso is an Italian writer, translator, editor, and publisher. Since he started writing in 1996, he has published novels including *Antidoti Umani*, *E-Doll*, *Livido*, and *Bloodbusters*, in Italy, the UK, Brazil, Russia, Spain, the USA, Australia, Romania, Peru and China, winning him two Urania Awards, two Italy Awards and three Europe Awards. His novels often deal with the relationship between body and technology, in a way that oscillates between symbiosis and ambiguity, where biopolitical approaches clash with the needs of personal freedom and community expression. In addition to writing, he established Future Fiction, a publishing house and cultural association, in 2014, dedicated to world science fiction. He has published narratives from over 30 countries and 10 different languages, with authors such as James P. Kelly, Ian McDonald, Ken Liu, Xia Jia, Liu Cixin, Chen Qiufan, Olivier Paquet, Vandana Singh, Lavie Tidhar, and Fabio Fernandes. This international endeavor is a testament to Francesco Verso's vision to peer into diversified possible futures by spreading stories about the ambiguous relationship between human beings and technology, transformations of personal identity and social organization, and the encounter between humanity and the scarcity or abundance of resources. Besides, he is an active public speaker and panelist to many science fiction conventions across the world, including WorldCons, EuroCons, and Chinese SF Conventions, in pursuit of making non-English SF heard by a bigger audience.

The 34th Chinese Galaxy Awards in 2023 gave Francesco Verso the Best Promoter of Chinese Science Fiction. He launched the editorial project of the Chinese Science Fiction series and has published more than ten anthologies in English or in Italian. He also cofounded Future Fiction Workshop, a Chinese SF Writers Workshop, in Chongqing College of Mobile Communication. In some of these efforts, I worked with him, so we took an opportunity to discuss the diversity in science fiction.

Li Yating: Last year, China hosted the World Science Fiction Convention.

The grand affair provided a platform for people to talk and witness scenes, machines, and other futuristic things from sci-fi novels come into reality. How do you feel about it? Do you think SF writers have the mission to predict and influence the future?

Francesco Verso: The Science Fiction Convention in Chengdu, the WorldCon, was really a wonderful experience, which was really unique. It was setting new and higher standards for science fiction conventions across the world. For me, it was really good to be back after the problems of the pandemic. It was also a very good moment to meet international science fiction authors and to get together with the international community.

When it comes to science fiction writers, I don't think that their mission is to predict the future, but surely, they can kind of create some scenarios and try to explore possibilities. These possibilities don't have to be the reality, but they can be some alarms, some warnings, some hopes, some projected trends, things we want to avoid, or things we want to achieve. They don't have to be like the weather forecast, but very interesting risk-free scenarios as you can play out the consequences of things going bad or things going well. It is a very nice thought experiment in the sense that the things that might happen in science fiction maybe will not be true or real, but they will in a way make us understand certain priorities, values and concepts.

Li Yating: We will see many possibilities through sci-fi novels. You also brought your Future Fiction series to China. Many Chinese sci-fi stories have been translated and published by your small press, Future Fiction. As a result, your efforts made you win the Galaxy Award (China) as the Best Promoter of Chinese SF. What attracted you to Chinese SF?

Francesco Verso: It's a beautiful story actually, because the first time I came to China, it was 2017, invited by Prof. Wu Yan. The reason was that I had just published the first-ever dual-language anthology in Italian and Chinese of Chinese science fiction. It was a very strange book indeed, because the book was in Chinese, and for most of the Italian readers, that was impossible to read, but we wanted to create something special in the sense that we wanted to unite the cultures. We wanted to show that another kind of science fiction existed and was written in a language which was not English which was the dominant culture at the moment influencing every kind of science fiction everywhere. For this reason, I started to explore more and more, including all the beauty, the freshness, and innovative themes of Chinese science fiction.

Over the course of seven years, I published more than fifteen books of Chinese science fiction and two comics. I have the biggest collection of Chinese science fiction in the world, outside of China, in one single series of books. That is why for all the work that I did, I was given a Galaxy Award and called Marco Polo of science fiction. China has everything to be interesting in the sense that together with thousands of years of tradition, history, and narratives, it has now the lead in and the edge on the technological innovation, and so basically Chinese science fiction has a very privileged point of view on the future.

China is a huge country with a huge influence and huge economic power to address some of the major trends of current technological development, whether it is the aging problem, using androids or robots for helping children or old people, whether it is the smart city, the development of urban planning, whether it is a near space exploration with the geoengineering project, and whether it is the sustainable environment or sustainable economy that invests in recycling and sustainable, renewable resources. All these things have a very important platform to be experimented, deployed, and developed in China. Thus, I think that Chinese science fiction and Chinese writers have the best tools to tell these stories about the next big thing, the next fifty years, the next hundred years, and how it will be.

I'm particularly interested in stories set on planet earth and the near future. There are wider scenarios or scenarios taking place in the galaxy and other planets, but I'm more interested in what is called mundane science fiction in the sense of a very close kind of futurism to our needs, our problems, and our hopes.

Li Yating: Apart from Chinese SF, you are dedicated to spreading stories from non-English-speaking countries to achieve diversity in science fiction. Consequently, what changes have taken place? What does the world map of sci-fi look like now?

Francesco Verso: This is a very important question. This is really what started me around fifteen years ago. When I was going to the bookstores in Italy and in other countries, whenever I was going to the science fiction bookshelf, I was always finding English written science fiction, or stories that were translated from English. I asked myself—is it possible that we tell the future just from one point of view, one language, one culture, one religion, and one economy? I thought that the world was bigger than that, and that is why I started this kind of quest of trying to decolonize the future and our imagination that has been occupied by some important platforms or industries like Hollywood, Disney, Marvel, or Warner Bros. My interest went in the opposite direction. I was really curious about what was happening in Africa, in Asia, in Latin America, and in other parts of Europe. The US and the UK have already a very long history and a privileged situation, so I want to give voice to underrepresented languages and cultures that have a very important role in shaping the future, so much so that we do not talk about our future in singular, but we talk about the futures in plural.

Everybody is entitled to look at the future from their point of view with their own tools, knowledge, wisdom, history, and language. We use English as a tool to communicate, but this tool does not have to become the only way we enjoy and experience life. For example, if I go to a restaurant, it is fine that the menu is written in English, but I don't want to find just English receipts. I want to find local ingredients. I use English to understand what is there, but the ingredients must be specific to the culture. When I go to a Chinese restaurant, I can read the English menu, but I want the Chinese products. The same applies for French cuisine, Italian food, Brazilian food, or Indian food.

Over these ten years, I have developed a number of concepts. One of the most interesting is indeed the Decolonization of the Future in the sense that we have to remove a bit of the influence that we had in order just to make room and space for other narratives. The most important thing for us is, for example, to translate from other languages, not just from English. I have been to many countries like India, Russia, Peru, France, Germany, Sweden, and I always ask the editors: what language do you translate from? The answer was always English, and I think there is room for improvement.

I'm very happy that Chinese sci-fi novels have the power to propose their narratives, because when it comes to Italy which is a small country, even though we have a long history and a long tradition, and our culture is very positioned and respected, but mostly for the past, so it is difficult. When it comes to China which has a big past and a big present, then I think that the future can be channeled through these narratives in a much more efficient way, so I think I played the role in trying to give other countries the awareness that they are entitled to tell their stories from the local point of view with their languages. They don't have always to go to the English market. They can also disentangle themselves. For example, we have a very few relationships between neighboring countries, like from Italy to France, but also China and Japan, China and South Korea, so we need to communicate with each other and let science fiction go also on the horizontal way, not always go vertical to the English market.

Through the community that we are building, also in China with the Fishing Fortress Science Fiction College or the FutureCon that I began to run some years ago during the pandemic, we are trying to create a more inclusive community with people that have never been to the US or the UK science fiction convention, just because they couldn't get a visa, or they couldn't get the flight because it's very expensive. My contribution is exactly in trying to facilitate the networking and communication among non-English-speaking countries and non-English-speaking editors and to make people understand that there are much more beautiful stories happening around the world.

Li Yating: There are many splendid cultures for us to see. Apart from "Decolonization of the Future", you have coined the concept, "Sense of Wander", to allow "Sense of Wonder" to travel around the world. While working on it, have you seen differences or similarities in sci-fi stories from different countries?

Francesco Verso: The "Sense of Wander" with "a" moves from "Sense of Wonder" with "o", which means that if you consider that when there is a new device coming out, it is the same device from Beijing to Mumbai, to Rome, and to Los Angeles—if it is the same kind of car or the same kind of smartphone—but what happens is that the local conditions are very different. The infrastructure, the economic situation can be very diverse, hence local cultures change, adapt, bend, and modify the global standard of technology in order to make it useful for them. This is my idea of "Sense of Wander". Wherever you go in the world, you will see the same device but use in a slightly different manner. For instance, one thing is to have 5G in Beijing, and another thing is to have 25K or 56K in some rural parts of Italy. We need to change this because the connection is not the same, because the networking is not the same, and because you need to change the apps and stuff. You need to apply what I call "Native Innovation" as a solution.

"Native Innovation" is exactly the creativity that every culture and every person have. It emerges from your needs. You develop it with your own wisdom, taking something from your neighbor, from your school, or from the things you try. You apply this to your problems, such as how to make a solar panel, how to recycle things better, how to clean the water in your neighborhood or stuff like that. Anything can be innovative. This is what I call the "Sense of Wander" because whether you are in India, or in Germany, or in Peru, things can be very different when it comes to innovation and technology if you remove the globalized layer of international technology. Even if you have it and give it to the people, they will change it and make it their own.

Li Yating: You have already known many cultures around the world, read their science fiction and helped to have the stories published. There are also wide-ranging and increasing themes or sub-genres of science fiction. From your perspective, as a publisher, how do you see the criteria for choosing sci-fi stories? What kind of stories do you think are worth spreading?

Francesco Verso: Stories are about human nature, about our relationship with ourselves, with our community, and with the universe. These three layers of interaction between the person and what is outside the person are the basic themes of the narrative and fiction. When it comes to science fiction, I really like to see a story that deals with these themes in an innovative way, in a cutting-edge kind of style, meaning that I'm more interested in the stories that have an impact on the self, on the identity, or on our community, for example. I'm more interested in stories that enable ourselves a possibility that without technology we would not have. It is important to have the technology in the story, but it doesn't have to be like physics, astronomy, or astrophysics. It could be a simple thing. It could be the way we deal with other people. It could be a new law. It could be a kind of changing system in the economy. It can be an app. It can be anything. It doesn't have to be the idea that science fiction deals exactly with some kind of sciences, like mathematics. No, I think that the future comes with more transformation in food, in fashion, in music, in architecture, in design, in anything. It comes to biology, chemistry, and everything. That's why I call my small press Future Fiction. It is a more general idea of looking at the future, in an entire way.

A good science fiction story for me is something that understands that the present is continually transformed by humans. It's not just a new engine but a new app that brings a new language, new words, new ways of doing things, new habits, if you think about how we were living just two hundred years ago. Can you imagine the level of transformation that is everywhere in transport, in housing, in services, in our life expectancy, and in the quality of our lives? If you project that into the next fifty years, I think you will understand the importance of taking the future together. When it comes to the stories that I select, it's about these. It's about having what is called a novel— something that has to be different from the present but in a way that has consequences, and it creates waves of transformation. Besides, of course it must be localized. I like the story that represents also a connection with the past, the present, and the future. We do not write in the emptiness. We write in our social contexts. All these things are important when I choose a story. It's not simple, but I have published more than two hundred and fifty stories, so there are very good things going on.

Li Yating: You are a multitasker. Future Fiction is not only a publishing house, but a cultural association that organizes meetings, workshops, and all kinds of activities about science fiction. What inspires you to do all of these, apart from publishing and writing? Over the years, you have also been active in promoting Solarpunk, which centers on ecological responsibility and serves as a reaction to the nihilism of Cyberpunk. The future envisioned by Solarpunk seems utopian. What is your idea of approaching such a brilliant future?

Francesco Verso: I really love it. I'm really passionate about the future, and especially when it comes to communicating with the young generation or to other writers. I want to spread some positive approaches to the future. I want to use the possibilities that we now have to influence the present. For example, I'm a big promoter of Solarpunk because I think that we have the responsibility to address some issues in a positive way and to make the future better than the present. Some things are going well in some parts of the world, but for many other parts of the world, things are not going very well. When it comes to recycling, wasting, or the way the economy doesn't address the issue of nature very well, I think we need to raise our awareness and change our behaviors. Through these conventions, panels, and book fairs that I organize, I try to give a good example of how things could be done. Of course, I don't have all the answers. I don't pretend to have all the answers, but I want to give a contribution in a very practical way. When you see our books, when you see our comics, these things are there. They are real. People can read these stories. It's not just a hopeful thinking. This is a practical thing.

I have organized really hundreds of panels and tens of conventions. Putting people together will have a very positive effect, because I believe that the culture is incremental. If I have an idea, and you listen to this idea, or maybe you contribute to that, and the idea becomes stronger and better. I don't have to keep the idea for myself, and I want to share it with others, because I believe that the more people listen to good ideas, the better the ideas will become, and will have an effect on them. I take these really as a mission, like a personal mission. I travel maybe five to six countries every year. Now, I'm relatively more known and famous in science fiction, so I want to use this little power that I have to try to include other people and try to show them that there is a positive way of looking at the future. Solarpunk is one of these positive approaches to the future. Of course, there are problems, a lot of, but with these approaches, things can be done a bit better.

Li Yating: These things are practical and useful for us to make a better future. I notice that science fiction has become more popular not only in literature, but in dramas, movies, and games. There are increasing sci-fi activities as well. What do you think of these trends?

Francesco Verso: The technology brings new devices and new ways of telling stories. As I have mentioned, for example, I started just with books, and then we did e-books. Then we did comics, and then we did audiobooks. Of course, the new and most important markets are the ones related to video games and movies, but I'm not there. I don't have much connection with that, but I see that the futuristic narratives, the science fiction narratives, are being taken by these industries. There is the idea of transmedia, or cross media, so that a narrative can be adapted to another media with very good results in terms of spreading the story and reaching out to wider audience, which are using more the electronic devices or the video games, then the books, because the book is a very slow experience. It's probably an experience that will remain flat and will not grow at all while the other media are much faster, and so they are growing much more rapidly. I hope that people will not give up reading for games and movies, because we need to be slow in some experiences, and because slowness is a value.

When it comes to understanding, and when it comes to grasping concepts that are complex, there is a process of over simplification of reality. It is always the right direction that books, video games, and movies will continue to talk to each other. The most important thing is to keep the quality. The higher the quality, the better the product will be, otherwise the risk is that we are just dumping down every kind of media, with the fast accelerating experiences that are not always very good.

However, in China, at this moment, the situation is really interesting. Last time I was in Chengdu, there were a lot of talks about IP—intellectual property, so I think it is a very interesting moment to understand how to develop these industries. I think that you need to build an environment, an environment that passes through the development of mini projects, small projects, middle projects, and big blockbusters. You cannot start just from the top. You need to build a pyramid on the building blocks of many different kinds of narratives—smaller ones. The smaller ones will give you the failing and successful experience. You need to fail to understand the right direction. You cannot always avoid failing and always go for the winning, because to win, you need to lose. It's just like that. It's a natural process. I hope that the

Chinese industry will structure itself in a more diverse and complex way, building an environment that also has different approaches to how to construct this industry.

Li Yating: *Bloodbusters*, one of your award-winning novels, has found a growing audience in China. The work, which imagines a tax system based on blood, has triggered thinking about ethics and humanity. What is your take on the social fabric of the future?

Francesco Verso: *Bloodbusters* is kind of a dark story, but is also funny and humerous, because it is a bit surreal, sarcastic, and ironic. The idea is exactly about how much the individual should contribute to the wealth of the state and how much the state can ask for a contribution from an individual, so it is about the relationship that we have with our extended community. Blood is also something very deep, something very important, and something that I think in our culture—Italian and Chinese culture—is kind of the same. We need blood ties. We have food cooked with blood in Italy, and I guess also in China, so it is something in our nature. It is really one of the most intimate elements of ourselves. That's why I wanted to play with this in a kind of funny, surreal way. Let's say grotesque.

Sometimes things are getting very strange, very weird in reality, and so we need to understand that when the situation changes, we need to adapt. We need to find a way to survive or find a way to get along. We need what is called resilience to changing but being ourselves, so I think that this story can really shed some light on how much we are prepared to give of ourselves, and what is then too much, what are the limits of our contributions, and what are the limits of the service in a way. It is also a love story. There are two philosophies about blood and about participating in society that are clashing. You will see that, together with bloodbusters—government workers to levy human blood as the tax by coercive measures—there are the blood Robins who take the blood from the rich and give it to the poor. Two different philosophies are confronting themselves in this story.

Li Yating: You have written and read about many possibilities for the future. You believe that the future arrives everywhere. However, we have only one reality. How do you think of the importance of the diversity of the future?

Do you prefer stories about the near or distant future?

Francesco Verso: The answer to the first question is relativity. We have one reality, but depending on who experiences this reality, we have infinite realities. The beauty and the problem arise indeed from this confrontation. If I say "horse", you have the picture of a horse, and I have a picture of a horse, which might not be the same. We understand the concept, but we are in a way related to our culture, tradition, and wisdom. I think that is a beauty, because without this relativity, we would have just one single concept. With that single concept, we would not have any development as the development comes from looking at the things in a slightly different way. This is the reality, but what if? So, the most important tool in science fiction is exactly to question that single reality and imagine a possible alternative. This is the way the sky looks like, but what if it looked like differently? This is the gravity we have on earth, but what if it was different? All these questions that we ask ourselves will have different stories, and we will let us understand that there is one reality, but there is a bigger picture behind it—that is the projected reality that we can imagine. That's why I like science fiction.

When it comes to the second question, I definitely prefer more near-future stories, because it is already very complicated for me to understand what will happen in ten years, so I cannot possibly imagine what can happen in five hundred or ten thousand years. This is one idea. Another reason is that I really believe in the power of transformation. I really believe that if we can understand something—a concept or a reality—we can put it into our lives, transform it, and make it something that we can experience. When it comes to reading a book, I don't want to read something that happens in ten thousand years, in another galaxy, because that is so far away from me that I cannot possibly relate to that. For example, when there is a story about artificial intelligence that can make me talk to my grandfather who died, or can make me be in relationship with my daughter in another continent, or can make me a hugger through haptic technology or through hologram, I think this will really make me feel more emotionally involved and make me believe that these things could happen.

There is a concept in science fiction, which is called "Suspension of

Disbelief". This was a thought originally proposed in the nineteenth century by an English poet and philosopher called Samuel Taylor Coleridge. He said, the idea or the story is like an agreement between the writer and the reader. We know that the dragon cannot fly because of the physics, but we make an agreement—you suspend your belief and I tell you a good story. You don't always have to believe in the things I write, but you just make do with it and pretend that you are believing in me. I think this happens in fantasy, but when it comes to science fiction, I think that we should do it the other way around. The reader should not suspend his own belief. He should really try to apply his knowledge and his understanding of reality. A good book becomes wonderful when I can really make you understand and make you believe that these things could happen. That's why I prefer to read stories that have a very high probability of becoming true in ten years, or twenty years, or thirty years. I could go for it, try to make it happen, participate in the process, and accelerate these futures to become realities.

Authors:

Li Yating, lecturer of Chongqing College of Mobile Communication, MTI of China Foreign Affairs University.

Francesco Verso, a multiple-award-winning Italian science fiction writer and publisher, with representative works including *E-Doll*, *Livido*, and *Bloodbusters*.

作者简介：

李雅婷，重庆移通学院讲师，外交学院翻译硕士。

E-mail：likatrina@163.com

弗朗西斯科·沃尔索，意大利科幻作家与出版人，获得多项大奖，代表作有《电子玩偶》《继人类》《猎血人》。

Intersectionality and Decentralized Narrative: The Creative Use of the Multiverse in *Everything Everywhere All at Once*

Cai Jingjing

Abstract: *Everything Everywhere All at Once* (*EEAAO*), a production by the esteemed American indie film studio A24, encapsulates an intricate web of themes within the narrative. In this paper the film's narrative ingenuity is analyzed, notably its adept use of the concept of the multiverse, a prevalent device in contemporary storytelling. I argue that the writer/director duo, Daniel Kwan and Daniel Scheinert, have skillfully employed the multiverse to explore diverse realities beyond the primary plot, tackling immigrant community conflicts and cultural clashes with the American power structure, making it a cultural milestone in multiverse storytelling. As a metaphor for the intricate intersectional identities emerging in contemporary society, the multiverse concept illuminates the liminal and queer experiences of Evelyn and Joy as women seeking identities within patriarchal social structures. By integrating the multiverse into its decentralized narrative, the film provides insights into Hollywood's evolving landscape, and this analysis is an exploration of A24's potential role in shaping the cinematic future. Thus *EEAAO* stands not merely as a film but as a spotlight on the film industry's evolution as a medium of storytelling and representation.

Keywords: multiverse; intersectionality; decentralized narrative; movie brats; Hollywood

交叉性和去中心化叙事：《瞬息全宇宙》对多元宇宙设定的创造性运用

蔡晶晶

摘　要：《瞬息全宇宙》（*EEAAO*）由美国知名独立电影工作室 A24 出品，以融合复杂主题的叙事为鲜明特征。本文剖析了这部影片的叙述逻辑，尤其对多元宇宙这一叙事设定的熟练运用。笔者认为编导双人组丹尼尔·关和丹尼尔·施因内特巧妙运用多元宇宙这个设定，来探索移民内部存在的种族和文化冲突以及他们与美国政府之间的冲突，这标志着多元宇宙叙事迎来了新的文化里程碑。此外，影片中的多元宇宙概念也是一种隐喻，深入探讨了父权社会中女性的边缘化和酷儿经历，揭示了伊芙琳和乔伊体现的复杂交叉性身份。最后，通过阐明多元宇宙与影片"去中心化"叙事的融合，本文探讨了 A24 在塑造好莱坞电影未来中的可能作用，并指出《瞬息全宇宙》不仅仅是一部电影，更是引领行业叙事和表现形式进化的灯塔。

关键词：多元宇宙　交叉性　去中心化叙事　电影新浪潮　好莱坞

The film *Everything Everywhere All at Once*（*EEAAO*），produced by the American indie film studio A24，was released on March 25th，2022，in the United States. The storyline centers on Evelyn，a middle-aged Chinese American woman residing with her husband，Waymond，and her father，Gong Gong，who is visiting from Hong Kong，China. Together，this diasporic family runs a laundromat and encounters issues with the Internal Revenue Service（IRS）concerning their business taxes. Besides these financial challenges，the film's narrative explores Evelyn's conflicts with her rebellious queer daughter，Joy. These interconnected problems are presented within a multiversal world-building context.

After its release, the film garnered acclaim during awards seasons, setting an exceptional record of over 300 nominations and making history as the first movie to sweep the Oscars across all major categories for which it was nominated (Bates & Cunanan, 2023, p. 126). It also had a profound and no doubt lasting impact on the broader American film industry, particularly within the realm of Asian American Cinema. In this paper, I have examined how the writer/director duo comprising Daniel Kwan and Daniel Scheiner, known as the "Daniels", has skillfully employed the concept of the multiverse, a recently prevalent storytelling device in media productions, to explore diverse realities beyond the main plot. I argue that the film reveals internal conflicts within immigrant communities and their clashes with the American government, thereby making it a noteworthy cultural milestone in multiverse storytelling.

Additionally, I posit that the use of the multiverse concept serves as a metaphor to explore the liminal and queer experiences of women in a patriarchal society. I further contend that the use of the multiverse concept exposes the roots of Joy's nihilistic worldview and in so doing reveals a way out of the existential void through the practice of kindness. Lastly, by highlighting the integration of the multiverse concept with the film's decentralized narrative logic, I explore the potential role that A24, the company that produced *EEAAO*, might play within the evolving landscape of the Hollywood film industry.

I. The Narrative Device of Multiverse: Origins, Advantages, and Limitations

The cinematic concept of multiple universes, or a multiverse, featuring the juxtaposition of two or more worlds within a single film, is a narrative device that has been extensively utilized in Hollywood films since the late 20th century (Insider, 2023). In his screenwriting manual, *The Anatomy of Story*, John Truby (2008) writes that each "key story structure step ... tends to have a story world all its own", with "its own unique subworld" (p. 191). This comment presages the notion of parallel realities of the multiverse, a term Truby doesn't use although his term "subworld" indicates an alternative environment, often defined by its distinctive visual construction, regardless of its affiliation or lack thereof with the world of reference (Boillat, 2022, p. 8). As special effects technology advanced to allow for increasingly convincing portrayals of worlds other than our own, New Hollywood filmmakers, such as Steven Spielberg, began employing its affordances to make popular movies that present these other worlds. [①]

According to Boillat (2022, pp. 12 − 16), most mainstream multiverse movies are adapted from either superhero comic books or video games. The concept of multiple universes debuted in DC Comics, initially serving to extend the lifespan of franchise characters and revitalize franchise themes within DC's comic book narratives (Wallace, 2008, pp. 20 − 21). For instance, Batman, a character with a relatively fixed persona as a superhero, undergoes generative adaptations within different universes to maintain novelty. In an alternate universe depicted in *The Batman Who Laughs*, Batman merges with the Joker, thus shaping a new image of Batman as an embodiment of both heroism and villainy within this fresh universe. [②] This move, which strategically generates high expectations among audiences for this new series, has proven to be exceedingly lucrative. [③] Marvel Comics, DC's long-standing rival, is also vigorously exploring the framework of the multiverse narrative. Following the immense success of the *Avengers*, the franchise encountered a critical juncture where its momentum seemed to falter. Therefore, in "Phase 3" of its cinematic repertoire, Marvel recurrently leveraged the multiverse concept to revitalize its cinematic

---

① Multiverse themed movies include but not limited to the following: *Terminator 2: Judgment Day* (1991), *The Chronicles of Narnia: The Lion, the Witch and the Wardrobe* (2005), *Spider-Man: Into the Spider-Verse* (2018), *Doctor Strange in the Multiverse of Madness* (2022), etc.

② The Batman Who Laughs, also known as Bruce Wayne, emerges as a supervillain featured in DC Comics' American-published comic books. He serves as the primary antagonist throughout the Dark Multiverse Saga, spanning from 2017 to 2021.

③ After its successful debut in DC comics, the Batman Who Laughs made subsequent appearances in video games, board games, and was even produced by McFarlane Toys as a 5-inch Superpower figure available for sale in 2022.

universe.① For instance, in the *Avengers:Endgame* (2019), the integration of the multiverse construct spurred an entirely new cross-dimensional crisis. The cataclysmic annihilation of half the population across universes infused the franchise's storyline with renewed vigor, injecting vitality into what had begun to feel like a narrative plateau.

The utilization of the multiverse in blockbuster movies serves both practical and somewhat clichéd purposes, constituting a pivotal aspect of narrative strategy. To begin with, the concept of the multiverse can be employed to construct paradoxes and collisions, pitting protagonists against alternate versions of themselves, as demonstrated in movies like *Looper* (2012) and *Cloud Atlas* (2012), thereby adding depth to their characters. Moreover, the multiverse concept can accentuate the uniqueness of a character, depicting a scenario in which all individuals mirror their counter parts across universes except for the protagonist. This singularity serves to underscore the exceptional nature of the protagonist within the narrative, as depicted in movies like *The Matrix* (1999), in which only the Neo in this particular universe stands out as the singular and genuine savior.

The concept of the multiverse, however, often succumbs to clichés and predictability, leading films down the path of formulaic and shallow entertainment. For example, the notion of multiple universes is often seamlessly integrated as an essential narrative setting in feel-good stories. Through the establishment of multiple universes, protagonists possess the ability to traverse a single time and space endlessly, accumulating hundreds or even thousands of times more experiences than others traveling linearly through the same temporal and spatial context. This enables them to easily acquire superpowers such as foresight into the future and the ability to produce viable solutions to future challenges. For instance, in movies such as *Groundhog Day* (1993) and *Source Code* (2011), the male protagonists find themselves perpetually trapped in temporal loops owing to the existence of multiple universes. This perpetual recurrence empowers them to achieve

① Phase 3 commenced in 2016, marked by the debut of *Captain America: Civil War*, and wrapped up in 2019 with *Spider-Man:Far From Home*. Notable entries within this phase encompass the crossover films *Avengers:Infinity War* (2018) and its sequel, *Avengers:Endgame* (2019).

an almost god-like dominion over the time-space continuum they inhabit, ultimately culminating in absolute control over their environment.

In brief, relying on the multiverse setup can be seen as a convenient shortcut in storytelling. Many creators adopt it without considering the inherent constraints within this framework and its themes. In my perspective, this superficial reliance on the multiverse as a plot device can strangle the narrative itself. For instance, when using the multiverse concept to escalate action, creators often introduce a crisis spanning dimensions, as seen in the Marvel universe where half of its population is wiped out. However, this multi-dimensional destruction is often an extravaganza that lacks emotional weight for the average viewer, whose point of reference is life on Earth, so their profound emotional reactions are to crises that directly threaten this planet. This orientation is notably evident in responses to movies depicting Earth's destruction, which may evoke memories of extreme war and natural disasters experienced in their lifetimes. [①] A cross-dimensional colossal catastrophe, however, is likely to be experienced as abstract, having failed to evoke in viewers a personal association with their own anxieties. Therefore, this easy reliance on the multiverse can impose limitations that undermine the impact of the storytelling.

On the other hand, the purposeful use of the multiverse setting in the film *EEAAO* does draw the viewer into the emotional chaos of the narrative. This intentional choice is evident in the introduction of a multi-dimensional entanglement of inherently human crises at the beginning of the movie. Nevertheless, the film's true brilliance is manifested in its resolution, which centers on the mother-daughter relationship. Evelyn, as the film's protagonist, remains emotionally detached from any cross-dimensional upheaval, prioritizing her daughter above all else. This deliberate emphasis on the mother-daughter bond fosters a profound emotional connection for viewers, transcending the inadvertent clichés often found in multiverse

---

① For example, such disaster or doomsday movies that performed well at the box office as *2012* (2009), *The Day after Tomorrow* (2004), *Armageddon* (1998), *28 Weeks Later* (2007), *Doomsday* (2008), and *The Road* (2009).

59

storytelling. The next section will delve deeper into examining the intentional and innovative application of the multiverse concept within this film, particularly through the lenses of gender and cultural studies.

II. Intersectional Identity Crises Across the Multiverse in *EEAAO*

In *EEAAO*, the multiverse concept is skillfully woven into an unpredictable storyline featuring a conventional Chinese immigrant family operating a laundromat while introducing novel elements within the family drama. This integration unveils and deconstructs traditional multiverse themes, commonly found in hard science fiction contexts but featured here in the familiar context of domesticity. *EEAAO* thus notably emerges as a pioneering film that confers cultural significance upon the multiverse concept, using it metaphorically to mirror a multicultural society and encapsulate its plethora of conflicts. Among other conflicts, the film portrays tensions between Chinese American immigrants and the powerful U. S. Internal Revenue Service; intergenerational frictions within Chinese American families, highlighting the strain between Evelyn, a traditionally strict mother and Joy, her rebellious daughter; clashes arising from Joy's identity as a lesbian in a conventional Chinese family adhering to time-honored values; and the juxtaposition of women's aspirations for personal autonomy and their socialization dictating that they compromise their ambitions to fulfill familial obligations.

In the first act of the film "Everything", the primary setting unfolds within the IRS building, representing the milieu into which individuals from diverse parallel universes jump as they begin their inter-dimensional space-shifting. The IRS building stands as a symbol of the authority of the United States, while the influx of individuals from other universes mirrors the arrival of immigrants from various countries all over the world. The unique orientations and abilities exhibited by these individuals, acquired in their alternative universes, symbolize the diverse cultures of various immigrant groups. Although the IRS building itself may lack inherent cultural significance, it acts as a stage for the demonstration of the distinctive cultural perspectives of these diverse immigrant communities.

Conflicts emerge within the immigrant community, sparking further tensions between its members and the U. S. government. In response to Evelyn's attempt at tax evasion, the IRS, serving as a representation of the U. S. government, initiates action, leading to conflict between the IRS's prioritization of tax collection and her pursuit of family welfare by reducing the resources surrendered to the government. However, for the U. S. government, payment of taxes remains strictly non-negotiable with zero tolerance for prolonged delays. Therefore, during the initial phase, Evelyn's family encounters several adversarial representatives of the U. S. bureaucracy, including IRS investigator Diedre, uniformed IRS security personnel, and subsequently law enforcement officers summoned to the IRS building to apprehend Evelyn, each representing a facet of American civil service. Even the unspoken regulations governing acts of verse-jumping, to which Evelyn adhered in the initial phase, satirically critique the American bureaucratic system. Consider, for instance, the notable scene involving the Butt Plug Trophy, an award officially conferred upon Diedre by the U. S. government in recognition of her diligent efforts. It is not intended as crude humor but rather to elucidate Diedre's unwavering commitment to investigating Evelyn's family's taxes and its alignment with the criteria of the American bureaucratic promotion and incentive structure, which rewards civil servants for meticulously examining citizens' financial matters. Until the conclusion of the film, none of the focal individuals, despite having successfully executed verse-jumping, manages to elude its confines. Even Evelyn's family, after enduring myriad hardships, must return to this building in the third act, "All at Once".

From a gender studies standpoint, the initial segment of the film presents a satirical reimagining of the heroic framework established by *The Matrix*. This film's storyline follows the journey of an underachieving protagonist (Neo), who is suddenly selected by a mentor from an alternate realm (Morpheus) to save the world. Aided by his true love (Trinity), Neo confronts adversaries and progressing through a series of challenges. In this narrative structure, the less accomplished a male protagonist appears at the beginning, the greater the likelihood he will evolve into a formidable savior. The first segment of *EEAAO* parallels this narrative structure, depicting Evelyn as the least accomplished individual in the primary universe yet unexpectedly emerging as the most promising. However, just as she approaches the level of Neo, capable of superhuman feats like dodging bullets, Evelyn suddenly experiences a mental breakdown, disrupting the white male heroic narrative of *The Matrix* and exposing the disparities and obstacles faced by Evelyn as a minority female hero.

Evelyn's decline mirrors her daughter Joy's descent into darker inclinations. As Joy succumbs to the influence of Evelyn of the Alpha universe, she transforms into the formidable antagonist, Jobu Tabuka. Simultaneously, Evelyn of the IRS universe experiences a journey fraught with exploitation and indoctrination, orchestrated by Alpha Waymond and Alpha Gong Gong of the Alpha universe. Initially mentors, they impose strict limitations on Evelyn's autonomy. During her training to become the universe's savior, she is allowed to borrow superpowers but barred from fully integrating into other universes as herself. Her aspiration to embody the glamorous persona of an action movie superstar from another universe is blocked by Alpha Waymond, whose insistence on her role as the universe's savior prevents her from adopting a more appealing alternate identity. These restrictions symbolize the gender dynamics of a patriarchal society, illustrating how women are socialized to comply with men's demands that they sacrifice their individual aspirations for the benefit of the family.

It can be contended that Evelyn's emotional collapse at the end of the film's first act introduces a subtle layer of cultural and gender significance. When initially united in an ethnic conflict with a bureaucratic system, the Chinese American family members, irrespective of gender, shared the common goal of minimizing their tax liabilities. Their engagement with the bureaucratic system exposed the society's racial biases, which subjected Evelyn's family, as a minority, to unwanted scrutiny. While facing the formidable IRS, familial unity prevailed. Yet, beyond the families struggles due to their ethnicity, both Alpha Waymond and Alpha Gong Gong, assume roles as mentors and, like their counterparts in the IRS universe, impose demanding gender roles and limitations on Evelyn and Joy, the mother-daughter duo. Alpha Waymond and Alpha Gong Gong impose the role of a savior on Evelyn, while in the IRS universe, Waymond demands more time from her. At one point, Gong Gong tries to persuade her to pursue a more advantageous marriage by threatening to sever their father-daughter bond otherwise. Meanwhile, Joy's lesbian identity has either remained unrecognized or been disapproved of in the IRS universe, leading to internal conflicts in her family. Within the Alpha universe, her mother imposes intense pressures on her, resulting in severe mental distress that ultimately steers her towards assuming the persona of Jobu Tabuka, a powerful antagonist across multiple universes.

However, when Evelyn fails to meet the expectations set by these male figures, their immediate response is to eliminate her. Alpha Gong Gong, realizing that Evelyn might break free from the imposed constraints and refuse to comply with his envisioned role, prepares to shoot her, which he rationalizes as necessary to preventing Evelyn from following in Joy's footsteps in defiance of patriarchal norms. Therefore, the unified ethnic struggle in the first act tragically disintegrates, emphasizing the societal message that gender hierarchies must endure within an ethnic narrative. Thus, the narrative's complexity extends beyond facing a single adversary like the IRS as gender norms compel the family to conceal Joy's sexual orientation. Similarly, Evelyn's discontent as a beleaguered wife and laundromat proprietor is a negative factor even though the IRS is viewed by the family members as their common enemy. Nevertheless, Evelyn must defer discussions about divorce until after the tax season. Notably, although ethnic and cultural conflicts are emphasized, no issues are resolved within this Chinese American family, leading to a complete breakdown by the end of the first act.

In the second act, the primary focus of the narrative shifts to the mother-daughter duo, Evelyn and Joy. Like her daughter, Evelyn gains the ability to freely hop from one universe to another, so as the section title suggests, she can be "Everywhere". As they traverse various universes the settings become considerably more diverse. Also, while the focus of the first act was mainly on ethnic struggles, in the second act it is on the pervasiveness of gender conflicts and features some reversals of roles between protagonists and antagonists. Most notably, Joy, formerly an antagonist, unexpectedly takes on a liberating role, while Alpha Gong Gong, who previously played an authoritative mentoring role, suddenly turns into an antagonist with intentions to harm Evelyn.

It is my position that intersectional theory offers a highly effective framework for analyzing the challenges encountered by Evenly and Joy in the film. In her 1989 paper, "Demarginalizing the Intersection of Race and Sex: A Black Feminist Critique of Antidiscrimination Doctrine, Feminist Theory and Antiracist Politics", law professor and social theorist Kimberlé Williams Crenshaw coined the term "Intersectionality" to conceptualize the interconnectedness of social identities and their associated systems of domination and oppression. Intersectional theory provides a framework for examining how various identity markers, including race, class, gender identity, sexual orientation, and religion, do not function independently but cohere to form a complex source of weighted oppression.

Evelyn and Joy embody a multitude of identities, together as low-caste immigrants and women of color, and individually, Joy as a queer individual and Evelyn as a subordinate to the patriarchy (Carrillo-Vargas, 2023, p. 5). In the second act, having faced intersecting forms of tyranny, these two women come to recognize the liminality of their existence within the IRS universe, which bears some resemblance to the oppression of the queer experience (Carrillo-Vargas, 2023, pp. 4 − 5). The reappearance of the antagonist Jobu Tupaki from a different universe, as an alternate version of Joy, introduces a nihilistic and anarchic perspective. This highlights the damaging consequences of navigating an unprotected zone in a fragmented state, rendering one's identity futile. Their recourse to exploring parallel universes represents an attempt to seize the worth of their existence amidst ongoing struggles.

In this act, Joy's rebellious influence ignites a cosmic-level nihilistic ideology in Evelyn as she rebels against gender injustices across nearly every universe in which she explores the prevalent gender narratives. For instance, in the IRS universe, she boldly signs a divorce agreement with Waymond without hesitation. In the chef universe, she exposes the male chef who has cheated his way to the top with the help of a raccoon, thus, it exposes the illusion that in the male-dominated work culture men are inherently endowed to be more competitive than women. In the female action star universe, Evelyn takes the initiative to pursue the wealthy businessman Waymond, thereby challenging the traditional narrative of female stars being passively under the thumb of affluent men. In the hot dog finger universe, Evelyn reconciles with her female partner Diedre, and, for the first time, engages in an intimate same-sex relationship in which they playfully feed each other hot dog fingers.

Nevertheless, the second act "Everywhere", clearly diverges from the recurring theme of self-sacrifice found in female revenge films throughout cinematic history, in which women often resort to suicide following their acts of resistance as an escape from gender exploitation and injustice. This theme is enacted in movies like *Thelma & Louise* (1991), *Promising Young Woman* (2020), and even in the ending of *Crouching Tiger, Hidden Dragon* (2000), where female protagonists either take their lives or remain in an ambiguous state between life and death (Chan, 2004), as if these heroines are confined by a storytelling structure that leads to "liberation through self-destruction" (p. 13), a form of freedom that ultimately proves annihilating, thus preserving the theme of female victimhood. In contrast, *EEAAO* vehemently challenges and rejects this prevailing pattern of suicide in female revenge narratives.

In the film, Joy creates a cosmic black hole resembling a bagel, which gives her immense power capable of destroying the entire metauniverse. Yet, her objective isn't universal annihilation, as she initially considers using the "bagel" to end her own life. This articulates the profound despair she experiences as she descends into a nihilistic void within the cosmos, where nothing holds significance. She seeks guidance from her mother, Evelyn, hoping to discover purpose and meaning in life, but this endeavor proves futile. Eventually, overwhelmed by despair, she proposes a joint suicide with her mother.

The film then features a poignant scene set in a primordial rock universe, where two rock embodiments of Evelyn and Joy engage in a conversation on the futility of existence at a cliff'sedge, from which they both metaphorically leap, reiterating the iconic final scene in *Thelma & Louise*. But instead, after intensely arguing with Evelyn, Joy, in a despondent state, heads to the parking lot alluding to self-destructive tendencies, satirically referencing the defiant cross-country road trip and its fatal climax in *Thelma & Louise*.

But in the second act's closing scene, the action swerves to a pivotal reconciliation between mother and daughter in the parking lot. Initially yielding to Joy's decision to leave, Evelyn has a change of heart and stops her, expressing her profound attachment to Joy as her mother in their journey across myriad universes, a realization that now becomes the cornerstone of her existence. It enables her to transcend nihilism and persuading her daughter to reconcile, culminating in a heartfelt physical and emotional embrace. While this reunion might seem like a conventional ending to a "love conquers all" narrative, at a deeper level it is an exploration of the simple yet profound concept of being kind. This concept enables the two protagonists to glimpse hope and perceive positive possibilities amid their journey across the multiverse, ultimately freeing them from the constraints of cosmic-level nihilism.

III. "Be Kind" as a Solution to the Multiverse Crisis

Prior to the reconciliation between the mother and daughter, there is a pivotal scene in which Evelyn confronts a group of verse-jumpers led by Alpha Gong Gong. Both sides engage in a prolonged standoff, and the potential for a full-blown battle looms. It is during this critical moment that a lateral turn takes the viewer to the universe of action movie stars. Here, the charismatic businessman Waymond addresses this universe's version of Evelyn, a female star, with the words, "I always see the brighter side of the world, not out of naivety, but out of necessity and survival; this is my way of life." Returning to the universe housing the tax bureau, Waymond earnestly urges Evelyn and her adversaries to embrace kindness, especially in uncertain circumstances, attributing their conflicts to fear and confusion. Initially skeptical, Evelyn has an epiphany in a flashback of her long companionship with Waymond and realizes that their shared memories, despite the mundane routine of running a laundromat, hold profound significance. For Evelyn, the path to being kind leads her away from the vast potential of multiple universes and toward reconciliation with the idea of persisting in the present universe alongside Waymond, including jointly managing the laundromat and addressing their tax obligations. Embracing this direction must be wholehearted for Evelyn to genuinely exhibit kindness, as any lingering resentment would hinder her ability to do so.

The use of the multiverse setting in this film is replete with real-world significance. In particular, the film presents various scenarios as possible lives within a multiverse, much as the ways in which social media provide windows into glamorous lives in real life. In an era dominated by TikTok videos and other social media, the internet exposes viewers to countless individuals showcasing their rich and glamorous lives. Ordinary people continually witness others living apparently abundant, renowned lives with seemingly little effort, and such observations often lead them to feel unfairly treated, fostering dissatisfaction and even resentment when they reflect on their own lives. The multiverse metaphorically represents how many idealize the lives of others, prompting a fundamental question: "Why? Why am I the worst, the unluckiest version of myself in the entire universe? Why is it always me who ends up at a disadvantage?"

In the finale of *Wonder Woman 1984* , Diana Prince emphasizes the value of truth over all else, asserting that the truth alone suffices and holds beauty. This message is an endorsement of embracing the world's reality. ①
However, *EEAAO* goes beyond promoting acceptance of the beauty of the real world by guiding audiences to uncover hope and positivity amid crises and challenges, thus dispelling feelings of resentment and nihilism. In the IRS universe, Evelyn responds to the attack by Diedre, the tax agent who, manipulated by Alpha Gong Gong, has abandoned kindness with a

---

① At the end of the film, Prince Diana delivers a reassuring message: "This world was a beautiful place just as it was, and you cannot have it all. You can only have the truth. And the truth is enough. The truth is beautiful." Her message is about accepting the world as it is.

transformative speech: "You are not unlovable. There is always something to love. Even in a stupid universe where we have hot dogs for fingers, we get very good with our feet." These words trigger a pivotal moment for Diedre, who, in the hot dog finger universe forms a same-sex couple with Evelyn, reversing her sexual orientation to align with Joy's as well as their love-hate dynamic in the IRS universe. Evelyn leverages their relationship in the hot dog finger universe to influence Diedre in the IRS universe, fostering a vision of hope amidst absurdity. This portrayal illustrates that even within such surreal circumstances, love endures, fostering hope—a sentiment that persuades Diedre to ultimately choose kindness.

At this pivotal moment, a parallel event occurs. In the universe featuring the female star, wealthy businessman Waymond expresses his enduring commitment to doing taxes and running a laundromat business with Evelyn, even in an afterlife. This heartfelt confession finally resonates with Evelyn, prompting her to acknowledge the value in what others perceive as Waymond's weaknesses. Confronted with adversities, Waymond consistently adopts a "be kind" attitude, resulting in positive outcomes. This realization prompts Evelyn to recognize the profound significance of envisioning positivity amid challenges as a valuable mindset and skill. Therefore, in the film's climactic encounter, rather than resorting to violence, Evelyn employs her borrowed superpowers to awaken vulnerability within everyone's heart, thus resolving conflicts in a non-violent manner, an action that can be interpreted as an embodiment of the principle of "be kind".

Numerous scholars have analyzed the "be kind" concept in the film, contending that it effectively incorporates ancient Chinese philosophical notions, such as the Taoist principle of non-action (*wu wei*), along with significant elements reflective of Buddhism, particularly emphasizing compassion, and acceptance. For instance, Wahyudiputra and Purnomo (2022) juxtapose the portrayal of violence in the film with the principle of *wu wei*, and argue that the film can be interpreted as an allegory for the Chinese American diaspora's liminal experience in the United States, with the concept of *wu wei* serving as the film's utopian antidote to the violence of discrimination. Huynh (2022) suggests that the film embodies the Buddhist value of compassion as the appropriate lens through which to perceive life's challenges, a purely nihilistic worldview. He further explains that Western audiences often overlook the film's philosophical depth and primarily focus on its multiversal scope.

In my interpretation, the concept of "be kind" and its Chinese cultural associations mitigate the tendency of Hollywood Asian American films to include elements of brutality, which can reinforce associations of Asian culture with violence, particularly when portraying Asian characters as members of the diaspora in America (Szeto, 2011, p. 96). This connection of Asian-American culture with physical violence has been established through the incorporation of Chinese martial arts narratives into Hollywood productions, where in recent decades they have become the hallmarks of popular Asian-American films. In the 1990s the trend is represented by John Woo's filmography, including *Hard Target* (1993), *Broken Arrow* (1996), *Face/Off* (1997), and *Mission: Impossible 2* (2000). The early 2000s are exemplified by the popularity of Quentin Tarantino's *Kill Bill* duology and Ang Lee's *Crouching Tiger, Hidden Dragon*. In the late 2000s and the early mid-2010s martial arts are showcased in the *Kung Fu Panda* trilogy (Nama, 2021; Yang, 2018), and one of the most recent examples is David Leitch's *Bullet Train* (2022).

The first half of *EEAAO* adheres to the traditional formula of Asian American cinema, influenced by Hong Kong action movies. Violent elements dominate the entire first act, extending into a significant portion of the second act. We witness Evelyn developing a "heroic" persona, gaining various superpowers from different universes, and driving the plot forward through confrontations and combat, making the film highly entertaining to action fans. However, if she had continued in this direction, her daughter Joy would have inevitably spiraled into complete nihilism. Relying solely on violence would never have helped her escape the abyss of a nihilistic worldview. Only through kindness could the escalating conflicts be resolved, ultimately paving the way for reconciliation between the mother and daughter, achieved through their mutual love and kindness toward each other.

Conclusion: "Decentralized Narrative" and the Emergence of A24 Universe

To summarize the previous three sections of this analysis, in the initial section, the prevalent use of the multiverse concept as a plot device in recent Hollywood cinema was critically reviewed as overused to the point of becoming a cliché. In the second section, the intentional and artistic use of the multiverse concept in *EEAAO* to depict the conflicts with state authority and struggles against intersectional mistreatments suffered by two female protagonists was highlighted. In the third section, an analysis of the film's introduction of the concept of kindness as pivotal in guiding Evelyn and Joy along with Diedre, a heretofore hostile character, out of existential nihilism, helping them come to terms with shared traumatic experiences and suggesting a way to resolve conflicts related to ethnicity, gender, and familial dynamics.

This fourth and final section begins with an analysis of the symbolic importance of the black hole "bagel" in the film, starting with a revisit to the scene in which the mother and daughter rocks engage in a dialogue about the insignificance and folly of humanity. In this discussion, they recapitulate the early human belief that the Earth was the center of the universe, only to later realize it wasn't. Then they thought the sun was the center, only to discover that it wasn't either. The sun was just another star among trillions in the universe. This seemingly sudden discourse on humanity's limitations of understanding ties intricately into the representation of the bagel-shaped black hole formed by Jobu Tabuki, a phenomenon aligned with fundamental principles of astrophysics that govern black holes resulting from stellar collapse. [1]

Specifically, a parallel is drawn between the narrative arc that begins

---

[1] According to Félix (2017), stellar black holes (BHs) can be formed in two different ways: either through the direct collapse of a massive star, bypassing a supernova explosion, or via an explosion in a proto-neutron star. However, if the energy released in the explosion is insufficient to fully disperse the stellar envelope, a significant portion of it falls back onto the transient neutron star. This process results in the delayed development of a black hole. See Mirabel (2017).

during the film's initial act, involving Evelyn's subordination to male mentors, and stellar narratives. At this point, her narrative consistently emphasizes the need for a paternal figure (akin to a sun) to steer her within the broad context of ethnic and cultural conflicts. This narrative subtly coerces her to suppress her own aspirations, resulting in an ambiguous state of existence. Conversely, in the subsequent act, Joy, having assumed the persona of Jobu Tabaki, boldly challenges the sun-centric narrative, thus asserting the dispensability of the patriarchal figure. However, upon the removal of this paternal influence (analogous to stellar collapse in the universe), a bagel-shaped black hole emerges, symbolizing the trajectory of female retribution and suicide as protest. This metaphorical black hole engulfs all entities, including the two female protagonists, elucidating the genesis of Joy's self-destructive tendencies subsequent to assuming the identity of Jobu Tabaki.

At this point, in both the first and second acts of the movie, there is still a narrative center. Yet, like the metaverse, the film's configuration is entirely decentralized, suggesting that all problems posed in its narratives, whether governmental discrimination against ethnic minority immigrants or gender-based injustices suffered by women, should be concurrently and equitably addressed. That is, film seems to suggest that when multiple issues are resolved simultaneously, unforeseen positive outcomes may emerge. An illustrative instance is Evelyn's decision to dismantle her hard-earned Laundromat, prompting her husband, Waymond, to disclose their impending divorce, to which he attributes Evelyn's bad disposition and lack of cooperation in filing taxes, to the tax inspector, Diedre. Unexpectedly, this revelation triggers Diedre's painful memories of her own divorce experience, resulting in a shared bond of trauma between these women, which prompts Diedre to relinquish her harsh governmental persona.

Thus, a resolution to the tax evasion incident, entangled with ethnic and cultural tensions in the first act, emerges intertwined with a gender-related incident in the subsequent act. Therefore, the film's ultimate message is to not sequence issues according to some measure of priority but to address them collectively in a decentralized manner. Analogous to the concept of a multiverse, where distinctions between principal and subordinate universes disappear, the film advocates acknowledging all contradictions within a diverse society without hierarchical ordering. Only through such an approach can a diverse society authentically embody the inclusiveness essential to its unity.

In concluding this analysis, I now shift my focus toward the film's production company, A24, and examine its correlation with the prevailing trend of decentralized development within the contemporary Hollywood film industry, which closely resembles the decentralized narrative of the film. In the 2023 Academy Awards, A24's *EEAAO* surpassed such formidable competitors as Steven Spielberg's *Avatar: The Way of Water* (2022) and Darren Aronofsky's *The Whale* (2022). These two directors, whose prominence within the Hollywood directorial landscape gives them particular significance as highly influential figures, represent the Movie Brats 1.0 and 2.0 cohorts, respectively.

According to Michael Pye and Linda Myles' (1979) seminal critique, the designation "Movie Brats" characterizes a pioneering cohort of film school graduates and cinephiles who ascended to significant positions of influence by revitalizing the beleaguered Hollywood film industry during the tumultuous 1960s and 1970s. Pye and Myles specifically identify six prominent directors as exemplars of this Movie Brats cadre: Francis Coppola, George Lucas, Brian DePalma, John Milius, Martin Scorsese, and Steven Spielberg. Symbolizing the emergence of fresh talent within the New Hollywood, this cadre departed from conventional career trajectories involving the traditions of theater and literature, having instead honed their cinematic sensibilities through immersive exposure to films on television from an early age. This immersive engagement fostered a profound appreciation for film as a distinct and nuanced artistic medium, leading to their collective influence on the industry.

In the context of this discourse, I propose categorizing this first wave cohort of influential directors as Movie Brats 1.0 to distinguish them from a subsequent equally important cohort, Movie Brats 2.0, which includes such figures as Quentin Tarantino as well as directors who gained prominence through affiliations with influential industry figures like Harvey Weinstein before his fall, including Steven Soderbergh, Darren Aronofsky, and Kevin Smith. This classification highlights the evolution and diversification of cinema within the original Movie Brats' legacy, acknowledging subsequent waves of influential filmmakers who have left an indelible mark on contemporary American cinema.

The term "Movie Brats", suggesting both youth and defiance of convention, accurately characterizes these individuals. Among their shared attributes, they are deeply instrumental in the evolution of the Hollywood film industry, demonstrating adeptness in both utilizing and reshaping its revered star system while adroitly infusing their films with spectacle, often using new technologies, a trend less commonly observed in European art cinema or auteur films. Moreover, the most prominent works by these Movie Brats significantly engage with and transform American popular culture. For example, Quentin Tarantino's *Pulp Fiction* (1994), while drawing on shooting techniques previously utilized by the Coen brothers, had groundbreaking impact both on the film industry, earning the prestigious Palme d'Or at the Cannes Film Festival, a hallmark of achievement in art cinema, and on American popular culture, evident in its 136 cultural references documented on IMDb. Moreover, films by Movie Brats often exhibit both homage to and rebellion against preceding cinematic generations, fostering a substantial dedicated fan base. Lastly, the most exceptional works by Movie Brats serve to assuage the aesthetic anxieties prevalent in the Hollywood film industry. Periodically, when Hollywood filmmaking becomes ensnared in routine and cliché, a new generation of Movie Brats emerges as a rejuvenating force, offering exciting new aesthetic experiences that renew the vitality of the industry.

Therefore, I argue that the great victory of *EEAAO* at the Oscars might signify a pivotal shift in the Hollywood film industry towards the inception of the Movie Brats 3. 0 epoch. Significant in this evolution, Movie Brats 3. 0, represented by A24, established in 2012 as the latest new paradigm film studio, diverges from the individual-centric leadership of Movie Brats 1. 0 and 2. 0. Much like the conceptualization of the universe as closed system governed by a single sun has expanded to the notion of a multiverse without known boundaries, A24 departs from a focus on a single director's oeuvre to the intentional nurturing of a lineage of auteur directors. For instance, the directors of *EEAAO*, the Daniels, previously collaborated with A24 on *Swiss Army Man* (2016), which, while it might not have garnered widespread critical acclaim, was noteworthy for its whimsical narrative and imaginative elements, leading A24 to grant the Daniels a broad canvas for creative cultural critique in *EEAAO*. By supporting such exploratory originality, A24 exemplifies robust ambitions in crafting films of substantial thematic depth. *Minari* (2020) stands as a pivotal marker in A24's production of significant works centered on the experiences of American ethnic minorities, recapturing their narratives, and engaging authentically with American subcultures. This deliberate shift in thematic emphasis underscores A24's commitment to evolving cinematic discourse by presenting narratives that ambitiously expose and redefine cultural landscapes.

As a film studio, A24, has embarked on a trajectory that embraces an auteur identity as exemplified in *EEAAO*. More specifically, I posit that A24 operates as a universe of auteur directors, notably distinguished by its diversity. Among the cadre of burgeoning talents under its patronage are directors such as Josh and Benny Safdie, renowned for *Uncut Gems* (2019), and Ari Aster, celebrated for *Midsommar* (2019). Each of these directors manifests exceptional creativity while preserving a distinctive, independent voice. This collective of diverse talents represents A24's commitment to fostering a film studio as an inclusive environment, epitomizing the highly productive symbiotic relationship between auteur directors and film studios within the contemporary cinematic landscape.

References:

Bates, T., & Cunanan, D. (2023). Film Review: *Everything Everywhere All at Once* by Daniel Kwan and Daniel Scheinert. In *California Sociology Forum*, 5 (1), 126−129.

Carrillo-Vargas, D. (2023). Bridging the Fragmented Identities and Experiences of Immigrant and Queer Women of Color: A Queer Analysis of the Film *Everything Everywhere All at Once*. *UC Merced Undergraduate Research Journal*, 15 (1), 1−28.

Chan, K. (2004). The Global Return of the Wu Xia Pian (Chinese Sword-Fighting Movie):

Ang Lee's "Crouching Tiger, Hidden Dragon". *Cinema Journal*, 3–17.

Crenshaw, K. (2013). Demarginalizing the Intersection of Race and Sex: A Black Feminist Critique of Antidiscrimination Doctrine, Feminist Theory and Antiracist Politics. In *Feminist Legal Theories*, New York, NY: Routledge, 23–51.

Huynh, B. (2022). The West Misses the Point of *Everything Everywhere All at Once*-It Gets the Asian Psyche. The Guardian. Accessed 2024, January 16. https://www. theguardian. com/film/2022/may/16/everything-everywhere-all-at-once-asian-hollywood-film.

Insider, D, (2022). Hollywood's Evolving Obsession with the Multiverse. DIRECTV Insider accessed 2023, December 28. https://www. directv. com/insider/hollywoods-evolving-obsession-with-the-multiverse/

Kwanm, D. & Scheinert, D. (Directors). (2022). *Everything Everywhere All At Once* [Film]. A24.

Mirabel (2017). The formation of stellar black holes. *New Astronomy Reviews*, 78, 1–15.

Mirabel, F. (2017). The Formation of Stellar Black Holes. New Astronomy Reviews, 78, 1–15.

Pye, M. , & Myles, L. (1979). *The Movie Brats: How the Film School Generation Took Over Hollywood*. London: Faber and Faber.

Szeto, K. Y. (2011). *The Martial Arts Cinema of the Chinese Diaspora: Ang Lee, John Woo, and Jackie Chan in Hollywood*. Carbondale, Illinois: SIU Press.

Truby, J. (2008). *The Anatomy of Story: 22 Steps to Becoming a Master Storyteller*. New York, NY: Farrar, Straus and Giroux.

Wahyudiputra, A. , & Purnomo, A. R. (2022). Chinese-American Liminality in *Everything Everywhere All at Once*. *ELS Journal on Interdisciplinary Studies in Humanities*, 5 (4), 643–655. https://doi. org/10. 34050/elsjish. v5i4. 24158.

Wallace, D. (2008). *Alternate Earths*. In *The DC Comics Encyclopedia*. London: Dorling Kindersley, 20–21.

Author:

Cai Jingjing, Ph. D. in Chinese Literature, assistant professor of Chinese at Centre College in Kentucky, United States. Her research interests include Sinophone literature and culture, gender studies, film studies, and language pedagogy.

作者简介:

蔡晶晶，毕业于印第安纳大学布卢明顿分校，获得中国文学博士学位。目前在美国肯塔基州的中心学院（Centre College）担任中文助理教授。她的研究兴趣包括华语文学与文化、性别研究、电影研究和语言教学法研究。

Email: jingjing. cai@centre. edu

批评理论与实践　● ● ● ● ●

《伦敦城下之城：街道下的秘史》：挖掘被遗忘的伦敦地方意识

黄天颖

摘　要：城市的地下空间往往不被人注意，即便是在现代社会中，人与地下的接触通过各种城市交通、公共系统的发展愈发密切，但大众对城市地下的认识依旧浅薄。在以往的印象中，地下往往是阴暗、肮脏、神秘甚至恐怖的存在。但一座城市的许多历史又往往埋藏在地表之下，形成了古老、神秘的特殊文化空间。阿克罗伊德注意到了地下历史的亟待挖掘，在《伦敦城下之城：街道下的秘史》中聚焦伦敦地下，绘制了另一幅不为人知的伦敦景观。对此，本文将对该传记进行分析，考察阿克罗伊德如何通过地下探究伦敦的地方性记忆，建构书写伦敦的传统，强化大众对伦敦的认可。

关键词：城市地下　伦敦　地方意识　城市认同

London Under: The Secret History Beneath the Streets: Unearthing the Forgotten Sense of Place in London

Huang Tianying

Abstract: The underground spaces of cities often go unnoticed by people. Even in modern society, although the interaction between people and the underground has become increasingly close with the development of various urban transportation and public systems, the general understanding of the underground in cities remains shallow. In past impressions, the underground is often seen as a dark, dirty, mysterious, and even terrifying place. However, much of a city's history is often buried beneath the surface, forming ancient and mysterious cultural spaces. Ackroyd has recognized the urgent need to explore underground history. In *London Under: The Secret History Beneath the Streets*, he offers a different, lesser-known perspective of London from underground. This article will analyze this biography, examining how Ackroyd explores London's local memory through the underground, constructs the tradition of writing London, and reinforces the public's recognition of London.

Keywords: urban underground; london; sense of place; urban identity

借伦敦来探讨现当代"英国性"一直是阿克罗伊德写作的重要目的。在他的眼中，伦敦几千年来的历史以及作为英国首都的地位，让其成为以"地方"窥探整个不列颠的重要媒介。对此，阿克罗伊德十分强调具有地方意识的书写方式。从时间上看，西方当代的"地方意识"（sense of place）概念与20世纪60年代的西方环境运动密不可分。在彼时全球化浪潮兴起的背景下，全球化的发展趋势也引发了一系列社会问题，影响到政治、经济、文化、环境等多个层面。特别是跨国企业的出现，让大众对"全球性经济垄断乃至政治、文化强权"（陈红，2015，p.70）感到担忧，其中跨国企业可能引发的环境问题是大众关注的重点之一。同时，全球与地方之间的矛盾也开始显现，形成了厄休拉·海斯（Ursula K. Heise）等学者眼中的全球与地方之争（2008，pp.28-29）。

虽然学界目前对"地方意识"的概念仍没有达成共识，但地方与全球化、人与环境这两个关键含义始终存在于其概念的发展中。例如挪威哲学家阿伦·奈斯（Arne Næss，1950— ）等学者关注地方意识在与全球化对抗过程中延伸出的一种与社会现代性的对抗性精神（1989，p.144）；美国人类学家塞萨·洛（Setha Low，1948— ）给"地方意识"下定义时，强调了地方为人提供的情感意义，从文化的角度肯定了环境对人的情感和社会文化观的塑造作用（1992，p.165）。在克朗眼中，"地方"代表着一套独有的文化系统，人们通过"地方"的定位，能够找到自己的文化与情感归属（2003，p.96）。

从这一角度看，地方意识更是"一种基于自然景观并在人地频繁互动中产生的情感意识和文化意识，它凝聚了人类的个体经验、情感体验、文化积淀和价值取向"（唐子尊，2023，p. 157）。

结合上述对地方意识关键内涵的梳理，可以看到阿克罗伊德在他的作品中书写伦敦时，无不在强调这座古老城市的特质。特别是在地方传记中，阿克罗伊德无时无刻不在突出他的"伦敦视角"，强调伦敦作为一个地方的重要性，以及伦敦能够以自身辐射整个英国文化的媒介作用。那么，阿克罗伊德如何具体地在作品中对上述的核心主题进行探究，又如何在他的一系列作品中借助伦敦来实现他对现当代"英国性"的建构？

从作品内容的特点来看，阿克罗伊德无论是在历史虚构作品、人物传记还是城市传记等作品中，都在借助城市中的古物、人和景观，来展现被遗忘的城市历史或记忆，从某种程度上打破大众对伦敦的固有印象，进一步挖掘伦敦。特别是在《伦敦传》《伦敦城下之城：街道下的秘史》等城市传记中，阿克罗伊德以"城市如人体"的视角构建了伦敦的全景图，呈现伦敦丰富多彩的历史，表现出伦敦的持久生命力。

当前，学界对城市传记的这一新兴文体的研究有限，但也对城市传记特点、重要研究视角和方法进行了梳理和归纳。首先，新兴的城市传记是以城市历史为基础，经过文学处理后的一种文体（何平，2022，p. 110）。该定义反映出城市传记要在历史与文学之间寻找到平衡点，在尊重历史的前提下对史料进行一定程度的文学想象。其次，城市传记在更大程度上是一座城市独特的性格史（p. 111）。每座城市拥有自己独特的历史、文化和人文氛围，这些构成了城市独有的性格魅力，在城市传记作家的笔下，"历史不再是抽象、孤立的事件与传统，而成为鲜活、生动、有血有肉的城市形象"（芦坚强，2016，p. 75）。最后，城市传记反映出作者个人对一座城市的独有印象。城市传记在一定程度上脱离了传统的"大"历史，从微观角度书写一座城市的方方面面，这其中掺杂了作者本人在城市中的经历、日常、情感与记忆，形成了私人化的城市印象。基于上述特点，不同学者对城市传记的主要研究层面进行归纳总结，均强调了下面三个研究层面：城市记忆和地方性精神、一座城市独有的书写传统建构以及对一座城市的认同感（Geertz，1983，p. 45）。

基于阿克罗伊德在城市传记中探索伦敦的重要视角以及城市传记研究的相关特点，下文将以《伦敦城下之城：街道下的秘史》为例，分别考察阿克罗伊德如何通过地下探究伦敦的地方性记忆，建构书写伦敦的传统，并最终强化大众对伦敦的认可。

一、在被忽视的空间中探寻遗忘的伦敦记忆

探寻伦敦不为人知的一面是阿克罗伊德撰写此书的主要目的。为更好地对伦敦的地下维度进行探索，阿克罗伊德首先着力于阐明伦敦地下具有的各种特性。结合全书可以看到，伦敦的地下在空间与时间上均展现出自身独有的特性，为城市和大众提供了一个记录与想象的神秘空间。对此，下文将详细阐释在阿克罗伊德眼中，伦敦地下的时空呈现出怎样的显著特征，并对地下空间之于城市记忆和想象的作用展开更细致的讨论。

（一）伦敦地下的特性

"它（地下）是城市的影子或复制品"（Ackroyd，2011，p.2），这句话很好地展现了阿克罗伊德对伦敦地下的看法与态度，即伦敦地下与地面相互映射、互为表里，地上的活动会一定程度地反映到地下世界的变化中。基于这个观点，可以看到阿克罗伊德十分强调地下空间与地面空间的对照性。但与空间不同，地下的时间在自然规律与人类活动的作用下，呈现不同时间片段交织的杂糅状态。这种空间上的对照与时间上的无序，令地下世界藏匿了无数被遗忘的伦敦记忆，充满了未知与神秘（Bhabha，1994，pp.3-4）。

在阿克罗伊德眼中，伦敦地下是对地上世界的不完整映射，它既随着伦敦的发展产生变化，但也拥有自己的一套独立系统。这种不完整的映射，首先体现为两者在空间上的有限对照性。例如伦敦现今的街道就与被掩埋在地下的古代街道形成一定对应关系，像是"在狗岛上发现了青铜时代的轨道。盎格鲁—撒克逊时期的砾石街道沿着少女巷和短裤花园、花卉街和国王街的路线"（Ackroyd，2011，p.14）。可以看到，伦敦现有的城市街道在一定程度上继承了古代街道的空间位置，而古代的街道则又在历史的长河中被掩埋在伦敦的地下，以此与地面形成一种不完全的对照。

进一步来看，空间上的有限映射实际反映出伦敦地下处在一种杂糅且无序的时间状态。引发此类时间状态的原因，一是在过去的伦敦被破坏、挤压并被遗忘在地下的过程中，地下空间中的融合引发了时间上的混乱。譬如随着对伦敦的考古挖掘，不同时期的地穴、古墓等会出现在相近的区域。二是随着不同历史时期人类活动对地下空间的探索和干涉，原本稳定的地下空间遭到破坏，进而引发了地下时间坐标的混乱。最典型的例子当属近代修建的伦敦地铁。修建地铁不仅是一种都市现代性的体现，其在破坏了原有地下空间结构的同时，又打通不同的时间坐标，最终使得地铁线路在某种意义上还

成为能够穿越时间的重要形式。

由于地下空间与时间的上述特性，伦敦地下具有了两类重要的功能，即伦敦记忆的承载体之一，以及大众对伦敦进行想象的主要对象之一。由于伦敦地下掩埋着城市几千年以来的古物，它们多以墓地、遗骸、古代遗迹的形式存在，城市过去的记忆附着在这些古物之中，考古挖掘可以再现部分过去的城市记忆。而地下、古物、遗骸等要素的存在，使得伦敦地下天然地与恐惧、黑暗、神秘等印象形成联系，令伦敦地下成为大众印象中一种令人畏惧又好奇的存在。

（二）伦敦地下与城市的记忆

伦敦地下时空体中遍布人类的活动痕迹与遗迹，它们在历史中被掩埋于地下，又在历史的发展中不断被后人挖掘并重见天日。在阿克罗伊德眼中，伦敦的地下自远古时期就开始记录伦敦的城市记忆，为大众更好地了解伦敦提供观测点。然而，阿克罗伊德也察觉到地下时空体的特点，即地下记录的记忆注定是残缺且片段化的，并且会随着人类活动在地下的不断扩大而受到影响。对此，下文将对伦敦地下记录的城市记忆特点进行阐述，讨论地下记忆在承担着记录、储存与再现记忆功能的同时，其本身如何受到地下时空体特性的影响而使记忆呈现出片段化特征，且随着人类在地下活动的开展，地下记录的记忆又受到了怎样的影响、发生了怎样的变化。

对于伦敦地下对城市记忆的记录功能，阿克罗伊德在开篇便以"复制品"与"自身的扩张和变化规律"（Ackroyd，2011，p. 1）进行了概述，这表明伦敦地下对城市记录的储存浓缩了伦敦几千年来的时间长度，但又因地下自然活动与人类干涉等原因，其储存的记忆出现了独属于伦敦地下的特殊部分。除开这种记录功能，伦敦地下的记忆也会主动或被动地展现在伦敦大众的视野中。譬如在第二次世界大战时期，伦敦人面临德国空袭的威胁，一度大量转移到地下躲避乃至生活。这时地下空间成为一个由"隧道、交换所、掩体、隔间和更大的指挥空间"（p. 158）组成的临时社会空间，但这一空间又与19世纪伦敦地下由贫民、流浪汉等社会贫苦大众构成的回忆空间产生交集，使得躲避战火的民众接收到绝望、恶臭与死亡的回忆，导致了这一时期对政府不满情绪的激增（p. 171，p. 175）。

诚如前文所提到的，伦敦地下承载的记忆是残缺的，在多数情况下成为一种时间片段。伦敦地下记忆的重现总是以稳固的空间遭受破坏为代价的。像是中世纪时期对地下水源的开凿，近代各类管道系统的铺陈，战争时期伦敦遭受的炮火，都在一定程度上破坏了地下世界对城市记忆的保护。此外，像是地下无数的墓穴、残骸、遗迹，都在人类开发各类地下系统时遭到破坏，让人们难以激活这些古物中储存的记忆。

地下承载的记忆存在残缺性，人们在对这些记忆进行修复时，也对它们做了一定的修改与干涉，并对原本位于地下的记忆框架进行了重新建构。例如伦敦地下电网的修建，就是在用线路、管道、沟槽、地下发电站等新的人工产物不断占据地下的空间，用象征着工业科技的电流取代了远古的遗迹（Ackroyd，2011，p. 97）。最显著的一个例子是阿克罗伊德关于地铁的论述，他提到历史上日益新建并扩张的地铁线路，对伦敦地下以线条的形式进行了某种简化，让大众对伦敦地下的认知停留在地铁地图上，在某种程度上篡改了原本地下世界储存的记忆，影响了伦敦民众所接收的记忆。

（三）伦敦黑暗神话的所在之处

伦敦地下时空体的特性，又注定了伦敦地下充满了神秘与未知，不断地等待大众进行探索与挖掘。这种神秘和未知，天然地令伦敦地下成为市民的想象对象。从古到今，伦敦人对伦敦地下的想象都充斥着死亡、污秽和恐怖的色彩，但也不缺乏极富浪漫色彩的想象和符号。在阿克罗伊德眼中，伦敦人对地下世界的想象塑造了无数个关于伦敦的黑暗神话，让伦敦的阴暗面直白地展现在伦敦人的眼前。对此，下文从阿克罗伊德的视角出发，分析伦敦人对城市的地下世界进行了怎样的想象，并且这种想象在历史的发展中产生了什么样的变化，最终又构筑起了何种黑暗神话。

在阿克罗伊德的讲述中，大众对地下的固有印象与冥界、恐惧、污秽等负面印象形成了天然的绑定。从远古时期开始，在丧葬仪式和死亡文化的影响下，大众会本能地将地下世界视为死者的世界，并以此编造出不少关于地下的神话、传说，这种对地下世界的原始想象，同样发生在了古代伦敦。但阿克罗伊德也注意到地下世界在大众眼中较为积极的一面。他谈到"它（地下）也可以被视为一个安全的地方……它是外界的避风港，它是免受攻击的避难所"（p. 4）。从整个伦敦的历史来看，随着城市对地下空间的不断开发，大众对伦敦地下的固有印象也有所松动（Pleßke，2009，p. 187）。比如在 19 世纪中期，随着城市排污和循环系统的修建，阿比米尔斯泵站（Abbey Mills Pumping Station）成为地下水道系统的中心，其在当时又因特别的建筑设计风格，获得了"污水大教堂"的名号（Ackroyd，2011，p. 78）。

地下世界的两面性，在近现代的文学作品中得到了很好的呈现，令地下世界的形象进一步丰富。但从总体来看，伦敦地下的黑暗神话构成一种彼此对照又彼此互补的神话体系。伦敦的地下神话按时间可以分为古代和现代的神话，前者是神秘、充满危险、古老未知的体现，后者则是充满梦幻、浪漫想象的未来憧憬。伦敦人对地下过去与未来的想象，让伦敦地下的黑暗神话脱离了传统的刻板印象，让伦敦的地下神话成为一种能够无限延伸、不断产生新神话的有机体系。

随着伦敦人对伦敦地下的不断探索，有关伦敦的黑暗神话也在不断地修正和变化，为伦敦的黑暗神话体系持续补充着新的内容。例如前文提到的线路、地铁、轨道以及相伴发掘的墓穴、遗迹，让伦敦地下的神秘面纱有所脱落，为世人对地下黑暗神话的想象提供了重要的参照物。这一黑暗神话正如阿克罗伊德在传记末所言："地下使想象力产生敬畏和恐惧。它（地下）在一定程度上是一个人类世界，由许多代人的活动构成，但它也是原始的、非人道的……伦敦建立在黑暗之上。"（Ackroyd，2011，p. 187）

结合上文的分析可以看到，阿克罗伊德在《伦敦城下之城：街道下的秘史》中首要强调的是地下空间存储的伦敦记忆，并试图从不同的角度，对这些记忆进行解读。他首先强调了伦敦地下世界所具有的特性，将其与《伦敦传》中的城市地表空间进行区分；随后对伦敦地下记忆呈现的特点进行分析；并在最后引出十分关键的一点，即地下对伦敦黑暗神话想象的意义。通过这种书写方式，阿克罗伊德成功地树立起地下独有的形象，并让大众领略到了伦敦历史的另一种风貌。那么，阿克罗伊德在具体书写过程中又具有哪些特点？对此下文将展开具体讨论。

二、《伦敦城下之城：街道下的秘史》的书写特点

阿克罗伊德在书写地下世界时显得更加克制，这是由于地下世界的古老和未知，使得书写地下的材料和角度受到颇多限制。但作者依旧为书写城市的地下世界提供了许多重要的观测点和角度。首先，从结构上看，阿克罗伊德呼应了地下与地上的对照性特点，呈现出从"自然－人文"的书写角度与地面的城市历史发展的对应；其次，在内容上，阿克罗伊德着重强调了地下与地面的互动，以加深读者对地下世界的印象；最后，阿克罗伊德十分突出人联系地上与地下世界的媒介作用，强调了地下世界与伦敦人之间关系的密切程度。对此，下文将分别从结构、内容以及人的媒介作用出发，对《伦敦城下之城：街道下的秘史》的书写特点进行阐释和分析。

（一）从自然到人文

阿克罗伊德将《伦敦城下之城：街道下的秘史》大致分为了两个对等的部分，前半段从地质、河流等自然角度书写，中间转变为从管道、线路、地铁等人文角度的书写。这种书写方式既兼顾了大的线性叙事框架逻辑，也契合了城市发展在驱动因素上的变化，符合地下的过去与现在的各自特点。对此，下文将根据这一线索，对阿克罗伊德在此书中的书写逻辑进行具体分析和讨论。

在全书的第一章，阿克罗伊德便向读者暗示了他书写伦敦地下时采用的结构与逻辑。他首先强调了伦敦地下充满着未知、危险与神秘，将其自然状态与古代关于地下的黑暗想象进行联系，像是"它不能被清楚地或全貌地看见"、"这是一个与世隔绝的禁区"（Ackroyd，2011，p.3）、生活在地下的神话生物等，都在不断强化读者脑海中的伦敦地下，描绘那神秘又危险的天然魅力。在讲述完伦敦地下神话的一面后，阿克罗伊德转移到地下作为"浪漫之地"（p.6）的一面，开始将论述的重心放到人与地下在历史上的互动。

遵循这一书写逻辑，可以看到从第二章到第五章，阿克罗伊德撰写伦敦地下的角度重点集中在石头、地下水、河流等自然物上。从第六章至第八章，阿克罗伊德借助"水"这一要素，将笔锋转向了地下水道系统等人造物，讨论人类社会对伦敦地下的开发所产生的社会效应、给相关工作领域的民众带来的变化、对城市地面的影响。从这三章开始，阿克罗伊德将书写重心过渡到人造物与人的维度。在接下来的第九章至第十三章中，阿克罗伊德把目光聚焦在各类地下城市系统上，包括各类管道、电网、暖气设施、地铁等地下设施上，最后以近代以来大众对伦敦地下所形成的想象内容作为结尾，与第一章开篇的神秘地下世界进行了跨越时代的呼应。如此，阿克罗伊德的书写逻辑很好地体现了"自然－人文"的顺序，很好地将伦敦地下世界的变化呈现在读者面前。

此外，"自然－人文"的顺序也是历时性的书写逻辑。《伦敦城下之城：街道下的秘史》前半段主要书写自然景观，其时间大多处于伦敦的古代和中世纪时期。例如第二章"崛起"中，构成地下的重要元素——岩石成为叙述核心，这不仅是因为"城市历史的全部层次紧密地堆积在一起，形成了由粘土、砾石、木头和石头组成的块状物"（Ackroyd，2011，p.16），还因为伦敦远古人类活动遗留下的痕迹，终将以石头的形式储存在伦敦地下。因此，通过伦敦地下的石头，可以窥见久远且不曾记录的过去。这也与阿克罗伊德的《伦敦传》以"石头"为开篇进行了某种呼应。在石头之后，于石头中出现的水源成为下一个书写的要点。因此我们看到，阿克罗伊德描绘了地下水具有的神奇功效（p.35），并自然地书写到贯穿于整个地下空间中的河流，最终借着"河水"将书写的视角投向与地下河关系紧密的地上河流。土地与水构成了伦敦城出现和发展的重要基石，也在某种程度上象征着未经工业文明染指的历史。随后，阿克罗伊德的书写对象从地下的河流转移到相关的设施——地下水道，以此开始过渡到近代以来，人类在伦敦地下的活动不断深入、活动类型不断复杂、关系越发紧密的逻辑上来，从地下的角度呈现了自中世纪结束后到 20 世纪末的伦敦发展史。

（二）地上与地下的互动

除去结构上的对称性，阿克罗伊德在内容上借用地下与地面的互动，来突显伦敦地下和城市相互影响、相互对照的关系，进一步强化大众印象中的地下形象。如前文分析，随着历史的发展，地下世界的变化越来越受到地上世界的干涉，并且这种干涉的范围越来越广，强度越来越大。换言之，在两者的互动中，地下世界愈发处于一种被动状态。但是，由于地下世界的广袤和未知性，地上在干涉地下的过程中，也会在无形中受到后者的影响，发生某些变化。对此，下文将具体阐释地上与地下的互动形式是如何发生的，是否存在着某种规律，这种互动模式在阿克罗伊德的书写中如何加深了读者对地下世界的认知。

从全书来看，地下与地上的互动模式主要可以被归纳为直接与间接互动，每类互动模式又可进一步细分为记忆层面的互动与想象层面的互动。首先，地下与地上的直接互动多集中在近代以后，类似地下挖掘、建设各类地下工程设施都属于这一类互动范畴。其中，记忆层面的互动主要集中在挖掘这一行为上（Pike，2002，p.107）。例如后人对伦敦地下的众多墓穴与古代遗迹的挖掘，必然会触发过去记忆的再现，进而受到这些记忆的直接影响。阿克罗伊德甚至将挖掘时使用的机器外形比作"蹲在一具弯曲的骨架上，生者含蓄地模仿着死者"（Ackroyd，2011，p.25），并强调伦敦就是建立在"死者的骨头上"（p.25）。正如阿克罗伊德所言，诸如对墓穴等地下古物的挖掘，使得大众能够通过附着在这些古物上的记忆，在一定程度上还原与再现过去的个人记忆与社会文化记忆（Pleßke，2009，p.176）。在想象层面上，地下与地上的互动表现在目睹地下空间后产生的情感波动与联想，这反映出人类在直接接触伦敦地下后的深层心理活动，引申出阿克罗伊德对伦敦地下与神话传说之间的联系。1960 年一位旅客走访皮卡迪利（Piccadilly）大街地下后，第一时间将其形容为"就像是穿越了冥河。雾气跟着我们从街上沉下来，像冥界的溪流那般在褪色、散发着刺鼻气味的河流上方盘旋"（Ackroyd，2011，p. 84）。"冥界""褪色""刺鼻"等词语的出现，与阿克罗伊德在第一章中提到的地下世界与亡者世界的神话想象存在联系，体现出大众在与地下接触互动时的本能反应。

地下与地上的间接互动方面，主要呈现为地下的自然物，诸如石头、地下水、河流，与近代以来人类在地下的活动所引发的连锁反应，以及地上与地下之间存在的不完全映射关系。例如伦敦的地下水早就以井水、泉水等形式出现在伦敦市民的生活中。这些地下水的衍生物不仅"连接着地下与地表，更连接着现在与过去，想象与现实"（p. 31）。在想象层面，诸如伦敦中世纪居民对井神、河神的敬畏与崇拜（p. 32），或是某些河流因地理因素被冠以"犯罪和疾病的代名词"（p. 62），抑或是在文学作品中对地下世界展开天马行空的想象，都是地上与地下间接互动的重要表现。

（三）突出人在地下书写中的功能性

从结构与内容上分析完阿克罗伊德书写伦敦地下的特点后，可以发现人类在伦敦地下的书写中扮演着最为核心的角色。很多对地下历史的讲述，往往透过不同时代的人类活动与视角展开。具体来看，人在阿克罗伊德对伦敦地下的书写中具有以下几类最为显著的功能：梳理地下世界的一个重要基准点；地上历史与地下历史相互贯通的重要媒介；以及人类对地下的想象是建构和记述伦敦地下世界的重要方式之一。下文将分别从这三个角度展开讨论，分析阿克罗伊德如何利用人的活动与世界来绘制别样的伦敦地下。

无论是从结构还是从内容来看，人在《伦敦城下之城：街道下的秘史》一书中都处在"中间"的位置。人类对地下的观察、记忆、想象以及干预活动，均在不断认识、揭露和改变伦敦的地下世界。例如，古代人们将地下视为冥界的所在，便与土葬存在天然的联系。正因如此，我们可以看到大众对伦敦地下的最初认知，依据便是埋葬在伦敦之下的尸骨与地穴。地下的死者成为伦敦地下世界的重要成员，它们共同构成了这座城市地下的一部分，大众能够通过这些遗骸去重现被掩埋在伦敦地下的城市历史。

在整个伦敦的人类社会文化史中，与地下相关的历史无论是在过去还是未来，都扮演着举足轻重的角色。例如在古代，伦敦地下便与市民的祭祀史产生了关联。无论是生者对死者的祭拜，还是对神明的崇拜，大众产生敬畏的对象都源自其脚下的土地。特别是伦敦市民在过去对井的崇拜，他们相信"许多井……是神圣的"，并由此诞生了"人类历史上最初的水崇拜传统"（Ackroyd，2011，p.30）。而这些井水来自伦敦地下的空间，人们对圣水的崇拜，以及"在附近（井水）衍生出各种形式的戏剧和仪式"，本质都是大众对伦敦地下力量崇拜的移情。

最后，人对伦敦地下的想象，是人类能够突破时间和空间的限制，去试图认知并发散伦敦地下形象的重要媒介。无论是古代将伦敦地下想象成死亡之地，还是近代将地下作为恐怖、绝望的等价物，或是战争时期将地下作为庇护所，抑或是现当代科幻文学将地下视为有待探知的神秘空间，伦敦地下形象在不同的时代借助人们的想象在不断发生变化，也因此引发了伦敦大众对地下世界的兴趣。

综上，阿克罗伊德在《伦敦城下之城：街道下的秘史》的书写中参考了城市地下空间的特性，强调了如何从自然过渡到人文、突出地上与地下世界的互动关系，并着意描写了人作为连接两个世界的媒介，如何在其中发挥关键作用。总的来看，阿克罗伊德利用章节结构、书写重点以及内容的选择，将伦敦地下的历史特点、空间特质以及与大众生活的关系很好地展现出来。那么，阿克罗伊德又是如何借助对地下空间的描写来强调大众对伦敦的认同的？对此，下文将展开详细分析。

三、借助地下空间强化大众对伦敦的认同

从书写的效果来看，《伦敦城下之城：街道下的秘史》以挖掘伦敦的未知地下空间，展现伦敦作为一座千年古城的多样性、可探索性和可塑性，试图通过帮助大众深入了解伦敦地下，增进他们与伦敦之间的联系，进一步提高民众对伦敦城市形象的认可度。基于此，本节将分析阿克罗伊德如何在《伦敦城下之城：街道下的秘史》一书中引导人们去了解伦敦的未知维度，来减少现代化伦敦与城市居民之间日益增生的距离感，通过对地下的记忆和想象，从情感、观念和互动等方面加强大众对伦敦的认可。

（一）挖掘伦敦的未知维度

伦敦地下对大众而言具有天然的神秘性与未知性，它不仅是世人眼中有待继续探索的空间，也是日常被大众忽视的空间。对于这样一处压缩并记录伦敦历史的重要场所，阿克罗伊德通过《伦敦城下之城：街道下的秘史》，向大众展现了伦敦地下空间中蕴含着无穷探索的可能性，从较为少见的角度展

现了伦敦的别样风貌，以此引起大众对伦敦的探索兴趣。

阿克罗伊德为了引导大众对伦敦的地下世界产生兴趣，首先在书中树立了伦敦地下存在的广袤未知空间，强调伦敦的地下"不能被清楚地或整体地看到……是一个与世隔绝的禁区"（Ackroyd，2011，p.2）。但在对伦敦地下做出"禁区"的界定后，又结合伦敦地下的神话、怪谈和古老传说，引发大众对伦敦地下的猎奇心理，将伦敦地下形容为一个有待大众发现的神秘文化空间（Döring，2002，p.33）。在对伦敦地下的形象进行铺垫后，阿克罗伊德对伦敦考古的城市地下挖掘进行重点刻画，借助"城市的整个历史被压缩到不足30英尺"（Ackroyd，2011，p.15）这一概念，让考古工作成为探索伦敦地下的一种重要形式。无论是挖掘因爆炸暴露出的遗迹，还是对古老的地下水域展开调查，对伦敦地下全方位的考古活动不仅修复着城市的历史，更是从多维的社会文化层面向伦敦市民重现了象征伦敦起源的伦底纽姆（Londinium），展现了伦敦精神的源头。

在为伦敦的地下形象进行铺垫后，阿克罗伊德在书中全方位地展现伦敦地下所具有的魅力，即无穷无尽的多样性。对此，阿克罗伊德在书中有过一个总结性的概述，他称呼地下是一个"恐惧和危险的地方"，但也能"被视为一个安全的地方"，同时，地下对伦敦大众又是"吸引人的对象，也可能是恐惧的对象"，地下可以成为恶魔的巢穴，也能成为一位温柔的母亲，成为"外界的避风港"。（pp.3-4）这一概述很好地突出了伦敦地下具有的多样性，地下世界在人类社会中的印象会随着人类的需求而发生改变。这种类似"魔像"一样的神秘空间中存在无穷的可能性。

上述提到的地下魅力，从心理上极大地满足了大众对未知空间的探索和征服需求。在展现完伦敦地下的独特魅力后，阿克罗伊德进一步在书中暗示和引导大众继续对伦敦展开探索，展示出伦敦地下是一处藏有秘密的"闪闪发光的宝藏之地"（p.79）。这里的秘密与宝藏，更多指向伦敦地下存在的那些悬而未决的未解之谜，或者是那些被淹没在历史之中的伦敦故事，还有观察伦敦的隐藏维度等。例如伦敦一些因事故和自杀事件而出名的死亡之站（dead stations），这些地方的车站在修建时发生过严重的死亡事故，或是常有人们选择在这些地点自杀。人们对神秘死亡事件的探究，引发了对这些地铁站和地下空间的无数猜测（p.144）。这些例子均表明地下作为一处秘密和宝藏之地，等待着伦敦人继续探寻。

（二）拉近伦敦与大众之间的距离

在引导大众对伦敦重新产生兴趣后，阿克罗伊德通过展现伦敦的地下，在一定程度上减少了民众对伦敦的距离感和陌生感。自工业革命高速发展以来，伦敦的景观、文化、社会氛围在 200 多年间发生了翻天覆地的变化，特别是在当代全球化以及互联网发展以来，人与城市之间的关系不再如在古代和近代时那般紧密，人仿佛成为存活在这座钢铁巨兽上的寄生体，与冰冷的现代城市之间保持着一种冷漠、畸形的关系。

阿克罗伊德通过让大众了解伦敦地下，来消除大众对未知空间的恐惧与误解，也展现了伦敦历史与大众之间的另一种深厚关系，突显出人和城市在历史发展进程中相互不可或缺的地位，借此来减少大众与伦敦之间的距离感。下文将讨论阿克罗伊德如何具体消除人们对伦敦地下空间的误解，如何通过展现伦敦地下来拉近大众与城市之间的关系以彰显城市与人的同等重要性。

首先，伦敦的地下世界注定了城市发展的未来，比如伦敦的地质"以黏土为基础"（Ackroyd，2011，p.9），使得伦敦处于一种"慢慢下沉"（p.9）的状态。这种地质条件不仅决定了城市的建设规划，也在一定程度上影响了伦敦市民的公众行为。其次，伦敦人日常生活中使用的能源，基本取自或运输于伦敦的地下，诸如地下水、电气、天然气，伦敦人的日常生活从一开始便无法离开地下世界的供给。最后，伦敦社会的权力系统早已遍布城市地下，无论是城市地下设施的建设，还是战时整个政府与民众往地下转移，人类的活动轨迹早已深刻地烙印在地下空间中。

从日常生活方面消解大众对伦敦地下的陌生印象后，阿克罗伊德又结合伦敦地下在时间和空间上的特点，向大众证明地下世界的变化发展也在一定程度上永久改变了地面城市的空间与时间系统结构。随着历史的演进，当时间来到近现代，人们对地下世界进行挖掘与建设后，永久地改变了地下世界，并在其基础上构建了支持城市运转的重要交通和服务系统设施。由于人们对地下空间的开拓与认识，伦敦大众对地下世界的印象也迎来巨变，启发了各种浪漫化的想象，由此永远地拉近了两者之间的距离。

（三）借助想象与记忆强化大众对伦敦的认可

在引导大众重新燃起探索伦敦的兴趣，拉进大众与现代伦敦的距离后，阿克罗伊德最终借助关于地下世界的想象与过去的记忆，来强化大众对伦敦的认同感。这种认同感的建构，主要通过对大众对地下世界情感的正向引导，让大众对地下世界形成一种更加具体、客观的认知，并强调大众与地下之间存在着日益牢固的互动关系。对此，下文将从情感、观念和互动层面上，分析阿克罗伊德如何具体地完成大众对地下认同感的建立。

情感方面，阿克罗伊德试图扭转大众对地下世界的负面情感，让大众对地下世界的印象由阴暗变成充满浪漫与未知，以此产生正面的积极情感。阿克罗伊德剖析了地下世界存在的恐怖意象，包括怪物、罪犯甚至神话中的地狱等形象的根源。

在情绪上做了铺垫后，阿克罗伊德又从观念入手，让大众对地下的印象从模糊转向清晰，并解释地下与地上的互动关系，来加深大众对城市地下的认可。具体来看，阿克罗伊德将过去伦敦地下的各个形象及其来源，明确且具体地呈现在大众的视野中。比如他谈到了地下之所以被称为"隐藏的罪恶之地"的源头，与伦敦人对部分区域的社会偏见以及城市发展使得部分人流离失所有关。归根结底，伦敦大众对地下的负面认知源于他们的传统观念以及对黑暗空间的过分想象。当阿克罗伊德揭开地下的神秘面纱之后，大众会发现地下世界的真实容貌及其历史，进而对伦敦地下世界形成一个全新的认知。

改变大众的认知后，阿克罗伊德又通过强调地下世界与地上世界互为一体、二者不可分割来让大众对地下世界产生认同感。在全书中，地下世界为城市运转提供的功能、地下世界对城市历史的记录以及地下世界为城市神话构建提供的想象均被阿克罗伊德强调。通过展现地下世界对伦敦生活具有的现实意义、历史意义与文化意义，阿克罗伊德让伦敦大众意识到地下世界的重要性。

结　语

结合前文的分析，阿克罗伊德在《伦敦城下之城：街道下的秘史》一书中不断地挖掘伦敦的未知面，让大众意识到伦敦地下对城市本身的重要性，并且以此来拉近城市与民众之间的距离，让大众意识到自己已经融入伦敦城市空间的所有维度。值得注意的是，阿克罗伊德还强调了地下的浪漫属性，改善了地下世界在大众心目中的印象。

综合来看，阿克罗伊德在《伦敦城下之城：街道下的秘史》中构建了大众与伦敦地下世界的联系。其中，阿克罗伊德很好地结合了地下空间的自然属性与人文属性的特征，做到了写作逻辑上的合理。同时，阿克罗伊德在全书中十分强调人的媒介作用，借此让大众对地下世界产生归属感，并以此为基础提高大众对伦敦的认可度。

引用文献：

陈红（2015）. 文学视野中的"地方意识"——以池莉的"汉味小说"为例. 东岳论丛，

10，70—77.

何平（2022）. 城市传记何以可能? ——以叶兆言《南京传》为例. 当代文坛, 2, 108—114.

克朗, 迈克（2003）. 文化地理学（杨淑华、宋慧敏, 译）. 南京: 南京大学出版社.

芦坚强（2016）. 昆明文学的地方性研究. 昆明: 云南大学.

唐子尊（2023）. 瓦·拉斯普京小说中地方意识的建构与破坏. 当代外国文学, 1, 156—163.

Ackroyd, A. (2011). *London Under: The Secret History Beneath the Streets*. London: Vintage Books.

Bhabha, H. (1994). *The Location of Culture*. London: Routledge.

Döring, T. (2002). "Of Maps and Moles: Cultural Negotiations with the London Tube". *Anglia*, 1, 30—64.

Geertz, C. (1983). *Local Knowledge: Further Essays in Interpretive Anthropology*. New York: Basic Books.

Heise, K. U. (2008). *Sense of Place and Sense of Planet: The Environmental Imagination of the Global*. Oxford: Oxford University Press.

Low, S. M. (1992). "Symbolic Ties that Bind: Place Attachment in the Plaza". In Irwin Altman and Setha Low（Eds. ）. *Place Attachment*. New York: Plenum Press.

Naess, A. (1989). *Ecology, Community and Lifestyle*（David Rothenberg, Trans. ）. Cambridge: Cambridge University Press.

Pike, D. (2002). "Modernist Space and the Transformation of Underground London". In Pamela Gilbert（Ed. ）, *Imagined Londons*. Albany: State University of New York Press.

Pleßke, N. (2009). "London Underground. Der Grenzraum einer Metropole". In Dennis Gräf and Verena Schmöller(Eds.), *Grenzen. Konstruktionen und Bedeutungen*. Passau: Stutz.

作者简介:

黄天颖, 四川大学外国语学院讲师, 研究方向为英美城市文学与欧洲研究。

Authors:

Huang Tianying, lecturer at the College of Foreign Languages and Cultures, Sichuan University, specializing in British and American urban fiction and European study.

Email: Alfredhty@163.com

文化符号与族裔身份认同：符号域理论视角下的《接骨师之女》①

邢延娟

摘　要：谭恩美的《接骨师之女》聚焦美国华裔移民的身份认同问题。女儿的身份追索和母亲的身份宣示都表明，文化符号作为特殊的意识秩序在移民身份的构建中提供了身份族裔性言说的关键手段。在符号域理论视角下，茹灵母女各自的精神境遇俨然是文化符号在身份言说中的代言。

关键词：《接骨师之女》　文化符号　族裔身份认同　符号域

Cultural Signs and Ethnic Identity: A Semiotic Reading of *The Bonesetter's Daughter*

Xing Yanjuan

Abstract: Amy Tan's novel *The Bonesetter's Daughter* incorporates her close attention to the issue of identity of Chinese American immigrants. Ruth's seeking and Lu Ling's demonstration of identity indicate that the cultural manifestation of ethnicity is critical to individual immigrants' self-identity. It is the cultural signs that provide the key device for the ethnic writing in the novel. From the theoretical perspective of Yuri Lotman's semiosphere, a comparison of spiritual circumstance between Ruth and Lu Ling illustrates clearly the close connection between cultural signs and ethnic identity.

① 本文系国家社科基金项目"英国新马克思主义'中国智慧'文化书写研究"（21BWW017）的阶段性成果。

Keywords: *The Bonesetter's Daughter*; cultural signs; ethnic identity; semiosphere

《接骨师之女》延续了华裔作者谭恩美（Amy Tan）对华裔家庭矛盾与文化冲突的关注，是作者关于种族文化、族裔身份的思考的呈现。在国外对该作品的研究当中，"离散""归属""记忆"等关键词聚焦于华裔群体在异域语境中的生存状态与心理向度。国内文章则呈现出更多元化的理论视角，除去对身份的探讨，更多聚焦于该作品里的自传体叙事以及移民家庭中"恼人的母女关系"（Beadling，2008，p. 887）。而笔者认为用符号域理论观察文化符号对族裔身份的形成的协助与巩固作用，更能突显文化符号与族裔身份的*丝丝入扣*的关联度，从小说所呈现的母女身份对比可以看出，核心稳定的传统文化符号对于母亲的身份建构有着积极的作用；而对作为第二代华裔移民的女儿而言，传统文化符号的缺失是导致其身份困境的根源。

符号学家洛特曼强调文化场域的民族性。他指出，民族文化场域就是民族的文化符号域，它"包容着一个民族深层的思维和意识结构，如：传统的思维方式、价值观、人格和心理结构等"（郑文东，2007，p. 82）。无独有偶，对于身份认同问题，霍尔提出，"我们的文化身份反映共同的历史经验和共有的文化符码，这种经验和符码给作为'一个民族'的我们提供在实际历史变幻莫测的分化和沉浮之下的一个稳定、不变和连续的指涉和意义框架"（霍尔，2000，p. 209）。洛特曼的符号域概念与霍尔所谓的指涉和意义框架具有共通之处。霍尔提到的有关身份界说的要旨被洛特曼纳入符号与符号域关系的系统阐释之中。符号与其背后的民族文化文本承担了洛特曼意义上身份认同的实际溯源之地。从这一理论角度下审视《接骨师之女》，茹灵母女身上的身份认同征候与族裔文化符号在谭恩美的艺术笔触下呈现出独特的关联性。

一、失语的女儿：符号的缺失与身份认同焦虑

"身份"一词具有两个层面的含义，即"人格"与"认同"，因此有学者认为该词的中译应该是"主体的认同"（赵毅衡，2011，p. 345）。在《接骨师之女》的故事叙述中，女儿露丝一直在试图寻求主体的认同。从文化场域视角看，故事里的女儿露丝对"我是谁"这一身份本质问题的追索一开始就面临不同文化相互间的影响甚至干涉。露丝貌似有在异质文化场域间游走的权利。但她的境遇表明，这种权利对个体的身份建构毫无帮助。她面对着无法确定自己文化场域归属的尴尬，实际上也就悬空于特定文化场域的身份塑造力量之外。詹姆斯（William James）在《心理学原理》中曾言："如果可行，

对一个人最残忍的惩罚莫过如此：给他自由，让他在社会上逍游，却又视之如无物，完全不给他丝毫的关注。"（德波顿，2014，p. 7）露丝身份的焦虑更多是来自身处异质文化所滋生的被忽略感。

露丝身为第二代华裔移民，非同寻常的人生经历注定使她在自我身份的建构与认同上麻烦不断。一方面，"由于和中国并无直接的关联，美国华裔二代对中国文化的经验与认知主要源于移民父母的叙述"（Chen，2006，p. 99）。另一方面，"他者"境况依然是横亘在华裔群体中的一道心墙。美国标榜文化多元，但瓦斯普（WASP，White Anglo-Saxon Protestant）意识形态的核心地位并未出现根本变化。涉及华裔族群的社会及文化地位，这意味着主流社会有限的认同与接受。事实上，"在美国族裔言说范式中，华裔/美国人话语将华裔族群摆在一个矛盾的构式中，他们既是少数族裔典范，同时也是永久的他者"（Feng，2000，p. 757）。无论是茹灵还是周遭的环境，都没有对露丝产生身份建构意义上的影响。露丝既受累于美国文化场域对她的封闭与拒斥，又受累于自己对身份追索的认识与措施偏差。

被关注的渴望贯穿了露丝的一生。小说中的失语现象隐喻了露丝在身份困境中无力与无奈的挣扎。不说话既隐喻露丝的身份缺失体验，也标志着身份建构充满稚气的开始。小时候的露丝把身份建构的希望放在自己的主体性之上。最初，露丝将身份等同于不被忽略，最好是能引人关注。从滑梯上意外摔下受伤后，"露丝越是不说话，妈妈就越努力地要猜测她到底想要什么"（谭恩美，2010，p. 70）。返回学校，继续扮演惜字如金形象的露丝被同学们"当作海伦·凯勒一样来对待，仿佛她也是个百折不挠的天才"（p. 74）。想办法获得关注的身份诉求延续到成年。露丝凭一己之力举办中秋家庭聚会。"这是她头一次主持中秋节家宴。她费了好多心思做准备"（p. 82）。聚会上，她能成为焦点并扮演操盘手的角色，煞费苦心的背后同样隐藏着获得身份认同的动机。利用特定情景的支持，露丝把自我身份的感知托付给行动与期待中的关注。但谋求个人主体性把控的身份操演本身有很大的偶然性和不稳定性。一旦情景退场或操演不力，其结果注定是"损坏身份感的心理断裂"（Schechtman，2003，p. 239）。在身份动机的驱使下，露丝的行动只能算作自我身份感的刻意营造，也必将面临随时而来的烟消云散。

莱姆克（Jay L. Lemke）提出，"在现象学的范畴内，身份提供了与历史经验的联系，在符号学的范畴内，身份提供了与持久文化及社会体系中有关信仰、价值以及意义生成的操演等的联系"（Lemke，2008，p. 21）。这一见解切中了露丝身份追索存在的重大缺陷。尝试向美国主流文化靠拢是露丝寻求自我身份认同的又一维度。她期待通过个人努力与人生成功来实现自我的身份认同。为此，露丝对主流文化尽量表现出驯服与迎合的姿态。但对于她的所有努力，现实给予的反馈并不如她所愿。

一方面，职业经历没有带给她对自我价值的认同。新客户泰德暗示露丝，她作为一名职业写手不过是一个随时可以被替换的角色。虽然与别人合作完成出版的著作数目可观，但在书上，"露丝·杨这个名字总是用小字体印在主要作者后面，有时甚至根本不出现她的名字"（谭恩美，2010，p. 38）。尽管百般不甘，但妥协与退让一直都是露丝的第一选择。失意背后浸满意欲融入美国主流社会而不得的苦涩。另一方面，在自己的"准"婚姻生活里，露丝同样饱尝妥协之苦。露丝在加入亚特父女家庭之后并没有迎来家庭话语权力结构的改变。尽管全力扮演妻子与继母的角色，但家中还是真正的美国人说了算。中秋晚宴，露丝不欢迎不请自来的米利安，米利安的出现在提醒她，"过去并非完美，未来也还不能确定"（p. 82）。但在亚特心中，此事无足轻重，"不过是大家一起吃个饭罢了"（p. 81）。露丝最终"不再表示反对"（p. 82）。她宽慰自己的理由是"不想显得自己太小心眼"（p. 81）。表面的大度掩盖了身份缺失而致的内心卑微。把懊恼藏在心里也证明，露丝已习惯性地认为自己的意志很少能实现情势的改变。

最后，在长期的身份焦虑与迷茫中，露丝没有意识到母亲对自己的身份建构有何意义。露丝眼中的母亲脾气暴躁，思想固执，举止怪异，让她难以忍受。母女之间异见频出，表现出巨大的意识形态鸿沟。露丝对文字秉持实用主义的观点，她承认，"大概是因为我一直靠文字吃饭，所以只想到它们的实用性"（p. 28）。茹灵始终拥抱着文字的神圣性。在她心中，"每个汉字都包含一种思想，一种感觉，各种意义和历史，这些全都融合在这一个字里"（p. 53）。对茹灵疑似患有阿尔茨海默病一事，露丝深信核磁共振检查报告的诊断。站在工具理性的阵营里，她实在想不出母亲的健康问题与她的个人精神境遇甚至族裔文化背景有什么关联。在露丝眼中，茹灵的占卜无比荒谬，于是经常待之以轻慢的应付甚至欺骗，而且不觉得有任何不妥。分立的文化视野致使露丝与母亲的交流隔膜深重。冲突的表象后面暗涌着露丝急于向美国文化靠拢的身份认同焦灼与努力。情急之下，露丝对母亲大叫，"我是个美国人……我活着不是为了满足你的要求"（p. 138）。愤怒之中，露丝撇清与母亲族裔文化关系的迫切心情溢于言表。不时从远处传来的"雾角低鸣"隐喻了露丝明确的身份诉求与迷茫的获取途径之间的撕扯，也隐喻了露丝在身份问题上的内心混沌与哑然。令她倍感困惑的问题是"为什么她总觉得自己不属于任何人"（p. 98）。这一追问暴露了露丝的自我身份建构一直处于摸索与未完成的境况。

在移民情境下，露丝身上的"他者"标签已然是美国文化场域给出的排斥性话语区分判断，她的主观意志无从左右。这决定了在美国文化场域内，露丝无法找到可以把握的持久和安全的身份认同内容。阿皮亚（Anthony Appiah）认为，身份的内涵首先在于将个人划归入所属群体。他提出，"在社会公共话语体系中，由话语掌控的身份划分无处不在，群体依据身份归属的话语准则完成对个体的区分和确认"（2005，pp. 67-68）。个体身份建构与认同的落脚点在于特定话语体系的接纳。对于露丝来说，对美国文化的亲近与遵从也是学习意义上的，并不会换来身份的接纳。

露丝身份的表述空洞说明，信仰、价值以及意义等文化场域中的文本没有构成真正的身份塑造力量。主观努力的身份建构缺少了先天的文化滋养。究其原因，露丝的身份追索鲜有文化符号的参与，存在符号意义上的失败。作为个人与群体表达文化同一性与历史连续性的连接工具，符号的缺场致使身份及其背后深厚文化内容的再现与传承失去了载体，也就意味着身份建构实际上没有发生。作为被排斥的文化"他者"和不愿接近母亲族裔文化的异见者，露丝的身份努力"因无法与过去相勾连而伴随着本身意义的塌陷"（Chin，2000，p. 271）。

二、自言的母亲：符号再现与族裔身份的建构及认同

茹灵对自己的身份归属不曾有任何的质疑和动摇，以其母亲宝姨为支点，传统文化的塑造力量深远而整体地作用于茹灵的身份建构，影响了茹灵的一生。她的身份境遇与露丝截然不同。她出生在中国一个手工业者家庭，父亲在她出生前意外身亡，母亲也在她十四岁时含恨暴毙。尽管家道中落，生活充满苦难，但茹灵的身份建构有清晰而密集的符号参与。伍德沃德（Woodward）认为，就身份与符号的关系而言，"符号系统与'我们到底是谁'的身份意义建构息息相关"（2002，p. 76）。符号的再现为价值、意义、信仰、法则等文化内涵的诠释与界说提供了强有力的手段。威廉姆斯（Raymond Williams）把文化看作"一个能指系统，正是通过这一系统，社会秩序得以传播、复制、实践及阐释"（1981，p. 18）。这一概念被洛特曼（Lotman）在符号学的范畴内具体地转化为符号域，即"符号存在与运作的空间"（1990，p. 123）。洛特曼观念中的符号是"以实物与非实物标记的方式"（p. 42）进行文本意义表达的形式修辞。符号首先肩负存储、记忆、传输

文本意义的基本功能，充当着"文化记忆的凝结器"（p. 18）。其次，符号是文化秩序、信仰、禁忌、价值律令等的标志（pp. 102-103）。最后，符号昭示人的"精神构成（spiritual make-up），是严谨与正当生活的意义前设"（p. 42）。在文化场域内表达个人和集体在精神秩序上的整饬与文化上的安顿，这是符号功能的核心价值。符号文本意义先在的元话语性与元结构性聚合文化场域内的话语权威与意识逻辑先导，为个体的身份建构提供清晰、稳定的内容与安全的路径。可以说，在中国文化场域里，符号文本早已为茹灵框定了何为"我们"的归属性文化言说。反过来，又是通过主动操演与再现符号的方式，茹灵确立并不断宣示自己与中国文化场域紧密的归属关系。尤其在移民情境中，作为文化上的"他者"，茹灵用自己符号化的"自言自语"画地为牢，时刻彰显着自我身份的族裔性特征，坚定的故国文化归属立场与行动使自己免于了身份建构的麻烦。

小说开场茹灵就说道，"这些事我知道都是真的"（谭恩美，2010，p. 1）。这句话暗示往事在茹灵心中留下的印迹难以磨灭。小说第二部分，以回忆形式完成的故国书写记述了茹灵的苦难成长经历，也勾勒出她在中国文化场域中的身份建构过程。民族文化的符号叙事参与在茹灵的回忆中分外醒目。作为"特殊的意识秩序"（Lotman，1990，p. 48）修辞，符号铺就了她对生活的特定认知路径。

汉字叙事代表民族文化的核心内容与特征。通过汉字学习，茹灵对自我身份的审视与把握一开始就处于民族历史与文化空间的核心位置。洛特曼指出，在符号域内，"处于民族文化符号域中心地位的，最能反映民族思想，传统和价值观的文本，是最不易发生改变的。具备这一特征的文本首推民族自然语"（p. 127）。在卡西尔的观念中，"语言宛如一种精神的气氛，弥漫于人的思维与情感，直觉与概念之中"（卡西尔，1988，p. 89）。教茹灵书法时，宝姨生动描述了汉字的象形特质及其丰富意蕴。"看到这一弯吗？这是心脏的底部，血液聚集在这里，然后流到全身各处，这三点代表着两条静脉和一条大动脉，血液就是通过它们流进流出。我（茹灵）一边学着写，她一边问道，是哪位先人的心脏赋予了这个字的形状？这个字是怎么来的呢？"茹灵不解地提问："我们干嘛非知道这是谁的心？"宝姨回答，"人应该知道凡事都有个来由，来由不同，结果就不同"。（谭恩美，2010，p. 131）从字的形意关系阐释出发，宝姨传递了深植于中华民族文化中的朴素因果逻辑意识，为茹灵的意识形态刻上最初的烙印。书写规则之下，汉字蕴藏着民族集体记忆中的经验总结，也透露出清晰的民族意识形态规则。

实体意象"骨"的叙事贯穿茹灵故国书写的始终。在洛特曼的符号观中，"骨"属于典型的聚合性（具象）符号，在民族文化场域中使"描写世界的语言与被描写的世界之间具有象形特质"（白茜，2007，p.46），重在用"视知觉济言语之穷"和"立象以尽意"（龚鹏程，2005，p.87）的视觉化表达手段凝结并再现文化文本意义。首先，"骨"传达了祖先敬畏之义。祖先遗骨必须安葬，不得擅自挪动，否则必遭诅咒。宝姨家擅动祖先遗骨而致家破人亡；宝姨惨死，尸骨无寻后，茹灵的生活连遭祸乱，重复了母亲的苦难。经过个人惨剧的效验，失骨的严重后果在茹灵心中格外有说服力。因果报应之说的意识形态权威因此越发巩固。其次，"骨"也是根脉传承之义的表达。即便沦落到身无分文的境地，茹灵也不肯用手中最后一片甲骨去换一张火车票，她说，"我怎么能把它卖掉呢？这东西曾经属于我母亲，我外祖父，它是连接我跟亲人祖先的纽带"（谭恩美，2010，p.232）。辈辈传承的甲骨在茹灵的意识里已上升为可资溯源自己身份的关键物证。

此外，宝姨冤魂的凝视构成符号化的鬼魂叙事。宝姨含恨惨死后，家中随即失火，生意尽数被毁，全家人陷于困苦，应验了宝姨冤魂不散之说。因果报应之说让茹灵相信，自己摆脱不掉宝姨临死前留下的诅咒："永世不得安生，注定一辈子不开心。"（p.202）必遭惩罚的念头盘桓在茹灵心中，带给她对前设的恐惧的稳定期待。只要有不幸发生，必是宝姨冤魂显灵。鬼魂的元话语效力由此被赋予超越并凌驾于现实之上的真实性。随着现实境遇反复"佐证"，民族文化的命定之说围绕鬼魂的再现被进一步放大，以特定的意识路径规制着茹灵心中世界图景的自我描述。经历过一番磨难后，茹灵接受了诅咒的安排，对于自己未卜的前程反倒安之若素，她说，"我想明白了，这就是命，不论发生什么事，这就是我的新命运"（p.263）。

移民美国，空间位移造成与民族文化场域的脱离，昭示着茹灵身份属性的变化。她成了少数族裔，文化上的"他者"。移民背景下的个人身份有遭消解的环境与可能，这是茹灵面对的主要问题。为抵制异质文化对个人身份肆意的话语拆解或拼凑，身份族裔性的明确宣示对茹灵而言至为关键。为此，重建与故国文化场域间的联系是茹灵唯一的选择。茹灵移民后的生活表现出浓重的仪式化色彩。对于仪式化行为（ritualized behavior）的功能，洛特曼视其为文化元话语的符号化修辞形式，特定仪式的表演与行为模仿充当了加载与解码文本意义的中介。通过仪式化行为的频繁操演，远离的故国文化场域跨越时空障碍，在茹灵的生活中重新成为具有当下性的在场。茹灵对中国的占卜术态度虔诚，占卜仪式的铺开就是她邀请宝姨鬼魂进行对话，进而勾连与故国文化场域关系的重要举措。露丝误打误撞被茹灵当作宝姨鬼魂的授话人。她觉得占卜可笑荒谬，每一次丢给茹灵的只言片语要么有口无心，要么出于自己的目的，有时甚至只为戏弄母亲，但茹灵却奉之为宝姨的"神谕"。根深蒂固的因果报应思维路径与视角以此为契机延伸进现实生活，茹灵遇到的各种问题在"报应"的话语框架内被一一合理化。通过占卜的仪式复演，茹灵打开了自己的移情通道（empathic access）。"原本的心理构成获得重现；原本的信仰、价值判断以及愿景等的合法性依然被确认，并且在个体的意义决策中保持着影响力"（Cote，2002，p. 273）。各种现象的鬼魂关联背后，茹灵继续沿自己固有的意识形态中轴进行主观勾连、话语设计或诠释。威廉姆斯曾指出，"神话是一种通过复杂的信仰话语体系为世界赋义的方式。围绕神话建构的社群以神话证明并维持自身存在的意义"（Williams，1981，p. 81）。依此见解，依据神话思维展开的占卜操演对茹灵而言是一个重要的身份表征。它表明在自己的世界里，茹灵掌握界说价值、意义等的权力。

对汉字书法的勤练不辍为茹灵提供了宣示身份族裔性特征的又一有效途径。自然语的不同是异质文化场域间差别的核心表征。茹灵体会到，"写中国书法跟写英语单词完全不是一回事。思路不同，感觉也不同"（谭恩美，2010，p. 52）。因此，茹灵持续的书法练习可以被视为民族文化场域核心符号的再现操演，是带有自我身份确认的仪式性事件。伍德沃德认为，"正是通过各种形式的再现，包括语言、日常行为实践、表演以及展示，我们才标记了身份的归属"（Woodward，2002，p. 74）。在异质文化场域中，书法研习的展示在异文化环境的衬托下特征尤其鲜明，相当于一张族裔身份名片。

记忆本身构成对文化空间的复原。借故国往事的书写，茹灵实现了对故国文化场域的重访。回忆录的撰写让茹灵揭开并复演了自己内心的伤痛历程。对于当下的生活，细致入微的疼痛翻检并非多余。在多恩斯吉斯看来，回忆"虽然只是一个过往的'废墟'，但表现力强大，事关历史、文化与道德等在当下的言说"（Donskis，2009，p. 199）。如其所言，在异质文化场域中，回忆录对茹灵的身份表述意义显而易见。以记述中的符号再现为手段，茹灵在自己的视野内完成了对民族文化场域的重新梳理、盘整与存储。这一活动象征着茹灵把当下的自我依旧归入故国文化中"我们"的行列，是她明确的身份立场宣言。对茹灵来说，故国书写连同各种形式的操演构成一个自我身份宣示与保护的闭环。对于"我是谁"的身份终极追问，茹灵心中有自己的完整答案。

三、对话：身份的认同传承与意识超越

相对于茹灵稳定、清晰的自我身份认同，露丝的个人身份追索陷入主客观的"他者"化泥沼长期无解。如何脱身而出是露丝解决身份问题的关键。多年的身份追索实践与挫折让露丝逐渐意识到，贴在她身上的"他者"标签几乎与生俱来，是美国文化场域给她划出的界限。个人身份认同所需的文化归属感与安全感无法与建构在"他者"言说基础上的隔离感并存共立。露丝最终觉察到，在身份问题上，母亲拥有的正是她所欠缺和苦苦追寻的。于是露丝的身份建构发生重要转向。一方面，借助茹灵的回忆录，露丝与母亲的人生经历深入对话，由此完成了自己身份的溯源、梳理与传承。另一方面，通过对话，露丝调整了自己与亚特的关系，并以此为契机结束了自己的妥协姿态。身份意识的淡化标志着两人关系的重启与好转。在审视彼此关系未来的可能性时，身份不再构成对露丝的羁绊。

人类学家怀特指出，"全部文化（文明）依赖于符号，……正是由于符号的使用，才使得文化有可能永存不朽"（1988，pp. 31-32）。可以说，符号是个体身份建构在文化场域中最可依靠的抓手。它的缺场足以解释露丝的身份认同困境。久悬未决的身份追索迫使露丝推翻了自己之前的选择与行动，将目光转向了母亲。毕竟，同样的移民生存环境，同样的"他者"境遇，茹灵并没有受到身份问题的挟制。露丝逐渐意识到，母亲的笃定、顽固和偏执背后有更多值得深入品评的身份意义和价值。

虽然冲突频发，但露丝和茹灵的情感纽带始终不断。情感关系的坚韧暗示了母女深层情感范式的一致。这本身就是包裹在情感关系中的一条文化认同暗线。尽管露丝的身份建构蓝图是"当个美国人"，但在家庭与家族观念上，来自母亲的中国文化属性隐约可见。生活的砥砺、现实的身份挫折和茹灵无条件的情感接纳让露丝越发看清楚，自己是母亲人生经历的自然接续，是母亲故国往事推进至异国生活情境中的有机构成；自己稳定、安全、可溯源的身份归属与母亲的生活经历息息相关。在与母亲故国往事的勾连与梳理中，露丝身份建构所需的文化整体感与归属感初现轮廓。

回忆录也是茹灵留给露丝与过往生活对话的关键文献。茹灵希望露丝看看她"是怎么成长起来，又是怎么来到这个国家的"（谭恩美，2010，p. 12）。围绕典型民族文化符号的再现，回忆录的故国书写将茹灵个人的家国记忆与民族集体记忆汇集一处。随着民族符号文本释义的不断进行，茹灵为自己和露丝的身份主体理出了清晰的历史脉络。露丝最终确信，中国文化为母亲的

身份提供了背书，而自己身份的根本必须由母亲说开去。个人的身份建构最终落脚于回归母亲的家族谱系，完成民族文化符号再现与接受的传承。在对话中的文化回归宣告露丝身份追索乱局的结束。

与亚特关系的调整表征了露丝身份缺失症候的退场。中止与亚特联系暗示露丝终结自己妥协姿态的开始，是身份建构转向迈出的重要一步。对于之前在亚特父女面前的个人姿态问题，露丝做了深刻的自我检讨，"她越发看清楚，自己已经习惯了，哪怕对方不提出要求，她也会主动妥协，迎合他的感受，这已经成了自己的情感模式"（p. 284）。妥协意味着露丝必须埋藏自己的诉求，进而扮演失语的被动执行者角色。因此，成为真正意义上的平等对话参与者，拥有表达自我诉求的畅通渠道成为露丝获得自我身份认同的又一重要衡量。在露丝转向母亲寻求自我身份建构的前提下，她与亚特重启的对话具有了异质文化间对话的属性。洛特曼认为异质文化间形成真正的对话有特定的规约机制，他指出"没有符号差异的对话无意义，同样，绝对相异且相互排斥的对话也无发生的可能。因此，异文化文本间发生真正对话的基础在于二者'共同语言'的唤起"（1990，p. 143）。对于露丝和亚特而言，确立真正对话关系的"共同语言"表现在双方对身份意识的淡化直至超越。二人达成跨越身份意识樊篱的共识，存异求同，回归响应各自内心最真切的需要并彼此协商关照。在亚特面前，露丝开始摆脱因一味妥协而致的身份不安。从与亚特相识开始，"很长一段时间以来，她第一次觉得比较有安全感"（谭恩美，2010，p. 286）。亚特退出基于身份的话语主导权是他赢回露丝情感认同的关键举措。露丝毅然离开使他不再无视自己内心作祟的"他者"意识给露丝带来的身份伤害。他承认，"我明白过来自己的确是自我中心，习惯于凡事先考虑自己"（p. 304）。亚特的反思表明，以"他者"意识为话语核心的身份二元对立长期戕害着露丝所代表的少数族裔的身份感受。小说结尾处，亚特放弃对少数族裔居高临下的身份俯视，并邀露丝一道重述人与人关系超越身份意识的价值永恒；在异文化间的碰撞、理解与交融中，回到人本价值的视野内重新商讨并升华个人在彼此生活中的价值与意义担当。

结　语

身份问题的核心可以被归结为个体对自我的定义以及对自身社会角色与群体归属的认知。表征功能体现着它的重要性所在。伍德沃德认为，"身份给予人们的是存在感，并且在相当程度上满足了内心对稳定与安全的需要"（2002，p. xi）。在更抽象的层面上，身份的意义被认为关乎个体生存，它

"对于精神世界的连续性与关联性至关重要"（Lewis，2003，p. 144）。这一见解表明，有关身份的意义必定在历时的传承及共时的环境两个维度间交叉融合。迈尔瑟（Mercer）提出，"只有当处于危机中时，身份才会成为问题"（1990，p. 4）。对于移民而言，首当其冲的身份危机在于"他者"化的境遇。小说因身份而起的困扰既是移民生活境况的写照，也为移民在危机中重新思考并修正自我身份的认同提供了契机。族裔性书写在小说中对个体的身份认同意义重大。这一书写的核心内容建立在族裔文化符号的再现与诠释上。符号架起了勾连族裔文化与自我身份认同的桥梁。

《接骨师之女》中个人身份认同问题的应对本质上反映着整个华裔族群的精神境遇以及为改善这种境遇所付出的努力。对族裔身份现象，谭恩美表现出更多文化层面的关怀。在她看来，身份绝不应该成为少数族裔先天背负的原罪。相反，个人身份的认同与身份安全的维护有赖于族裔身份殊异性的明确表达与宣示。为此，谭恩美格外强调族裔文化符号对于昭示自我身份审视轨迹的途径。文化符号是个人身份有关历史文化正义性与合法性表述的有效凭借。族裔文化符号的再现与传承赋予个体克服自我身份认识盲点，梳理身份历史文化源流，勾连身份认同与家国记忆、民族情怀之间密切关联的根本依据。

引用文献：

白茜（2007）. 文化文本的意义研究——洛特曼语义观剖析. 北京：中国社会科学出版社.

德波顿，阿兰（2014）. 身份的焦虑（陈广兴，译）. 上海：上海译文出版社.

龚鹏程（2005）. 文化符号学导论. 北京：北京大学出版社.

怀特（1988）. 文化科学（曹锦清，等译）. 杭州：浙江人民出版社.

霍尔，斯图亚特（2000）. 文化身份与族裔散居. 罗钢、刘象愚. 文化研究读本. 北京：中国社会科学出版社.

卡西尔，恩斯特（1988）. 符号·神话·文化（李小兵，译）. 北京：东方出版社.

谭恩美（2010）. 接骨师之女（张坤，译）. 上海：上海译文出版社.

郑文东（2007）. 文化符号域理论研究. 武汉：武汉大学出版社.

Appiah, A. (2005). *The Ethics of Identity*. New Jersey: Princeton University Press.

Beadling, L. L. (2008). "New Visions of Community in Contemporary American Fiction: Tan, Kingsolver, Castillo, Morrison." *MFS Modern Fiction Studies*, Baltimore: Johns Hopkins University Press.

Chen. L. L. (2006). *Writing Chinese: Reshaping Chinese Cultural Identity*. New York: Palgrave MacMillan.

Chin，S.-Y.，Peter，X. F.，Josephine. D.（2000）. "Asian American Cultural Production." *Journal of Asian American Studies*，Baltimore：Johns Hopkins University Press.

Cote，J. E.，& Levine C. G.（2002）. *Identity Formation，Agency，and Culture: A Social Psychological Synthesis*. Mahwah，NJ：Lawrence Erlbaum Associates，Inc.

Donskis，L.（2009）. *Troubled Identity and the Modern World*. New York：Palgrave MacMillan.

Feng，P. X.（2000）. "Asian Americans and the Modern Imaginary." *American Quarterly*，Baltimore：Johns Hopkins University Press.

Lemke，J. L.（2008）. "Identity，Development and Desire：Critical Questions." Carmen Rosa Caldas-Coulthard and Rick Iedema. *Identity Trouble: Critical Discourse and Contested Identities*，New York：Palgrave MacMillan.

Lewis，D.（2003）. "Survival and Identity." Raymond Martin and John Barresi. *Personal Identity*. Oxford：Blackwell Publishing Ltd.

Lotman，Y. M.（1990）. *Universe of The Mind*. Trans. Ann Shukman. New York：I. B. Tauris&Co. LTD Publisher.

Mercer，K.（1990）. "Welcome to the Jungle." In Rutherford，J. *Identity，Community Culture，Difference*. London：Lawrence and Wishhart.

Schechtman，M.（2003）. "Empathies Access：The Missing Ingredient in Personal Identity." Raymond Martin and John Barresi. *Personal Identity*. Oxford：Blackwell Publishing Ltd.

Williams，R.（1981）. *Culture*. Glasgow：Fontana.

Woodward，K.（2002）. *Understanding Identity*. London：Arnold publisher.

作者简介：

邢延娟，青岛大学公共外语教育学院副教授，研究领域为英美文学与大学英语教学。

Author:

Xing Yanjuan, associate professor of School of Foreign Languages Institute, Qingdao University. Her academic interest covers the fields of British and American literature, and college English teaching.

Email：xingyanjuan@163.com

从私密走向公共：伍尔夫日记研究①

何亦可

摘　要：伍尔夫日记所折射出的不仅是她的个人世界，更是整个时代的缩影。日记一旦走出私人空间进入公共领域，参与现代文化生产和舆论空间建构，就具有了社会属性，体现了伍尔夫勇于担负起一个作家的社会责任。伍尔夫日记中的大量史料纠正了以前许多研究者认为伍尔夫不关心时事政治的看法。她将所参加的各种政治活动都通过日记记录下来，并明确表明了对这些政治事件的态度和立场，其社会批判意识也最先在日记中得以体现。首先，伍尔夫始终保持对工人阶级和劳动人民的同情，她在日记中两次集中记录和讨论伦敦工人大罢工的情况，认清了政党内部斗争丑恶的一面。其次，伍尔夫把战争给整个人类社会所带来的巨大伤害——写进了日记之中，表达了对战争的强烈控诉和批判。最后，伍尔夫考察了妇女解放运动史，还认为日记能够书写女性历史、参与重建女性文学传统。

关键词：伍尔夫日记　公共叙事　反战　女性文学传统

From Private to Public: A Study of Woolf's Diary

He Yike

Abstract: More than an individual's limited space, Woolf's diary draws a microcosm of the human world, which once moves from the private sphere into the public sphere, and is involved within the construction of

---

①　本文为教育部人文社会科学研究规划基金项目"弗吉尼亚·伍尔夫日记研究"（18YJC752009）的阶段性成果。

modern culture production and social networks. It soon takes on social attributes and illustrates that Woolf is an intellectual with conscience who is able to take her social responsibility. The archival documents in Woolf's diary reveals her slow growth from a woman who was fairly apolitical and concerned mainly with art, to an artist who realizes that art and politics are inextricably linked. Thus, it changes the view that Woolf is elite who pays no attention to the society. She records the political events and the fascinating development of her personal political thought, so that her critical awareness of politics first appears in her diary other than her other works. Woolf shows great sympathy for the working-class people in the diary, and utilizes the diary to record and discuss two great London workers' strikes, which make her recognize the dirty inside of partisan battles. Woolf is acutely conscious of the war, and she reflects upon it continually. While keeping a detailed account of the two World Wars, Woolf writes the terrible disaster the war has caused to the human beings into her diary entries, and strongly voices her criticism and indictment of the war. Woolf investigates the history of Women's Liberation Movement. She believes that diary could reconstruct and rewrite women's own history and the tradition of women's literature.

Keywords: Woolf's diary; public narration; anti-war; the tradition of women's literature

在伍尔夫的日记、书信等私人资料尚未面世之时，评论家们普遍认为她脱离现实生活、疏离下层民众，只是一名远离尘世、为艺术而艺术的作家。她的丈夫伦纳德也说她是"自亚里斯多德创造了'政治动物'一词以来，最不具有此特点的人"（伍尔夫，2001，p. 8）。伦纳德的评价对早期的伍尔夫研究影响很大，以利维斯（F. R. Leavis）教授为首的一些评论家指责她只会躲在象牙塔里借助荒诞的小说胡思乱想（1942，p. 296）。就连她的好友爱·摩·福斯特也曾评论说："如何改进这个社会，她可不愿考虑。"（1988，p. 5）随着伍尔夫研究的逐渐深入和对她以前未面世作品的不断发掘，不少学者开始从政治和社会学的角度分析伍尔夫的作品，并提出了与原来主流批评相反的观点。如亚历克斯·兹沃德林（Alex Zwerdling）认为，除了读书和创作，伍尔夫还积极参加一些自己感兴趣的社会活动。她的所有作品都具有强烈的社会性，战争、教育、性别歧视等社会问题一直是她竭力要表现的主题

（1986）。弗·詹姆逊也曾指出："对包括英国 20 世纪意识流小说家弗吉尼亚·伍尔夫在内的现代主义文学的研究，必须要在帝国主义的总体框架内，并联系帝国主义的政治、经济现象，才能够进行深入细致的探讨。"（王逢振，2004，p.189）学者们旗帜鲜明地肯定了伍尔夫作品深刻的社会现实意义，为后来的研究者开辟了一条新的思路。

　　日记是记载作者见闻和感悟的文字，要想窥知一个人的政治思想和处世态度，最直接的办法莫过于细读其日记。伍尔夫正是利用日记的实录性、持续性等特点，记录下社会历史事件以及自己的看法，她的社会批判意识也最先在日记中显现。于是伍尔夫日记不再是单纯的私人写作，而是从私密空间走向公共领域，更是通过大范围的出版，参与到了社会文化生产之中。本文将通过考察伍尔夫日记文本，从阶级冲突、暴力战争和女性主义这三个方面来考察日记的公共叙事，并探究她的社会理念，剖析她对当时英国社会生态的关注、对战争的控诉、对父权专制的批判、对妇女解放运动的重视，以及她对未来社会发展的良好愿望。

一、伍尔夫日记中对英国政党的态度

　　事实上，伍尔夫一直处于英国社会政治旋涡的中心。她的丈夫伦纳德是当时著名的政论家和社会活动家，曾在妇女合作社、费边社、工党关于帝国和外交事务咨询委员会，以及公务员仲裁法庭等组织和机构工作多年。在伦纳德的影响和带动下，伍尔夫参与社会政治活动的热情逐渐高涨。但她并不像伦纳德那样具有坚定的左翼政治倾向，她虽不属于任何政党派系，但有自己明确和坚定的政治信念。伍尔夫经常随丈夫参加各种集会、政治演讲，与一些党派的关键人物一起进餐交流，获得第一手的政治信息，因此她对政治时局非常熟悉。伍尔夫经常接触的有费边社的核心成员韦伯夫妇[①]、萧伯纳等。1915 年伍尔夫旁听了由费边社在埃塞克斯大厅（Essex Hall）举办的题为"和平的条件"（The Conditions of Peace）的会议，之后在日记中表达了想加入费边社的愿望。1918 年 5 月 1 日，伍尔夫夫妇与韦伯夫妇一起用餐，席间结识了卡米勒·胡斯曼[②]，他们就人民与政治等话题进行了广泛深入的交谈（Woolf，1977b，p.145）。虽然伍尔夫与费边社成员交往密切，但她并

---

　　① 锡德尼·韦伯（Sidney Webb，1859—1947）和贝特丽丝·韦伯（Beatrice Webb，1858—1943），英国社会改革学家，共同创办《新政治家周刊》。他们和伦纳德在费边社共事多年。

　　② 卡米勒·胡斯曼（Camille Huysmans，1871—1968），比利时社会主义作家，社会主义领导人。

没有不加甄别地盲目接受费边社的理念，而是持批判或保留的态度。随着对费边社和工党的日益了解，她感到费边社的改良社会主义理念是她无法接受的。通过分析伍尔夫的日记，我们可以发现，她在日记中隐晦地表达了这种看法和态度，1917 年 11 月 11 日，伍尔夫通过韦伯夫妇结识了 R. H. 托尼[①]和他的妻子。席间他们探讨战后重建的问题，伍尔夫描述了这次交谈的过程：

> 他们来之前，我被告知托尼夫妇是理想主义者。当我接触了之后，我认为他是个一嘴黑牙的理想主义者。这是我吃过最糟心的一顿饭，韦伯夫人一坐下就高谈阔论，详细讲解她参与的战后重建协会。席间她一口一个"协会"，目前她建立了婴儿协会、残疾人协会、精神病患者协会等无数个协会，并且还打算继续。我全程缄默，午饭过后，我们迅速离开了。（Woolf，1977b，p.74）

显然，伍尔夫对这对"理想主义者"夫妇的观点不感兴趣。费边社反对社会革命，主张以改良的形式实现社会主义。虽然伍尔夫肯定了费边社务实的社会建设和互助互爱的社会服务，但她也清晰地看出费边社的改良社会主义理念只不过是"有教养"的资产阶级的幻想。事实证明，费边社对英国工业和工会运动起了负面的作用。伍尔夫在日记中以戏谑的语气调侃他们，从他们身上看到社会改良主义的弊端，于是放弃了加入费边社的打算。

尽管伍尔夫属于英国上流阶层，但她对上流阶层的自私贪婪和骄奢淫逸极为不满，并始终保持对工人阶级的同情，持续关注他们的命运。她在日记中详细记录并讨论了两次伦敦工人大罢工的情况。1919 年 9 月 27 日到 10 月 6 日，英国全国铁路系统员工大罢工，包括矿工、邮递员等都参加了这场声势浩大的工人运动。伍尔夫对工人阶级发动的罢工运动表示同情，她在那几天的日记中一直都在密切关注这一事件的发展。1926 年 5 月 5 日至 5 月 13 日，伍尔夫追踪记述了英国第二次总罢工的情况[②]，这次罢工暴露出英国工人阶级与资产阶级之间不可调和的矛盾。她在连续 8 篇关于工人罢工的日记中表达了对工人的同情，以及对罢工中各股政治势力的看法。5 月 6 日，伍

---

① R. H. 托尼（Richard Henry Tawney，1880—1962），英国著名历史经济学家、教育家，曾任工人教育协会的主席。

② 各工会执行委员会（Trades Union Congress）的代表会议于 5 月 1 日通过举行总罢工的决议。5 月 12 日，工会代表大会总理事会宣布停止总罢工。此后，矿工又单独坚持罢工近 7 个月之久。

尔夫在日记里描写了伦敦工业区萧条的场景："漫步滨河区，看到运货车里挤满了老人和女孩，他们像是站在三等车厢。小孩们到处乱跑。商铺开着却没有人，那里给人整个印象是阴沉压抑。"（1977b，p. 80）当时的英国保守党领袖鲍德温坚决抵制和破坏罢工，拒绝与工会进行任何接触。伍尔夫在日记中表达了对鲍德温政府的不满，7日听完鲍德温的演讲后，伍尔夫在日记中写道："首相的讲话令人印象深刻，却丝毫无法引起我的崇拜和支持。我一想到那些将世界扛在肩上的被压迫的劳工们，就觉得他的那股子自负有点可笑。他变成了自大狂。我是不会相信他的。"[①]（p. 81）伍尔夫夫妇态度鲜明地支持工人罢工，但右翼势力的破坏最终导致罢工失败，这让伍尔夫对当时的政府感到十分失望。

或许从大罢工开始，伍尔夫就认清了政党内部斗争的丑陋面貌，并对这场斗争感到无望。杰西卡·伯曼（Jessica Berman）认为后期伍尔夫之所以与工党和费边社拉开距离，"是因为二者没能完全致力反帝国主义、和平事业和妇女解放运动"（2001，p. 109）。1931年，以拉姆齐·麦克唐纳为首的工党与保守党和自由党组成联合政府，并另组国民工党，导致与独立工党关系决裂。而当时的费边社在内阁中的影响降低，只能靠工会联盟的资助运作。伍尔夫认为工会联盟以男性为中心，对妇女运动的支持不够，因此逐渐远离二者。更重要的是，工党领袖在两次世界大战中推行绥靖政策，对纳粹德国采取妥协安抚的态度，从而助长了德国的侵略欲望和军事扩张野心，这让伍尔夫彻底失望。[②] 在《伯爵的侄女》一文中，伍尔夫指出："不同等级之间也许并无敌意，但也没有交流。我们被圈围、被分隔、被断绝。"（2001，pp. 425－426）英国社会各个阶级之间的交流受阻，导致产生很多社会问题。她所希望实现的理想是："再过大约一个世纪，所有这些阶级差别都可能不再有什么意义……人与人之间只剩下头脑和性格等方面的自然差别。"（p. 429）因此她建议成立以"所有的男人和女人的公正、平等和自由为目标"的"局外人"协会，它游离在所有政党之外，"不会有办公室，不会有委员会，不会有秘书；它不召开什么会议，也不举行正式大会"（p. 1137）。伍尔夫希望在这个"局外人"协会中，不同国别、不同阶层、不同性别的人能够互助合作、和平友爱，实现她所向往的世界主义。

---

① 鲍德温在广播里说："请相信我，因为18个月前你们把票投给了我。我做了什么失去了你们的信任？请相信我会做出公正的决断。"

② 麦克唐纳于1911年出任国会工党主席，但由于持反战立场，最终因1914年爆发第一次世界大战而宣布辞任主席，鲍德温在1939年大战爆发之前，没有做充足的军事准备。

二、伍尔夫日记中的反战意识

伍尔夫在短暂的一生中经历了两次世界大战的浩劫，她的很多亲友在战争中殒命，这些残酷的事实给她精神上以巨大的打击，她把战争给整个人类所带来的巨大灾难一一写进了日记中，表达了对战争罪恶的强烈控诉、对和平的向往以及对百姓的无限同情。

从 1915 年到 1941 年，伍尔夫日记中的反战意识逐步增强。自 1914 年一战爆发之后到 1916 年之间①，日记鲜少提及战争，直到 1917 年战火蔓延到英伦三岛，她才亲身体验到战争的无情和残酷。卡伦（Levenback）指出，"这是因为伍尔夫作为一名普通民众，对主战场不在英国的一战只能通过媒体来了解前线的战况，所以不会有直观的感受"（1999，p. 12），直到她目睹了战争对人身财产造成的巨大损害，才会油然升起"一股爱国之情"（Woolf，1977b，p. 5）。尤其是当得知身边朋友，如儿时的伙伴鲁伯特·布鲁克（Rupert Brooke，1887—1915）在一战中阵亡的消息时，她感到十分痛心，"布鲁克的死直接将战争幻象转变为现实"（Levenback，1999，p. 13）。日记恰恰是伍尔夫在真正经受了战争伤害之后所记录下的真实感悟，她在之后日记中对战况的记录也逐渐增多，例如 1917 年 10 月 22 日，她描述了伦敦街头被袭击的景象："皮卡迪利大街被炸出一个大洞，商铺的玻璃被震碎，妇女们四散逃跑"；1918 年 1 月 29 日："听到邱园有轰炸声，9 个人被杀害了"；1918 年 3 月 9 日："夜晚 11 点半，听到空袭和枪声，击中了外面的公交车，我们迅速躲到了厨房里"。除此之外日记还为小说写作提供素材，例如伍尔夫将 1918 年 1 月 3 日所描述的一个细节："我们不得不在地窖里用餐，外面都是枪声"（Woolf，1977b，p. 65，p. 116，p. 124，p. 93），经过改编融入《岁月》的"1917 年"这一章节里。

一战之后，伍尔夫敏感地意识到战争远远没有结束，战争给人民造成的创伤会很快显现出来。1919 年 7 月 19 日，庆祝战争胜利的活动在全英国范围内举行，伍尔夫也去观礼。在第二天的日记里，伍尔夫描述了和平纪念日的盛况。在游行的队伍中，"令人伤感的是看到那些落寞的老兵们，他们背对着我们，低头抽着烟"（p. 294）。一战后，英国政府对那些牺牲在战场上的士兵表示最高的敬意，将他们视为"光荣的战士"。而那些活着回来的士兵却怀着"活着的罪恶感"（Survival Guilt）（Niederland，1971，pp. 1—9），他们因

---

① 1915 年只记了不到两个月，1914 年、1916 年没有日记。

没有像同伴们一样战死沙场而感到内疚和焦虑，性格发生改变，并期望受到惩罚，甚至产生自杀倾向。[1] 伍尔夫身边就有这样一个老兵，1917 年 12 月 3 日她写道："我们在周日得到了塞西尔·伍尔夫（Cecil Woolf, 1887—1917）牺牲的消息，菲利普·伍尔夫（Philip Woolf）也受伤了。"（1977b，p. 91）塞西尔和菲利普是伦纳德·伍尔夫的两个弟弟，两人在一战爆发的第一天就参加了战争，被分配到法国战场。在 1917 年 11 月 29 日的康布雷战役中，塞西尔被炮弹击中死亡，菲利普身受重伤。塞西尔的遗体被埋葬在法国，而菲利普则带伤返回英国，回到亲人身边。当他于 1919 年 3 月到阿什汉姆拜访伍尔夫夫妇时，伍尔夫敏锐地发现了菲利普的"内疚感"："当菲利普过来之后，我突然感到非常不适，我想是因为他自己表现得像一个多余的人，一个局外人，一个旁观者，他仿佛被世人遗弃，身上的孤独感令人心中一凉。"（p. 248）伍尔夫还注意到，菲利普经常表达出想回法国的意愿。

相比一战，伍尔夫更是时时关注着第二次世界大战的临近和进展，并在日记中频繁写下自己的战时经历和感受。"伦纳德告诉我，K. 马丁（首相）说我们这次会参战。希特勒正在摸着小胡子深思。但一切都开始摇晃了，我的书会像一只在火焰上飞舞的蛾子，顷刻间就烟消云散。"（伍尔芙，1997，p. 218）伍尔夫预感到战争的脚步临近，言语中既充满对贪婪残忍的法西斯政权的轻蔑和憎恨，更担心那个战争狂人会把整个欧洲卷入战火纷飞的硝烟之中，甚至还担心自己也可能会在飞机炮火的狂轰滥炸中死于非命，而她的生活和写作计划也将彻底被打乱。"哈罗德在广播中以他那老于世故的口吻暗示说，这可能是战争。战争不仅导致了整个欧洲文明的彻底毁灭，而且也毁了我们的余生。昆汀已经应征入伍，我已不想提这些了——结束了。"（pp. 222-223）广播中不时传来各种令人心惊胆战的消息，英国政府的绥靖政策并不能阻止希特勒企图称雄世界的脚步，战争似乎一触即发。"战争带来的压力迅速将伦敦整个儿毁了，这是最难熬的一天。我在想，投降意味着置所有的犹太人于不顾，意味着集中营。我害怕听到法国政府撤出巴黎的消息。"（Woolf，1984，p. 292）因为伦纳德是犹太人，所以她曾与丈夫约定，一旦希特勒的军队攻占英伦三岛，他们宁可一起自杀，也绝不苟且受辱。

伍尔夫在 1940 年 9 月 18 日的日记中曾写道："我家所有的窗子都被震得粉碎，麦肯贝广场附近的家中，碗碟大多成了碎片，炮弹爆炸了。……我们需要有勇气，昨晚伦敦遭到了猛烈的轰炸——还是等着无线电中的消息吧。

---

① 这种精神疾病也是战争留下的心理创伤的一种表现，或被称为弹震症。

可我不管怎样，仍在不停地写着《波因茨邸宅》。"（伍尔芙，1997，pp. 246—247）这段日记记载了她的住宅被炸毁的真实状况，就是在隆隆的炮火声中，伍尔夫仍然奋笔疾书："难道不该写完《波因茨邸宅》吗？难道不该将事情做个了结吗？生命的终结倒给日常随和的生活带来了些生气，甚至是些喜气和无畏。昨天我就想过，这段日子或许会是我生命中最后的一段旅程。"（pp. 241—242）面对死亡的威胁，伍尔夫表现得异常勇敢和淡定，当意识到生命的旅程即将到达终点时，她反而心情平静，无所畏惧地与时间和生命赛跑。

传统的战争叙事往往通过描述一个或多个战争场面，集中塑造一个或几个英雄人物，并赋予他们骁勇善战、不怕牺牲、保家卫国的崇高品质，塑造高大光辉的形象，以歌颂战争的伟大、正义和英雄大无畏的精神。传统战争叙事模式是线性的叙事结构，按照时间和逻辑顺序勾勒出明显的情节线条。但伍尔夫日记却具有明显的反战争叙事的特点。首先，日记很少正面记录真实的战争场面，更多的是着眼于普通民众的身心和财产在战争中受到的摧残和战争过后的心理创伤。伍尔夫的反战争叙事不是为了展现战争的宏大场面，而是痛诉战争的残忍和罪恶。其次，日记的反战争叙事没有塑造一个战斗英雄，而是刻画了受到伤害的弱者群像。在伍尔夫看来，战争中没有胜利者，也没有所谓的英雄，只有受害者，这颠覆了传统战争叙事的英雄主义价值观，也体现了伍尔夫一贯反对任何形式的暴力的思想。最后，日记的反战争叙事模式没有明显的情节线，没有因果关系推动的起伏发展，呈现出的是破碎凌乱的战事叙述，反映出战争的荒谬和残酷。

伍尔夫日记中的反战争叙事的核心是利用日记的形式和内容特点始终保持反战的态度。相对宏大历史叙事，日记可看作个体的口述历史。例如 1935年，对于墨索里尼对阿比西尼亚的军事进攻[①]，国际联盟（League of Nation）做出让步。这件事发生之后，伍尔夫注意到英国法西斯联盟（British Union of Fascist）开始在伦敦频繁活动，于是她在日记里写道："政治新闻充斥着报纸的整个版面，标题有如：'不要为外国人而战。英国管好自身即可。'墨索里尼的势力开始蠢蠢欲动。"（1982，p. 337）伍尔夫敏锐地发觉英国法西斯联盟与德国纳粹相互勾结的事实，认为是法西斯在英国政治极端主义的表现。她在 1936 年的一篇日记里通过一件个人小事继续深化了对该观点的认知。该年 11 月 24 日，伍尔夫夫妇开车穿过东伦敦时发生了轻微事故，她在日记这

---

① 1936 年，墨索里尼攻占了阿比西尼亚。

样写道："雾很大，一个人影突然出现，为了躲避他，汽车撞到了旁边的墙上。行人都在围观，一个手拿报纸的好心人把我扶到一旁。我看到那是《黑衫报》（*The Blackshirt*）①。"（pp. 35−36）这段描述中出现一个强烈的对比：好心人的善行与他手中宣传法西斯主义的《黑衫报》，伍尔夫得到了一个与自己的政治倾向敌对的人的帮助。更具讽刺意味的是，极端主义就这样诡异地暴露在日常生活中。虽然这则日记只是对事故的简单记录，但字里行间透露出潜伏在普通民众之间的纳粹分子让人感到不安。伍尔夫通过讲述个人所经历的小历史，折射了整个欧洲的大历史。

　　伍尔夫还通过日记叙事来解构法西斯情景剧式演讲，揭穿纳粹的丑恶嘴脸和谎言，打破其所营造的幻境，最终表达反战的意愿。法西斯主义者声嘶力竭的演讲往往极具欺骗性和煽动性，令观众群情激动，将他们麻醉甚至洗脑，最终达到其政治目的。尤其是希特勒精心准备的演讲如情景剧，营造出一个虚幻的世界，让观众深陷其中。1919 年到 1933 年，希特勒通过演讲赢得了大批德国普通民众的支持。夸张的肢体动作、煽动性的表演、高昂的声音和语调是他表演的法宝。1938 年 9 月 5 日伍尔夫在通过电台广播听到希特勒的政治演讲时写道："我的脑子无法正常接收他的演讲，如果是真声，或许还能听懂一些，但收音机传来的是一阵模糊不清的噪音，大概想象他在疯狂地宣布纽伦堡大集会开始。"（p. 166）1938 年 9 月 13 日，伍尔夫在日记中再次描述了她通过电台收听的希特勒在纽伦堡大集会的演讲，指出演讲具有情景剧的特点："希特勒夸夸其谈，但毫无意义。他只会大喊大叫，如同一个将被行刑的人的野蛮嚎叫。然后听到观众的长嚎，如此反复再三，像是有人拿指挥棒引导一样。隔着无线电波都能感到他们声音的恐怖，我无法想象他们的面部表情是多么的狰狞。演讲的后半部分虎头蛇尾，突降法（anti-climax）是他惯用的伎俩。"（p. 169）1939 年 11 月 9 日她再次表示无法听懂希特勒的歇斯底里："无线电波传来希特勒在啤酒馆的演讲，他一会儿压抑地啜泣，一会儿又激动地大喊大叫。真不明白，这些演讲者们是怎么做到的。"（p. 245）伍尔夫的日记是反法西斯主义叙事的一种策略形式，她消解了希特勒情景剧式的演讲，甚至嘲讽他的演讲风格，暗示他只会通过渲染气氛来影响台下的观众，而重复的主题、空洞的语言、随意的承诺说明"表演"背后的虚伪。华而不实的语言、夸张的动作、不切实际的表达只为传递恐怖、暴力元素。伍尔夫在日记中一针见血地揭穿了希特勒小丑般拙劣的把戏，把他看作"好

---

① 一种为纳粹服务的报纸。

战、暴虐、丧心病狂地追求权力的化身"（2001，p.1373），她通过这种"暴力"演讲认清了纳粹疯狂残忍的本质。

三、伍尔夫日记中的女性主义思想

伍尔夫被尊为西方女性主义的先驱，她"虽然不喜欢这个标签，但毫无疑问，她是一位女性主义者"（Zwerdling，1986，p.210）。从1910年对当时如火如荼的激进女权主义产生兴趣，到20世纪三四十年代提出"局外人"和性别差异的理念，伍尔夫对妇女解放运动的辩证认识是不断深化发展的。综观伍尔夫日记，可以发现她时刻关注当时女性的生存状态，记录下所参与的各项妇女活动及感受，从日记中能一窥其女性主义思想的发展历史。

20世纪的英国进入妇女运动的高潮，女权主义者们为争取与男性平等的权利采取激进的手段斗争。年轻的伍尔夫对这场声势浩大的妇女运动非常关注，并以自己的方式回应和支持妇女解放事业。她在1905年5月27日的一则日记中列下了一个阅读清单，其中有：穆勒的《论妇女的屈从地位》和丁尼生的诗歌《公主》等。可以看出，伍尔夫开始试图从历史和法律的角度考察女性的地位和权利变化（Woolf，1990，p.127）。1910年伍尔夫写信向她的希腊语教师珍妮特·凯斯（Janet Case）请教："如果我通过给成人选举组织（Adult Suffragists）写信来查询会得到帮助吗？你能否寄给我一些相关资料，或者告诉我他们办公室的邮寄地址？我既不会辩论也不擅长演讲，但我可以做一些其他力所能及的事情。上次你跟我讲到，那些被关押的女性所遭受的暴行令我深表同情，我在想，能改变这种状况的方法到底是什么呢？"（1975，p.421）可以看出，刚刚步入社会的伍尔夫受到妇女运动的鼓舞，决定为争取妇女权益贡献自己微薄的力量。只是她对极端的暴力行动不感兴趣，不像其他女权主义者一样采取激进的做法。在这封信中，伍尔夫用的是"suffragist"，而非"suffragette"，两者虽然都被译为"妇女参政权论者"，但在英语中仍有细微区别，前者指采取非暴力手段争取选举权，后者是通过暴力措施获得选举权。这说明她并不赞成当时"妇女社会与政治联盟"的某些政治观念和做法。

1910年初，伍尔夫参与了"妇女选举权协会总工会"。尽管她所从事的只是分发各类信件的简单工作，但她仍希望通过这种方式为争取妇女选举权的运动做出自己的贡献。1916年伍尔夫加入了"妇女合作协会"（Women's

Co-operative Guild)①，还是该协会里士满分会的负责人。她每个月在霍加斯的住所主持一次集会，负责召集参会的妇女，邀请主讲人，选择关于社会、文学、和平等内容的会议主题（Wood，2014）。伍尔夫主持的这个协会维持了4年的时间（Woolf，1977a，p.54），她经常在日记中描述会议的情况，例如1918年4月的日记中写道："总是令我奇怪的是，这些女性为何过来，难道是为了在冬日里享受免费的暖气？她们很明显注意力并不在演讲上面，除了主讲人，没有任何人说一句话，结束后，也没有人提问。"（Woolf，1977b，p.76）虽然伍尔夫有时不满于参会妇女的缄默，但也会为她们在谈论中偶尔冒出的闪光点而感到欣慰。伍尔夫在19世纪20年代多次为"妇女联合服务会"（The National Society for Women's Service）、剑桥大学的纽汉姆女子学院和格顿学院做演讲。她在日记中写道："我刚冒着瓢泼大雨，从格顿学院演讲归来。那些年轻女士渴求知识而大胆无畏——那是我的印象。聪明、热切、窘迫的女孩注定将被大批培养为女教师，我和颜悦色地告诉她们，要喝些酒，要有间属于自己的房子。经过像这样一个晚上的交谈，我感到兴奋，全身充满活力，身上的锋芒与孤僻都不见了，我茅塞顿开。"（1997，p.110）伍尔夫为女学生的聪明、热情和对知识的渴求所感动，自己也变得活力四射。她给那些女孩子提出了殷切的希望，希望她们要有一间属于自己的房子，争取自己的权利，要唤起自我意识，要有独立的人格和思想。

一战结束前后，英国女性相继获得参政权、投票权和选举权，伍尔夫在日记中记录下这一系列政策的颁布和自己的感受，日记体现出她对历史事件的个人立场。1918年伍尔夫得知年满30周岁的妇女获得投票权的消息后非常高兴地在日记中写道："今天因为被赋予这样的权利，我感到无比自信和荣耀。"（Woolf，1977b，p.207）她认为这为以后的妇女解放运动开辟道路。但伍尔夫对妇女运动的某些做法一直持有自己的看法和批判的态度，并时刻与某些激进者保持距离。1918年2月3日，女权运动领袖皮帕·斯特雷奇（Pippa Strachey）②到伍尔夫家拜访，两人在某些观点上产生不同的看法，皮帕批评"伍尔夫置身于女权运动之外"（p.118），伍尔夫对此不置可否。当得知英国妇女获得选举权时，她比起其他激进女权主义者更冷静和克制，她在日记里写道："我并没有觉得有那么重要。"（p.104）她认为这只是一个初步的

---

① 妇女合作协会的秘书长是玛格丽特·卡洛琳·戴维斯（Margaret Caroline Davies，1861—1944），她致力妇女健康和权利问题。妇女合作协会于1883年成立，隶属于社会主义互助合作社。

② 皮帕·斯特雷奇（1872—1968），当时女权运动的核心人物，利顿·斯特雷奇的姐姐，全国妇女服务协会的秘书长，1907年组织了英国第一次妇女选举权游行。

胜利，妇女获得真正解放的道路还很遥远。紧接着 3 月 9 日，日记记录了伍尔夫夫妇参加由女权主义者为了庆祝年满 30 周岁女性获得选举权而举办的授奖集会，她描绘了集会的状况："大厅挤满了人，吵吵嚷嚷的，观众基本都是女性，这令人有些沮丧。为了庆祝胜利，每个演讲都是溢美之词，令人生厌。"（p. 125）接下来伍尔夫讥讽了几个发言人："我看到劳伦斯夫人（一名与会者）激动地不停起立坐下，好像她的腿是弹簧做的。"（p. 125）她之所以在日记中对妇女获得选举权表现出冷静甚至冷漠的态度，是因为她认为单纯以获得选举权为目的的女权运动太狭隘。虽然伍尔夫肯定这一胜利成果，但政治上的平权并不代表在意识形态、教育观念上的平权。当所有女权主义者为之狂欢的时候，伍尔夫则看到胜利背后仍有艰难的道路要走。

伍尔夫认为女性在人类历史和文学史的长河中始终是缺席的，"英国的历史是男性家系的历史，而不是女性的历史"（伍尔芙，2001，p. 1627）。女性作品的题材往往侧重于家庭生活，但在男性批评家看来过于狭隘，因此她们的历史和文学传统被男性历史编纂者和文学批评家忽略或贬低。伍尔夫认为，这是以男性为中心的价值观在作祟，导致无数女作家在文学史上被抹去。因此她强烈呼吁女性必须有自己的历史，必须重新构建女性文学传统。在此，伍尔夫是一位勇敢的拓荒者："写作的妇女就是通过她的母辈往回进行思考。"（伍尔芙，2001，p. 577）这是伍尔夫在女性主义宣言《一间自己的房间》中提出的解决问题的关键，女性作家必须通过挖掘"母亲"的历史来了解女性的历史和传统。只有考察了普通女性的生活情况，才能构建她们的历史谱系。

伍尔夫坚信女性日常生活叙事是女性文学传统的重要组成部分，日常生活是女性经验的源泉。记录日常生活和内心情感的日记是承载女性经验和历史的最佳写作形式之一，阅读日记和写日记是了解和重构女性历史的有效方式。除了伟大女作家的日记，伍尔夫对无名女性的日记也非常感兴趣。不仅如此，她还身体力行坚持日记写作。日记是她最长的作品，既展现了她的生命轨迹，也是她毕生思想的结晶。多达 30 本的手写日记不仅记录了伍尔夫的家庭生活和社会交往，还记载了一位女作家的写作生涯。

首先，伍尔夫通过挖掘女性先辈的日记来重建女性文学史，因为女性日记同样遭受被男性文学史撰写者刻意贬低和忽视的命运。佩内洛普·富兰克林（Penelope Franklin）考察了大量史料之后，发现已公开发表的日记大部分都是男性所写，虽然有大量女性日记，但为人所知的非常少，要么遗失，要么被遗弃在某个角落不见天日（1986）。伊丽莎白·汉普斯顿（Elizabeth Hampsten）道出了其中的原因之一：日记被公认的价值是史料价值，男性相对女性而言有更多参与历史的机会，因此他们的日记因"更有价值"而获得保留；女性日记侧重日常的生活琐事，被认为没有史料价值，所以被世人嫌弃（1982）。而男性文化体系对文学的审查机制则限制了女性日记的出版，男性批评家对女性日记的贬低和忽视，致使大量宝贵的女性日记被冷落。例如亚瑟·庞森（Ponsonby）比曾如此评论："奈特莉·福斯利夫人（Lady Knightley of Fawsley）写了 60 卷日记，但没有一则有价值。"（1923，pp. 26 -27）斯伯丁（Spalding）则直接将女性日记作家剔除在外，缘由是"她们的日记无法与男性作家媲美"（1949，pp. 69-70）。因此女性主义者的任务之一便是寻找、收集、整理这些失落的女性日记，让更多的女性日记作家逐渐走入公众视野，这是伍尔夫一生都在做的工作。她的目的就是更正被歪曲了的女性形象，重塑女性的历史。例如玛格丽特女士（Lady Margaret Hoby，1571—1633）是英国第一位女性日记作家，却不如后期的佩皮斯出名。正是伍尔夫发现了她的价值，并高度赞赏了她的日记，才让后人重新认识她的文学地位。英国第一位女小说家范妮·伯尼在女性文学史中的地位之所以非常重要，正在于伍尔夫重新发现其日记的价值，并将她视为自己日记的启蒙者。

再者，书写女性历史是对女性历史、女性文学传统的重建与再构，一个女性作家个人的自述，是对女性自我意识、生活经历与感悟的陈述，只有靠写作才能最终重建女性文学的历史。伍尔夫几十年来经年累月地写日记，对她而言，日记已然成为与呼吸和喝水同等重要的事情，写日记便是撰写她的个人史，便是书写大写的女性史。伍尔夫将自己所发生的大大小小的生活事件都记录在日记之中，还原了女性的日常生活，总结了女性经验，重现了女性的历史。

结　语

伍尔夫无论是在日记中还是在小说中，都旗帜鲜明地反对任何战争、霸权和暴力行为。正如兹沃德林（Zwerdling）所言，"对于伍尔夫，反暴力是她的政治信仰，而非暂时的策略"（1986，p. 274）。通过对日记的分析，我们发现，伍尔夫看到的是社会制度和文化传统中最根本的问题，超越了狭隘的党派、阶级和性别之争。反暴力思想在当时是超前的，因此引起同时代人对她的误解。她反对因战争、阶级冲突、权利运动所产生的暴力，让当时的主流评论误认为她不爱国、不支持女性运动和工人运动。这让她感到自己与这个父权社会格格不入，所以自称是"局外人"。事实上，伍尔夫的政治理想是实现全世界范围内的自由、平等、和平的世界主义，与狭隘极端的爱国主义和民族主义是不相容的。她认为全人类都属于同一精神共同体，国家之间和民族之间更应该同舟共济，建立良好的相互促进的经济和政治关系。也许有人会认为伍尔夫的社会思想太过于宏大和理想化，但要认识到她本身是一位作家，"而非政治家"（p. 274）。伍尔夫试图通过文学介入公共领域，推动广大读者反思野蛮专制、尚武强权和狭隘民族主义，并深入探究人性与文明。而日记帮助伍尔夫表达其政治观点，让她可以随时记录并表达对政治事件的看法。日记中既有她对社会的批判，也有对未来的美好寄托，展现出文学与时代精神的丰富性与多层次性。和平是人类的共同向往，战争是人类的大敌。只要父权主义、暴力思想还存在，伍尔夫日记的公共叙事和社会意义就不会消失。

引用文献：

福斯特，爱·摩（1988）．弗吉尼亚·伍尔夫//瞿世镜．伍尔夫研究．上海：上海文艺出版社．

王蓬振（2004）．詹姆逊文集——现代性、后现代性和全球化（第四卷）．北京：中国人民大学出版社．

伍尔芙，弗吉尼亚（1997）．伍尔芙日记选（戴红珍，宋炳辉，译）．天津：百花文艺出版社．

伍尔夫，弗吉尼亚（2001）．达洛卫夫人/到灯塔去/雅各布之屋（王家湘，译）．南京：译林出版社．

伍尔芙，弗吉尼亚（2001）．伍尔芙随笔全集（石云龙，等译）．北京：中国社会科学出版社．

Berman，J. (2001). "Of Oceans and Opposition: *the Waves*, Oswald Mosley, and the New Party." In Merry Pawlowski（ed.）, *Virginia Woolf and Fascism*. New York: Palgrave.

Franklin，P. （ed.）(1986). *Private Pages: Diaries of American Women*, *1830 s—1970 s*, New York: Ballantine.

Hampsten，E. (1982). *Read this Only to Yourself: the Private Writings of Midwestern Women*, 1880—1910. Bloomington: Indiana University Press.

Hussey，M. (1991). *The Singing of the Real World: the Philosophy of Virginia Woolf's Fiction*, Columbus: Ohio State University Press.

Leavis，F. R. (1942). "After to the Lighthouse", *Scrutiny*, (10).

Levenback，K. L (1999). *Virginia Woolf and the Great War*. Syracuse: Syracuse University Press.

Niederland，W. (1971). "Introduction Notes on the Concept, Definition, and Range of

Psychic Trauma". In Henry Krystal and William G (ed.), *Psychic Traumatization: Aftereffects in Individuals and Communities*. Boston: Little Brown.

Ponsonby, A. (1923). *English Diaries: A Review of English Diaries from the Sixteenth to the Twentieth Century, with an Introduction on Diary Writing*. London: Methuen & Co..

Spalding, P. A. (1949). *Self-Harvest: A Study of Diaries and the Diarist*, London: Independent.

Wood, A. (2014). "Facing Life as We Have Known It". *Virginia Woolf and the Women's Co-operative Guild Literature & History*. Vol. 23, No. 2.

Woolf, V. (1975). *Letters of Virginia Woolf, vol. 1*. N. Nicolson and J. Trautmann (eds.). New York: Harcourt Brace Jovanovich.

Woolf, V. (1977a). *Letters of Virginia Woolf, vol. 3*. N. Nicolson and J. Trautmann (eds.). New York: Harcourt Brace Jovanovich.

Woolf, V. (1977b). *The Diary of Virginia Woolf, vol. 1*. Anne Olivier Bell (ed.). New York: Harcourt Brace.

Woolf, V. (1982). *The Diary of Virginia Woolf, vol. 4*. Anne Olivier Bell (ed.). New York: Harcourt Brace.

Woolf, V. (1984). *The Diary of Virginia Woolf, vol. 5*. Anne Olivier Bell (ed.). New York: Harcourt Brace.

Woolf, V. (1990). *A Passionate Apprentice: The Early Journals, 1897—1909*. Mitchell A. Leaska (ed.). New York: Harcourt Brace Jovanovich.

Zwerdling, A. (1986). *Virginia Woolf and the Real World*. California: The University of California Press.

作者简介：

何亦可，英语语言文学博士，硕士生导师，现就职于山东师范大学外国语学院，主要研究方向为英美文学、文学理论与文类研究。

Author:

He Yike, Ph. D. of English language and literature, lecturing in English Department, School of Foreign Languages, Shandong Normal University. She mainly focuses on the study of British and American Literature, literary theories and genres.

Email: heyike8638@163.com

跨学科研究 ● ● ● ● ●

Immersed in the Air: A Phenomenological Approach to *Spring in a Small Town* (1948)

Dou Miao

Abstract: Drawing from the concepts of "film's body" and "cinesthetic body" proposed by Vivian Sobchack and Jennifer Barker, the current essay contends that a phenomenological approach to *Spring in a Small Town* (*Xiaocheng Zhi Chun*, 1948) opens up new grounds to apprehend the tactility behind Fei Mu's aesthetic subversion of the slogan-solution filmmaking paradigm in the 1930s and the 1940s. In examining Fei Mu's idea of "*kongqi*" (Air) as the key notion to enable a phenomenological approach, this essay investigates Fei's experiment of Air in *Spring in a Small Town*, which was inspired by the Confucian doctrine "released from the affections and stopped within the bounds of propriety" (*fa hu qing, zhi hu li*) and Su Shi's song lyric "A Spring Scene" (*Chunjing*). The current essay demonstrates that this seemingly restrictive doctrine was in fact repurposed to communicate an air that alternately suppresses and seduces.

Keywords: film's body; cinesthetic body; *Spring in a Small Town*; Fei Mu; phenomenology

现象学视野中的《小城之春》（1948）

窦　苗

摘　要： 受电影学者维维安·索布切克（Vivian Sobchack）和珍妮弗·巴克（Jennifer Barker）的"电影身体"和"观影身体"概念启发，本文用现象学的方法来探究费穆《小城之春》的审美观。1948年，费穆有意颠覆20世纪三四十年代以来社会批判派电影中采用口号来提出解决社会问题方案的拍法。对于《小城之春》中"空气"的营造成为这一颠覆性实验的关键。本文通过对"发乎情，止乎礼"以及苏轼《蝶恋花·春景》的重新解读，试图对《小城之春》中既"发"又"止"，既压抑又诱惑的"空气"进行阐释，细究其如何突破当时口号式拍法的局限。

关键词： 电影身体　观影身体　《小城之春》　费穆　现象学

In 2005, *Spring in a Small Town* was voted the greatest Chinese film in history by one hundred film scholars and critics, as invited by the Hong Kong Film Awards Association (Daruvala, 2007, p. 171). Five years ago, as I was re-watching *Spring in a Small Town* in my room at night, I found myself deeply touched by the scene of boating on the river. As Dai Xiu sings "In a Distant Place" (*Zai na Yaoyuan de Difang*), an intangible shiver ran down my spine, as if a thousand ethereal fingers had gently grazed my skin. I was emotionally and sensually touched by the air of the scene. As I began to read essays on the film, I realized that such a moment of tactile immersion could not be easily reduced to the discussion of the film's narrative, the thematic significance and the techniques of long takes, as examined by previous scholarship (Fan, 2015; FitzGerald, 2013; Udden, 2012; Li, 2009; Daruvala, 2007; Chen, 2000).

Drawing from the concepts of "film's body" (Sobchack, 1992; Barker,

2009), and "cinesthetic body" (Sobchack, 2004), the current essay contends that a phenomenological approach to *Spring in a Small Town* opens up new grounds to apprehend the tactility behind Fei Mu's theorization of cinematic aesthetic. The key notion to enable such phenomenological approach is Fei Mu's idea of "*kongqi*" (air, hereafter referred to as Air). *Spring in a Small Town*, Fei Mu's most acclaimed work, creates a particular kind of Air that was inspired by the "Confucian" doctrine "released from the affections and stopped within the bounds of propriety" (*fa hu qing*, *zhi hu li*). This seemingly restrictive doctrine, however, was in fact repurposed to communicate an Air that alternately suppresses and seduces. It is precisely this kind of Air in *Spring in a Small Town* that experiments and amplifies the tactility potential of Air theorized by Fei Mu. Focusing on the concept of Air allows us to explicate Fei Mu's aesthetic subversion of the slogan-solution filmmaking paradigm in the 1930s and the 1940s.

While Victor Fan considers Fei Mu's Air concept as part of Fei's theorization of cinema ontology (Fan, 2015, pp. 140−141), this essay reads Air as an aesthetic choice for cinematic production. In "A Brief Discussion of 'Air'", Fei Mu writes: "To arrest the audience in a movie, it is necessary to assimilate the audience with the environment of the characters in the plot. To achieve this goal, I believe that creating the 'Air' (*kongqi*) within the plot is essential" (Fei, 1934 [1998], p. 8). This description suggests that the intended function, if not the definition of Air, is to immerse the audience into the film's world. Although Fei cites his first three films *Night of the City* (*Chengshi zhiye*, 1933), *Life* (*Rensheng*, 1934), and *Sea of Fragrant Snow* (*Xiang xuehai*, 1934) as examples of practicing his Air theory, these films, unfortunately, were lost in the political turmoil. Without concrete examples of the Air theory, scholars could only find traces of the concept from Fei's short 1934 essay. Chen Mo interprets Fei's proposition to "create Air" in cinema as Fei's innovation of a new cinematic form that transcends conventional "solid forms" —film narrative and their dramatic structures, namely, relatively fixed and cognizable elements of the film—and presents a "gaseous form" of cinema. This "gaseous form" refers to a type of cinema that ingeniously emphasizes props, the film set, and ambience (Chen, 2000, p. 53). Presenting a similar understanding, Victor Fan cites Fei Mu's proposition to "use the dramatic events and objects around the main theme in order to foreground the subject matter" (Fei, 1934 [1998], p. 8) and interprets the creation of Air as putting together "dramatic events and objects around the main theme so that the absence of the main theme would be crystalized as an air that lingers in the cinematographic image" (Fan, 2015, p. 161).

Expanding existent insights from both Fan and Chen, I find Fei's 1948 essay on *Spring in a Small Town*, "Director, Screenwriter: To Yang Ji" (*Daoyan, Ju Zuozhe: Xiegei Yang Ji*), best illustrates the evolved meaning of Air fourteen years after the proposition of the term "Air" in 1934. Film critic Yang Ji critiqued the film's elision of the important depiction of the economic plights experienced by a landlord family (Yang, 1948). In response to Yang's critique, Fei Mu humbly reflected on the "shortcomings" of *Spring in a Small Town*. The greatest drawback, according to Fei, was that "In order to convey the grey mood of ancient China, I constructed my film (without any techniques) using 'long shots' and 'slow motion,' making a bold and presumptuous experiment. The result is that the film became excessively dull" (Fei, 1948 [1998], p. 73). Calling the use of "long shots" and "slow motion" in the film a "bold and presumptuous experiment" indicates the status of *Spring in a Small Town* as a milestone in Fei's experimentation of creating the cinematic Air. As for what distinctively sets this film apart from Fei's prior works and those of his contemporaries, Fei wrote: "The screenplay writer Li Tianji's proposition is: regarding the subject matter [of *Spring in a Small Town*], the film refrains from having characters shout slogans or forcefully present solutions. I concur with him; however, I find that in the process of film production, it is far less easy and potent than shouting out slogans or presenting a way out." (p. 73) Here, Fei compares his daring experiment of conveying "grey mood of ancient China" in *Spring in a Small Town* with a conventional practice amongst serious works of his contemporary filmmakers, namely, the practice to highlight the main theme of the films with slogans, oftentimes as a way to propose a solution to social problems.

This slogan-solution filmmaking paradigm appears to characterize what Pang Lai-kwan identifies as "Chinese left-wing cinema", through which she theorizes "films that display the filmmakers' strong sense of social mission and ethical commitment to the nation and its people" and "contains [sic] elements of class consciousness or revolution" (Pang, 2002, p. 5). To take Fei Mu's own film as an example, in the anti-Japanese film *Blood on Wolf Mountain* (*Langshan Diexue Ji*, 1936), the slogan "all I know is that fighting wolves requires everyone's concerted effort, planning, and preparation" is proposed as the solution to the Japanese invasion. However, what Fei meant to subvert via the construction of Air in *Spring in a Small Town* includes his own films that aren't usually categorized into the politically specific term "left-wing cinema". For instance, his 1941 film *Confucius* (*Kongfuzi*) presents the last words of Confucius "rectify the mind, cultivate sincerity, self-cultivation, regulate the family, govern the state, and bring peace to the Under the Heaven" (*Zhengxin, chengyi, xiushen, qijia, zhiguo, pingtianxia*) as a slogan to advance an anti-war agenda.

In *Spring in a Small Town* Fei Mu relinquished the conventional style of thematic display that relied on slogan-driven solutions. Instead, he experimented with a type of cinema that dissolves and transcends the substance of slogans and solutions by foregrounding subtlety, insinuations, and atmospheres, which instantiated his earlier Air theory. On the surface, in stating that "the result is that the film became excessively dull" and "it is far less easy and less powerful than shouting out slogans or presenting a way out", Fei appeared to identify the drawbacks of this new experiment of his earlier Air concept: its insipidity and lack of immediate power. Nevertheless, if we consideed Fei's reflection a gesture of humility rather than a declaration of regret, calling *Spring in a Small Town* a "bold and presumptuous experiment" was in fact Fei's valiant affirmation of the innovativeness of his work. There was a sense of pride hidden beneath the guise of self-critique.

Set in 1946, *Spring in a Small Town* tells a story of the human struggle among desire, matrimonial duties, and friendship. Such a story about human relationships and unfulfilled desire is built against the postwar background composed of bombed ruins, instantiating what Carolyn FitzGerald and Paul Pickowicz termed "victory as defeat" as exemplifying the postwar disillusion of the lasting civil war (FitzGerald, 2013, p. 171; Pickowicz, 2000). The film features a melancholic narrator, Zhou Yuwen, a housewife of a declined landlord family. She spends her days walking along the shattered city wall and procuring Chinese herbal medicine for her ailing husband. The husband Dai Liyan, who suffers from lung and heart disease, resides in their bombed-out estate with his estranged wife, his sixteen-year-old sister Dai Xiu, and his manservant Old Wang. Their uneventful life is disrupted by the unexpected visit of Zhang Zhichen, Liyan's old friend and a physician who practices Western medicine. Unbeknownst to Liyan, Zhichen has had a romantic relationship with Yuwen. Caught between her marital obligations to her husband and her suppressed desire for Zhichen, Yuwen faces a profound struggle between *qing* (affection) and *li* (propriety). Dai Xiu's affection for Zhichen further complicates the love triangle, as Liyan suggests a marriage between his sister and his good friend. When Liyan discovers the rekindling of Yuwen and Zhichen's love, he commits suicide. Bounded by a sense of responsibility and guilt towards her husband, Yuwen chooses to stay with Liyan as Dai Xiu and Old Wang see Zhichen off to Shanghai. Narrated by Yuwen's dispassionate voice and set against the backdrop of architectural rubble, the film is shrouded in an air of "grey mood" (Fei, 1948 [1998], p. 73).

The specific Air enacted in *Spring in a Small Town* deserves further discussion. This essay proposes to apprehend the Air of the film through the association between the Confucian doctrine "released from the affections and stopped within the bounds of propriety" (*fa hu qing*, *zhi hu li*) and Su Shi's song lyric "A Spring Scene" (*Chunjing*). What is shared by both the Confucian doctrine and Su Shi's lyric is the rhythm of *qing* (affection or emotion). Wei Wei, who plays Yuwen in the film, recollected that Fei Mu told her to perform according to "*fa hu qing*, *zhi hu li*" in Jia Zhangke's documentary *I Wish I Knew* (*Shanghai Chuanqi*, 2010). Victor Fan's analysis of the film accentuates propriety's (*li*) regulation of emotions (*qing*) (Fan, 2015, p. 168). What I try to emphasize here, however, is the alternation of being released (*fa*) and stopped (*zhi*), which echoes the emotional pattern and rhythm portrayed by Su Shi's "A Spring Scene":

The petals have fallen and their red faded, but the green apricots are still small.

When the swallow takes flight, green water winds around the homestead. Catkins on the willow branches dwindle with the blowing wind;

Where at the ends of the earth is no sweet grass to be found?

Within the walls a swing, outside the walls a path.

Outside the wall a wanderer; within the walls a beautiful woman laughs. Her laughter gradually grows faint, the sound dies away.

One who cares is troubled by one who cares not.

花褪残红青杏小。燕子飞时，绿水人家绕。枝上柳绵吹又少，天涯何处无芳草！

墙里秋千墙外道。墙外行人，墙里佳人笑。笑渐不闻声渐悄，多情却被无情恼。

According to the screenplay writer Li Tianji, Fei Mu built the atmosphere, or Air, of *Spring in a Small Town* around the aesthetic ambience of "A Spring Scene" (Li, 1985 [1998], p. 157). Written during the poet's second exile to Huizhou, the opening line "The petals have fallen and their red faded, but the green apricots are still small" laments the lack of vitality in the late spring. This decaying scene of the spring fading away echoes the sense of suppression implied by the "*zhi*" (stop) of "*zhi hu li*". The swallow and green water in the next line, however, turns to suggest the release of suppression, resonating the "*fa*" (release) of "*fa hu qing*". Contemplating on the alternation between suppression and release, the wanderer consoles himself with "Where at the ends of the earth is no sweet grass to be found?" The second stanza reverses the pattern and starts with "*fa*" (release). The depressed wanderer is lightened up by the laughs of the beautiful woman within the walls. This delight is soon called to a halt as "her laughter gradually grows faint, the sound dies away". What is left with the wanderer, subsequently, is the emotion of vexation because the proliferation of his *qing* was stopped by apathy. This alternation between "*fa*" (release) and "*zhi*" (suppression, stop) informs and collaborates with the following phenomenological analysis of the sensual scheme in *Spring in a Small Town*.

The first connection between Fei Mu and the phenomenological approach of Barker and Sobchack's lies in their shared emphasis on the inseparability between the viewer and the film. Fei Mu aspires to create a kind of Air that are meant to simultaneously grasp the viewer and be immersed. Barker and Sobchack similarly theorize a reciprocal interaction between two sides of the screen—the onscreen and the offscreen, the viewed bodies and the viewing bodies. They anchor this two-way sensual paradigm between the viewer and the film in the viewer's capacity to perceive the world onscreen, as well as the cinema's capacity to touch—not instruct—and emotionally move the viewer offscreen. The current essay contends that Fei Mu fosters a paradoxical Air of reluctant stillness and self-restrained stirring in *Spring in a Small Town*. This "Air" is not content with simply using long takes, but instead demands multi-sensory immersion from the viewer. Barker's and Sobchack's phenomenological approach, recognizing the senses-related bodily experience as informing and coexisting with the meaning-making process of moviegoing (Sobchack, 2004, p. 63, p. 75), provides theoretical depth for my discussion of *Spring in a Small Town*'s Air from two paradoxical aspects: the film's Confucian body and the solicitation for the cinesthetic subject. These two aspects will be examined in the following two sections of this essay.

Ⅰ. The Film's Confucian Body

Drawing on film scholars such as Vivian Sobchack and Gabrielle Hezekiah, Jennifer Barker in *The Tactile Eye: Touch and the Cinematic Experience* develops her notion of the film's body. Vivian Sobchack in her *The Address of the Eye: A Phenomenology of Film Experience* defines film as "a dynamic and synoptic gestalt that cannot be reduced to its mechanisms" (Sobchack, 1992, p. 169) and the film's body as "the film's means of perceptually engaging and expressing a world not only for us but also for itself" (p. 168). For Sobchack, then, the concept of the film's body applies Maurice Merleau-Ponty's phenomenological descriptions to open up a new understanding of film's ontology. In Barker's interpretation of Sobchack, the film's body is "a lived-body (but not a human one) capable of *perception* of expression and expression of perception" (Barker, 2009, p. 9). For Barker, the film's body is then "a concrete but distinctly cinematic lived-body, neither equated to nor encompassing the viewer's or filmmaker's body, but engaged with both of these even as it takes up its *own intentional projects* in the world" (p. 8). In Barker's conceptualization, the film's body too sees and feels the world onscreen, as the viewer offscreen would do. This film's body cannot be reduced to the pure representation of the filmmaker's vision, that is to say, the film has its own (if human enabled) "subjectivity" (p. 10) or personality, through which it engages with the viewer physically and therefore emotionally: according to Barker, we as viewers could be "pulled into" a certain style of engagement that "viscerally produces" feelings and emotions (p. 16) through certain camera movements (e. g. a dazzling movement of simultaneously pulling away and reaching forward). Those "gestures of the camera", for Barker, are the evidence of the film's way of embodied perceiving of the world. And these "gestures" might be "thematically relevant" (p. 14).

What characterizes the gestures of the camera and subsequently the way the film's body of *Spring in a Small Town* perceives the world is of a specific kind: a relatively undemonstrativeness and, correspondingly, the seemingly self-restrained motion of the camera. This is less representative in the relatively frequent long takes (Udden, pp. 268 − 273) than the likewise relatively frequent long shots and self-restrained movements of the camera in the movie. Long shots guarantee a safe distance that is meant to be less intruding. The self-restrained movements, then, represent the almost-literati gesture of the film's body of *Spring in a Small Town*—the gesture of the well-educated Confucian gentleman or the gesture of the well-behaved Confucian gentry woman. This kind of Confucian gestures resonates with Fei Mu's instructions to Wei Wei, that is, the Confucian dictum "released from the affections and stopped within the bounds of propriety" (*fa hu qing*, *zhi hu li*).

The introduction of the male protagonist, Liyan (where the "*li*" in

"Liyan" is the same character as the "*li*" in "*zhi hu li*"）, begins with garden shots. This occurs as the voiceover of the female protagonist，Yuwen，which has been ongoing for 9 shots，starts discussing her sick husband's solitary habit of spending time in the garden. Accompanied by Yuwen's dispassionate narration，the camera maintains a distance，situated behind the corridor's fence. It tracks the servant Old Wang's movement towards the garden with a slight pan to the right，then to the left again. In the second shot，the camera continues to keep a distance from the characters. It first positions itself behind a cluster of rocks and weeds，as Old Wang calls out to his master Liyan from our side of the wall，through a hole on our left. Only when Old Wang moves to the hole on his right does the camera dare to reach towards the left hole in the wall to reveal Liyan. As Old Wang walks into the garden to speak with Liyan，the camera—handheld by the cameraperson—moves towards the hole on the left，revealing Liyan sitting about 20 feet away from the hole. It's hard to tell with the naked eye whether the camera zooms in or it's simply the handheld camera moving closer. What the viewer does witness is a kind of physical approach executed by the camera that mimics a human gesture：the film's body behaves like a paradoxical Confucian person，observing the characters from a safe distance，yet unable to resist peering into the unfolding situation. This stirs curiosity within the viewer's body，tempting them to take a closer look as well.

The Confucian body rife with curiosity best manifests itself in the scene where the love between Yuwen and Zhichen is rekindled，a moment that exemplifies "*fa hu qing*". In a medium close-up shot，the camera captures the Yuwen and Zhichen leaning on a ruined city wall and reminiscing about their prewar relationship. The camera follows Zhichen's motion and pans slightly the left. During this reminiscence，Zhichen's affection for Yuwen resurfaces. "If I asked you to come away with me，would you still say 'whatever you like'?" Asked Zhichen. Rather than responding with a passionate kiss，Yuwen retorts with another query， "Do you really mean that?" Lowering her head，Yuwen smiles，delighted by Zhichen's declaration of affection. The camera refrains from tracking Yuwen's steps as she moves away. Instead，it pans to the left，the gap between Yuwen and the camera gradually widening. Zhichen joins Yuwen in strolling along the city wall. The camera remains stationary, careful not to intrude too closely on the sudden surge of their affection. As Zhichen hops down from the wall's bricks, he stumbles, prompting the camera to slightly jolt, as if startled and concerned for Zhichen. The shot then dissolves into a long view of Zhichen and Yuwen walking side by side in a bamboo forest. The camera stands still, observing them separate and then come together again, with Yuwen grasping Zhichen's arm. Next, the camera captures a moment of intimacy with an extreme long shot: Yuwen releases Zhichen's arm and starts running playfully, with Zhichen chasing her fervently, as if the two were childhood sweethearts. No voiceovers or sounds accompany this long shot, as the film's body intentionally maintains a respectful distance, reluctant to delve too closely into the intimate details of their rekindled romance.

Ⅱ. The Cinesthetic Subject

In addition to the dispassionate voiceover and restrained camera movement that can be understood as part of the film's Confucian body, or its polite and respectful personality, in the creation of Air in *Spring in a Small Town*, the film's body also solicits what Vivian Sobchack defines as the cinesthetic subject, namely, the subversive body of the film viewer who both *senses* (my emphasis) and makes sense of what is onscreen (Sobchack, 2004, pp. 70−71). The neologism "cinesthetic", coined by Sobchack, drives from a combination of "cinema", "synaesthesia", and "coenaesthesia". The cinesthetic bodies are subversive because they "subvert their own fixity from within, commingling flesh and consciousness, reversing the human and technological sensorium" (p. 67). In other words, in perceiving what the film's body perceives and expresses, the cinesthetic body of the viewer possesses the capability to transcend the locality, or "fixity", of the viewer's sensory experience. In Sobchack's conceptualization, seeing the film viewer as the cinesthetic subject highlights the way different senses (including touch, seeing, hearing, smell, taste ...) collaborate to contribute to a reversible sensual structure at the movies that makes the film viewer "feels" what is onscreen, what is felt by the film's body (pp. 59−82). This structure refers to a process where, as "I" am in the theatre, the onscreen figural objects—such as a wool dress—sensually provoke me, but because my body cannot literally touch, or taste them, my body seeks "a sensible object to fulfill this sensual solicitation" (p. 76) by reversing the direct of sensing to my own *lived body*. Sobchack repurposes Maurice Merleau-Ponty's concept of the lived body to describe the "foundational grounds for the cinesthetic subject": the lived body is a "field of conscious and sensible material being on which experience is gathered, synopsized, and diffused in a form of prelogical meaning that, even as it is diffused, nonetheless 'co-heres'" (pp. 71-72). In other words, the lived body of the cinesthetic subject renders the boundaries of human skin and sensorium porous. As a "field", the lived body borrows, gathers, diffuses perceptions experienced by other bodies, including the film's body. In the re-directed fulfillment of the sensual desire, my sensual experience is enhanced because now it is "reflexively doubled" — I can "touch myself touching, smell myself smelling ... sense my own sensuality" (pp. 76-77). In other words, the way the film's body perceives the world *seduces* me (the film viewer) to engage sensually with the film's body, and the bodies and the objects onscreen, resulting in a peculiar type of immersion.

This sense of seduction is ubiquitous in *Spring in a Small Town*. It is most prominent in the boating scene, where the viewer's senses are most intensely engaged. The scene commences with a close-up of the water's rippling surface, mirroring the sky and clouds. Yuwen's voiceover dominates the soundtrack in this initial shot. This then cuts to multiple angle shots of the characters on the boat. To facilitate my discussion, I shall enumerate them as follows:

1. A long shot capturing the four characters from the front as they paddle the boat together. (Lyrics: In that distant land)

2. A medium close-up of Zhichen, Yu Wen's former lover, standing and maneuvering the largest paddle. (Lyrics: There lives [a lovely maiden])

3. A medium-long shot of the four characters taken from the front of the boat. (Lyrics: [There lives] a lovely maiden/As people pass by her tent/

They can't help but glance back [with lingering affection])

4. A medium close-up of Yuwen paddling, stirring the rippling water to her left, the camera then moves upwards towards Zhichen. (Lyrics: [They can't help but] glance back with lingering affection/Her rosy smile/Is like the radiant sun/Her beautiful, charming eyes)

5. A medium-long shot of the four characters, with Dai Xiu and Liyan singing. (Lyrics: Are like the brilliant moon at night/I wish to be a little lamb/Sitting by her side)

6. A close-up of the water's rippling surface. (Lyrics: I hope [she holds a slender whip])

7. A medium-long shot of the four characters, with Dai Xiu and Liyan singing. The camera moves upward and frames Dai Xiu in the front, with Zhichen and Yuwen in the background. (Lyrics: [I hope] she holds a slender whip/And lightly, continually lashes it onto me)

8. A close-up of Yuwen paddling. (Lyrics: humming, no lyrics)

A medium-long shot of the four characters, with Dai Xiu and Liyan singing. (Lyrics: humming, no lyrics)

9. A close-up of Liyan's paddle as it dips into the water. (Lyrics: humming the melody, no lyrics)

10. A medium close-up shifting from Zhichen to Yuwen. (Lyrics: humming the melody, no lyrics)

11. A medium close-up of Liyan and Yuwen's sister, with Yuwen visible in the background. (Lyrics: humming the melody, no lyrics)

12. A long shot featuring the four characters. (Lyrics: humming the melody, no lyrics)

13. A close-up of the water reflecting the image of the cloud. (Lyrics: humming the melody, no lyrics)

The soundtrack accompanying these multi-angle shots consists of two parts: the sister Dai Xiu's graceful and melodious singing voice, and the sound of the water being stirred by the paddles. The sound of the disturbed water, symbolizing the stirred desires and thoughts of the clandestine lovers, is emphasized in the soundtrack, being nearly as prominent as the enchanting singing voice. The singing voice and the song's repetitive, catchy melody stimulate our minds and desires, seducing us to sing along and sway our bodies like the characters do with their paddling. This is getting close to (but not quite yet) the moment of solicitation for cinesthetic subject that Sobchack discusses: we sway as we observe the swaying, we sing as we hear the characters' and our own singing, we stir ourselves as we watch the characters being stirred. Synchronizing with the paddling sounds and singing voice are the visually depicted stirring and rippling of the water. From every shot angle, we either witness the rippling water, the characters' movements as they paddle, or the paddles touching the water, disrupting the otherwise placid, mirror-like surface. This paves the way for a cinesthetic moment: we are enticed by the sounds, the water, and the swaying to become part of the film's body at this moment. We are drawn to sway the paddle (as a person), to sense ourselves swaying (as the melody), to touch the water (as the paddle), and to feel ourselves touching (as the water)... In the boating scene of *Spring in a Small Town*, our senses are multi-dimensionally mobilized by the film's seductive body.

As a cinesthetic subject myself, I find the entrancing potential of the boating scene extends beyond the physical boundaries of the screen and the temporal confines of the film. Its resonance lingers, even as I hit the pause button and close my laptop. The lyrics of the song, sung by Dai Xiu and Dai Liyan, contribute to this seductive potential. Titled "In a Distant Land", the song was composed by Wang Luobin around 1939. Wang was traveling in Qinghai province at the time, collecting local folk songs. According to Wang's assistant, Zhou Yikui, Wang based the initial draft of "In a Distant Land" on a Uyghur folk song called "The Shepherd's Song" (*Muyang Ren zhi Ge*) (Li, 2015, p. 177). As I, the cinesthetic subject, sing with Dai Xiu and Liyan, I comprehend the lyrics multi-sensorily. As Dai Xiu sings "There lives a lovely maiden", Liyan turns back and look at his wife, smiling affectionately. As Dai Xiu and Liyan sing "They can't help but glance back with lingering affection", Yuwen couldn't help but turns back to glance at Zhichen, drawn in by Dai's melodious voice. I, the cinesthetic subject, look at Yuwen's look at Zhichen, feeling the paddle touching the water, singing the song as though I am sitting on the same boat. In so doing, I simultaneously express and embody the line "glance back with lingering affection" as I watch and hear the characters express and embody the same lyrics. My sensorium is pulled multi-directionally towards the world perceived by the song, the world perceived by the film's body, and the world saturated with my own voice. As Dai Xiu and Liyan sings "I hope she holds a slender whip/And lightly, continually lashes it onto me," I, the cinesthetic subject has been so immersed in synaesthetic and coenesthetic experience of perception on-and off-screen that the "slender whip" enters my imagination, its imaginary lashes brushing against my skin in synchrony with the sound of the stirred water. The boating scene hence exemplifies the way that the seductive film's body actively solicits the subversive cinesthetic body to immerse themselves in the desire-laden Air produced by *Spring in a Small Town*.

Conclusion

As demonstrated above, the film's body of *Spring in a Small Town* is a paradoxical combination of the self-restrained Confucian body and a seductive body. This seemingly conflicted characteristics of the film's body of *Spring in a Small Town* aligns with the release-suppression rhythm inherent in Su Shi's "A Spring Scene" and the Confucian doctrine "*fa hu qing, zhi hu li*". As Fei Mu's bold experiment, the Air created for *Spring in a Small Town* radically challenged the paradigm of serious cinematic works at the time. It was precisely through Fei's investment in the Air rather than the slogan-solution formula that *Spring in a Small Town* transcends its contemporaries and continues to resonate with audiences across time. The charisma of the film is intricately tied to the nature of the Air: the Air has to be relatively stable, otherwise one cannot breathe and live within it; yet it can never be too stable—it desires to be stirred and threatens to stir up the already subversive bodies on- and off-screen. In Barker's sense, it is through this Air that the film's paradoxical body completes its intention to perceive the spring in this small town, its peculiar way to direct the moviegoer's sense of the movie. Sobchack helps us to *describe* the next step—following Maurice Merleau-Ponty's assertion that phenomenology is a philosophy dedicated to describing our experience—the actual functioning effect of the Air on the body of the cinesethic subject, that is, how the moviegoer is touched, sensually and emotionally, by the simultaneously confining and seducing Air.

References:

Daruvala, S. (2007). The Aesthetics and Moral Politics of Fei Mu's Spring in a Small Town. *Journal of Chinese Cinemas*, 1 (3), 171−187.

Fan, V. (2015). *Cinema Approaching Reality: Locating Chinese Film Theory*. Minnepolis: University of Minnesota Press.

Fei, Mu. (1934 [1998]). Luetan "kongqi" (A Brief Discussion of "Air"). In Ain-Ling Wong, Shiren daoyan: Fei Mu (Fei Mu the Poet Director) (pp. 7−8). Hong Kong: Hong Kong Film Critics Society.

Fei, Mu. (1948 [1998]). Daoyan, ju zuozhe—xie gei Yang Ji (Director, Screenwriter—To Yang Ji). In Ain-Ling Wong, Shiren daoyan: Fei Mu (Fei Mu the Poet Director) (pp. 73−74). Hong Kong: Hong Kong Film Critics Society.

FitzGerald, C. (2013). *Fragmenting Modernisms:Chinese Wartime Literature, Art, and Film*, 1937−1949. Leiden: Brill.

Li, Guoshun. (2015). Gequ Zai Na Yaoyuan de Difang zhi chuangzuo kaoyuan (The Song 'In that Distant Place': A Study of Its Origin). *Northern Music*, 35 (20), 177−179.

Li, Jie. (2009). Home and Nation Amid the Rubble: Fei Mu's "Spring in a Small Town" and Jia Zhangke's "Still Life". *Modern Chinese Literature and Culture*, 21 (2), 86−125.

Li, Tianji. (1985 [1998]). Sanci shoujiao, shuran yongjue (Three teachings received, and then suddenly parting forever) (1985). In Ain-Ling Wong, Shiren daoyan: Fei Mu (Fei Mu the Poet Director) (pp. 157−161). Hong Kong: Hong Kong Film Critics Society.

Minnepolis: Chen. Mo. (2000). *Liuying chunmeng: Feimu dianying lungao* (Spring Dream of the Oriole: on Fei Mu's Film). *Zhongguo dianying chubanshe*.

Pang, Lai-Kwan. (2002). Building a New China in Cinema: The Chinese Left-Wing Cinema Movement, 1932−1937. London: *Rowman & Littlefield*.

Pickowicz, P. G. (2000). Victory as Defeat: Postwar Visualizations of China's War of Resistance. In Wen-Hsin Yeh, *Becoming Chinese: Passages to Modernity and Beyond* (pp. 342−365). Dakland: University of California Press.

Sobchack, V (1992). *The Address of the Eye: A Phenomenology of Film Experience*. Princeton: Princeton University Press.

Sobchack, V (2004). *Carnal thoughts: Embodiment and Moving Image Culture*. Dakland: University of California Press.

Udden, J. N. (2012). In Search of Chinese Film Style (s) and Technique (s). In

Yingjing Zhang, *A Companion to Chinese Cinema* （pp. 265－283）. West Sussex：John Wiley & Sons，2012.

Wei，Wei. (n. d.). Xunfang laoban Xiaocheng Zhichun sanwei zhuyan Wei Wei，Zhang Hongmei，Liwei (Visiting the Three Main Actors of the Old Version of Spring in a Small Town，Wei Wei，Zhang Hongmei，and Li Wei). http://ent. sina. com. cn/2004－08－13/1552472499. html?from＝wap.

Yang Ji. (1948). Xiaocheng Zhichun shiping (An Attempt to Comment on Spring in a Small Town). Dagong bao.

Author:

Dou Miao, Ph. D. candidate at Washington University in St. Louis, USA. Her research interest includes women's studies, youth studies, and modern Chinese culture.

作者简介：

窦苗，美国圣路易斯华盛顿大学博士研究生，主要研究方向为妇女研究、青年研究、中国现代文化。

Email：doumiao@wustl. edu

The Work of Theater in the Season of Politics: A Study of Kara Jūrō's Situation Theater

Zhao Xinyi

Abstract: This article examines postwar Japanese avant-garde playwright Kara Jūrō's praxis and writings by situating him in the rising angura (underground theater) movement in the late-60s and a broader global cultural context. Borrowing from French philosopher Jacques Rancière's discussion of the relationship between art and politics, I argue that Kara's theatre not only blurs the boundaries between the actor and the spectator, art and life, but also provokes a radical rethinking of theater as a corporeal and affective engagement in politics. By changing the meaning of viewing and acting as well as the position of the spectator, Kara's theater is not so much a representation of politics as an attempt to redefine politics, which also played into the larger transformation of post-war biopolitics in Japan.

Keywords: Kara Jūrō; Situation Theater; art; politics; body

多事之秋的戏剧艺术：唐十郎的状况剧场研究

赵心怡

摘　要：本文通过将戏剧置于20世纪60年代末兴起的地下剧场运动和更广阔的全球文化背景中探讨了日本战后前卫剧作家唐十郎的创作与表演。借用法国哲学家雅克-朗西埃关于艺术与政治之间关系的论述，笔者提出唐十郎的戏剧不仅模糊了演员与观众、艺术与生活之间的界限，还是一种兼具具身性和情动性的政治

参与。他的戏剧不仅表现政治，更通过改变观看和表演的意义
以及观众相对于剧场的位置重新定义了政治，同时其对身体的
重视也引发了对日本战后生命政治的思考。

关键词：唐十郎；状况剧场；艺术；政治；身体

On January 3, 1969, at Shinjuku's West Gate Plaza in Tokyo, the public crowded into a red tent for play Koshimaki Osen: Furisode Kaji no Maki. Led by Japanese playwright Kara Jūrō, director of the famed and then scandalous Jōkyō Gekijō (Situation Theater), the Rent Tent had already become a sensation in Tokyo. Yet few audiences expected that the theatrical event would escalate into an extremely violent bodily encounter with the police. For the audiences sitting at the periphery, there was only a layer of canvas between them and the police. The riot police brandished truncheons on the audiences, while trying to stop the performance by yelling over the loudspeaker. It was a cacophony of the audiences' cries, policemen's curses, actors' shouting out the lines, and police siren. The "dramas" inside and outside the theater intertwined to become a tension-ridden spectacle. Kara, along with several other leads of Situation Theater, was arrested by the riot police afterwards.

Fig. 1 Kara Juro's Situation Theater and the Red Tent

From NHK documentary Transborder Red Tent: Kara Jūrō's Grand Adventure (2021).
Photo credit to Ide Jyōji.

More than an isolated episode of "mob violence" against police order, the incident bears complex aesthetic and political implications and raises more questions than the city law could answer. It fostered an active and affective spectatorship to such an extent that the myth of realism at the heart of modern theater art encountered its demystification at its own expense through its destruction. Is it theater's nightmare or its ideal realization? What, then, is theater? Is it a drama performed on stage based on a written script, a built environment, or an embodied event and encounter that ultimately transforms the spectators' perceptions and actions? Placing Kara's performances in the rising angura (underground theater) movement in the late-60s and a broader global context, can we say that the theatre's moving toward the streets reflects a smooth expansion of theater art in blurring actor/audience and art/life boundaries? Furthermore, what perspectives about concepts of politics are opened up through theater? Drawing on Kara's theatrical praxis and French philosopher Jacques Rancière's discussion of the relationship between art and politics, this paper provokes a radical rethinking of post-war Japanese theater arts as a corporeal and affective engagement in politics. Kara's Situation Theater, as I will argue, is not so much a representation of politics as an attempt to redefine politics by changing the meaning of viewing and acting as well as the position of the spectator. As I examine in light of Kara's writings on the human body, in bringing previously suppressed bodies and senses to the fore, his performances also play into the larger transformation of post-war biopolitics in Japan.

A closer scrutiny of Kara's performances cannot afford to overlook the burgeoning field of artistic innovations worldwide in the 1960s. As some scholars have pointed out, Japanese avant-garde arts of the era displayed a heightened sense of kokusaiteki dōjisei, or "international contemporaneity" (Havens, 2006; Tomii, 2009). Against the backdrop of the social, political and cultural upheavals, heightened social disengagement and commodification of art, artists in Europe and the US resorted to politicized, reactionary and socially engaged practice. Employing street performances and theatrical experiments, Fluxus, Happenings and Situationist artists sought to refine art not as a finished object but as an event, a site-specific and time-based experience. As Claire Bishop observes, "the audience" evolved through three stages in the twentieth century, from demanding a role in the early avant-gardes, to "enjoy[ing] its subordination to strange experiences devised for them by an artist, to an audience that is encouraged to be a co-producer of the work" (2012, p. 277). One common goal of Fluxus, Happenings, Situationist events and Kara's performances, therefore, is to transform the spectator into an active participant in generating meanings as opposed to a passive receiver of generated meanings.

As I will elaborate in the remainder of the essay, Kara's theater not only integrates the spectator into an essential part of the artwork/event by allowing them to participate, but also prompts us to rethink such terms as spectacle, performance, and even "the political" itself in both literal and metaphorical senses. My point of departure is that the theater—Kara's artistic platform—provides a fundamental and illuminating vantage point to engage with Jacques Rancière (1999)'s discussion of politics, in which such metaphors as stage, performance, and theater are omnipresent. In a recent interview, for instance, Rancière accounts for the operation of politics as follows:

> Politics is always about creating a stage ... politics always takes the form, more or less, of the establishment of a theater. This means that politics always needs to establish those little worlds in which ... forms of subjectivation can take shape and stage or enact a conflict, a dispute, an opposition between worlds. For me, politics is about the establishment of a theatrical and artificial sphere (qtd. in Hallward, 2009, p. 142).

For Rancière, every political subject acts in the theatrical sense, and politics is a matter of creating a theater to stage conflicts and inequality. In what follows, I will try to examine various aspects of Kara's theatrical practices in light of Rancière theatrical conception of politics to consider what makes Kara's theater political. A subsequent section *will take up Kara's* appearance in Oshima Nagisa's *Diary of a Shinjuku Thief* (1968), a film that playfully juxtaposes Kara's performance with documentary footage of student protests to reveal the theatricality at the core of journalism and more broadly politics per se. This paper closes with a section that brings into a comparative dialogue Kara's theoretical writing on the body and senses and Rancière's idea of "distribution of the sensible". The affective potential of the body alluded in both Kara's and Rancière's works, as I will demonstrate, creates contact zones between actor and spectator capable of developing models for the direct exchange of affirmative, political, and social energies.

I. *Angura* and Political (In) Visibility

Angura, the Japanese contraction for the term "andaaguraundo engeki", literally "underground theater", itself encapsulates the tension between art and politics. As noted by Peter Eckersall, the dimensions of space, time, and equally importantly, darkness, are constituent features of the angura movement (2005, p. xii). It should be stressed that the darkness here signifies not only the dark theatrical space or the sense of darkness and turmoil encapsulated in Kara's performances as suggested by Eckersall, but also its status as a counter-cultural art form not officially recognized by the state.

In what follows, I will illustrate the ways in which Situation Theater was engaged in producing alternative regimes of the sensible against sovereign power and the domination of ideology. They adopted a more confrontational stance against the state from the time they were driven out of the Hanazono Shrine in 1968 until they performed in the West Gate Plaza under police surveillance. It is remarkable that the "police" here goes far beyond the narrow definition as an agent of law enforcement and surveillance. To recall Rancière's useful distinction between the general order of "police" and the act of "politics", the term "policing" refers to a wide spectrum of the institutionalized activities of governance, regulation, and the exercise of power commonly understood as "politics": "Politics is generally seen as the set of procedures whereby the aggregation and consent of collectivities is achieved, the organization of powers, the distribution of places and roles, and the systems of legitimizing this distribution. I propose to give this system of distribution and legitimization another name. I propose to call it the police." (Rancière, 1999, p. 28)

For Rancière, the police predetermines what one can see, say, and do, as well as who can speak for a given political community. By contrast, politics for him is defined as a wide range of activities that upset this regulatory order of sense perception and distribution of social roles and bodies in society: "Political activity is whatever shifts a body from the place assigned to it or changes aplace's destination. It makes visible what had no business being seen, and makes heard a discourse where there was only place for noise." (Rancière, 1999, p. 29) The relationship between aesthetics and human is therefore not only a cognitive one, but also a social and political one. In other words, Rancière's conceptualization of politics centers on the logic of visibility; politics entails making visible of forms of existence that are otherwise rendered invisible. If, for Rancière, the major function of the police within a community is summarized in the phrase "Move along! There is nothing to see here!" then this motto equally applies to the riot police that continuously attempt to render the red tent invisible. The police order embodied by the riot police establishes a distribution of the sensible, or in Gabriel Rockhill's words, a "division between the visible and the invisible, the audible and the inaudible, the sayable and the unsayable" (2004, p. 8). In contrast, Kara's performances—not through the plot of drama or through dramatic characters who represent them but rather through the theater itself as an art form granted a dazzling visibility—constitute an aesthetic disruption of the circulation of state-sanctioned sensations and perceptions, thus are fundamentally political in nature.

Kara's theater provides an intriguing example to consider Rancière's conceptualization of political visibility and equality in more fully theatrical terms. In *The Emancipated Spectator* (2009), Rancière problematizes the binary opposition between the passive spectator and the active actor. In conventional theater-going experience, viewing is opposed to knowing and acting as the spectator is chained on the seat and assigned the passive role of contemplation. The asymmetrical nature of the relationship between theatrical action and the audience, according to Rancière, "specifically defines a distribution of the sensible, an a priori distribution of the positions and capacities and incapacities attached to these positions", hence symptomatic of, and in some ways a metaphor for sociopolitical inequality (Rancière, 2009, p. 12). The possibility of emancipation, in Rancière's formulation, begins when we "challenge the opposition between viewing and acting; when we understand that the self-evident facts that structures the relations between saying, seeing, and doing themselves belong to the structure of domination and subjection. It begins when we understand that viewing is also an action that confirms or transforms this distribution of positions" (p. 13). To create the conditions for emancipation from state power and capitalist sovereignty, from Rancière's perspective, artistic practices must change the meaning of viewing and acting, not just the position of the spectator. Then, how do Kara's theatrical practices pave the foundation for emancipation? I propose to consider this question by turning to Kara's creative treatment of the Red Tent, the theatrical space of his performance. The Red tent grants Kara's theater troupe three features that would be impossible otherwise, namely mobility, alterity, and interchangeability of inside/outside, as I will elaborate in the following pages.

First, the itinerant nature of Situation Theater evokes kabuki in the Edo period (1600 − 1868) by itinerant troupes of actors who were rejected by bourgeois society as outcasts, or "riverbed beggars". The reference to premodern theatrical tradition allows Kara to make a potentially political statement. Associated with the days when theater was not yet institutionalized as part of the ideological state apparatus, Kara gestures towards an absolute rejection of the present and thus an emancipation from the structures of domination that condition everyday life.

The mobility of the Red Tent further enables Kara to embark on a journey across Asia and beyond. While majority of contemporary artists in Japan were more interested in arty bourgeois festivals in the West, Kara took a road less taken. Partly influenced by his Zainichi-Korean ex-wife Ri Reisen, a member of his troupe, and Kim Sujin, one of the most significant contemporary figures in the considerable Zainichi artistic community, Kara staged plays—in both Tokyo and Seoul—that question Japanese imperial actions while advocating better Japanese-Korean relations. His concern for marginalized or outcast social groups culminated in 1972, when Kara brought his Red Tent to Lebanon and Syria and performed in Palestinian refugee camps. Kara adapted his Matasaburo the Wind Imp into Palestinian Matasaburo the Wind Imp, not only translating the stage play from Japanese to Arabic but also changing the setting from Japan to Palestine. The play was performed nine times, attracting over two thousand refugees each time (Senda, 2007, pp. 193 - 195). Kara's incentive to forge connections with marginalized social groups was encapsulated in a speech he gave prior to his departure to Palestine:

> In this globalizing world, it is meaningless to be biased toward Asia; it goes without saying that Palestine, at the crossroad of Asia and Western Europe, harbors the dynamism of dreams and reality. Believing that culture is an outcome of struggle and a panorama of memory, we wish to present to the people of Palestine the Red Tent Theater in the spirit of "riverbed beggars," and we hope it brings them enormous courage. (Higuchi, 2011, pp. 105-106).

Likening his troupe to "riverbed beggars", Kara seems to identify himself as an "outcast" from contemporary Japanese society. Kara's "outcast" status, the nomadic nature of his Red Tent theater, and his presence as "other" in Palestinian community find resonance in the refugee's own existence. For the refugees, Kara's theater hence assumes the function of an alternative public sphere; in opposition to the bourgeois public horizon claimed by Jürgen Habermas, the space of theater is proletarian in nature for it enables marginalized people to encounter each other, create social bonds, and share experiences. Amid rapidly growing tensions between Arab and Israeli, the refugees' experience of Kara's performances becomes deeply emmeshed in the displacement and discrepancies in their experience of the war as a whole.

Second, browsing through articles by people who have seen Situation Theater's Red Tent, one would be struck by the frequent recurrence of the word maboroshi. With poetic ambiguity, maboroshi can mean illusion, vision, dream, or apparition, suggesting an ethereal, utopian, and haunting place. Appearing and disappearing mysteriously, the Red Tent itself encapsulated a now-you-see-it now-you-don't theatricality. Occupying the intersection of reality and fantasy, it becomes a radical alterity of the urban space, interrupting the everyday flows of the city while creating disturbances that ultimately questioned the taken-for-granted use of the urban space.

Meanwhile, the illusory and ethereal qualities of the Red Tent metaphorically coordinated with the texts of Kara's works. Blending past and future, reality and fantasy, Kara's plays are replete with surrealist imagery, bizarre characters and creatures, and incongruous elements (eg. a nurse smoking in the operating room, a girl with a womb made of glass, and a puddle in contemporary Japan which turns out to be the a teleporter to wartime China). Featuring surrealistic, astonishing, absurd, even baffling plots, Kara's plays stress the imaginary, transhistorical, and experiential over the logical, realistic depiction of social reality. The stories flirt with the audience's desire to interpret, while the audience realizes only at a later point that the effort to "interpret" the lines as "meaning" per se is not at all what is called for. Kara's works thus propel us to rethink such categories as "sense" and "nonsense" that are all too often constructed antithetically; "sense" and "meaningfulness" are habitually equated, and given a positive valuation in an opposition that makes nonsense the purely negative term. His plays, however, do not set "nonsense" and "sense" in opposition, but rather show that the possibility of meanings can be recognized within nonsense—it is only within nonsense that one can begin to look for signs of meanings, not against it.

Therefore, Kara's engagement with surrealism adds an additional player in which the idea of (in) visibility comes into play. With its promise to liberate the mind fettered by rational thinking and brings the unconscious of everyday life—normally hidden beneath the conscious mind—to the surface, surrealism not only allows Kara to reveal the invisible while articulating the unspeakable, but also opens for reconsideration of the human psyche—the profound psychological disorientation in post-war Japan, for instance—as one among the many discourses (political, ideological, economic, etc.) that intersect to form the social field, thereby redefining "the political" itself. In short, Kara's anti-cultural, anti-establishment angura practices open up new ways of engaging with multiple registers of the invisible (political, historical, material, imaginary, sensory, and allegorical) and to shift thought beyond what seems given, natural, or necessary—in other words, visible.

Third, Kara's creative treatment of the theatrical space very often collapses the rigid boundary between art and life, spectator and spectacle. The dissolution between art and life is first made possible by the porous texture of the Red Tent. Made of canvas, the tent virtually had no sound-proof function. During the performance, the audience would hear noises of automobiles, nearby construction sites, rain and wind, and occasionally riot police outside intermingled with actor's voices inside the tent. These ambient sounds, normally perceived as a distraction to be eliminated, became an integral part of the soundscape of Kara's theater. The co-existence of inside/outside space also meant that each performance could differ wildly even should it be the same work, as it was impossible to predict what would happen during that day's performance.

The relationship between inside and outside is not only porous but also reversible, and such reversibility culminates in the following scene in Koshimaki Osen:

> Osen: Come back! Let's build a hut in this town and live together.
> Hoichi: Where?
> Osen (Pointing to the direction of Shinjuku): In Shinjuku!

As Osen finished the line, the curtain behind the stage was lifted, revealing the view outside the tent. According to Ide's recollection, he was struck when he saw the curtain lifted and the group of riot police gathering outside the tent. At the same time, the riot police were transformed into a spectacle on the stage and an essential part of the unfolding narrative, while audiences inside the tent were invited to gaze upon critically, alongside the actors on the stage, the on-going event outside the theater that was, in Kara's words, "summoned into (yobikomu)" the tent. More than a visual gag, Kara's creative treatment of the theatrical space turned the Red Tent into a site of concrete politics, a space not for consensus but divergence, for active disagreement via a fundamental disruption of an existing distribution of the sensible. Not only did the actors—at the verge of being rendered invisible by the police order—reassert their visibility, but they also bring the structure of domination—the police that rendered them invisible—to light.

More importantly, the police's involuntary participation in the play provides a polemical ground to rethink the very definitions of "participation" and "participatory art". As Bishop points out, as contemporary arts display an obvious tendency toward collaboration and participation, artists' and curators' blind faith in participatory art implies an "ethical" turn, promoting a model of collaboration, process, and equality in order to rule out other "unethical" practices that might be more politically radical and aesthetically complex (2012, pp. 20 − 30). Put differently, the democratic potential of participatory art may paradoxically become hegemonic and risks narrowing the scope of the arts. A good art by Bishop's standard is something predicated upon the logic of relational antagonism, which "would be predicated not on social harmony, but on exposing that which isrepressed in sustaining the semblance of this harmony" (2005, p. 79). Instead of naturalizing the relations of conflict within society or achieving a harmonious reconciliation between Situation Theater and the riot police, Kara's play incorporates what it considers its "other", while sufficiently sustaining the tension among different parts of its own internal makeup.

To push it further, such dramatic reversal not only radically collapsed boundaries between any world clearly labeled either "inside" or "outside", "fictional" or "real", but also partook in a fundamental reconceptualization of the hierarchical relationship between the artist and the viewer and the boundary between art and life. Life as experienced in his theater was no longer a mere reproduction or symbolic interpretation of our existential reality. Rather, his theater itself arranged the conditions for an active confrontation of reality, a reality not illustrated by but actualized in the inter-subjective and embodied encounter between the artist, the viewer, and the police as "intruder". The theatrical space of the tent is itself a representation as well as a methodology that provided the condition of possibility for emancipation, so to speak.

Ⅱ. Media, Event, and Politics as Performance

In theater as much as in politics, the idea of performativity is essential to its actualization. Politics during this era displayed strong performative tendencies, especially in 1968 and 1969, when the anti-Anpo movement reached a peak. Notably, the season of politics also coincided the rise of television, which was quick to turn student movement and other sensational events—including Kara's performances—into media spectacle. His performance at Shinjuku West Gate Plaza, for instance, was immediately classified by the Japanese media as worthy of description as an "incident" (jiken): Shinjuku Nishi-Guchi Koen Jiken, literally "Shinjuku West Gate Plaza Incident". Massive mediation of protests and marches and the growing presence of street-theatres led to a conflation of artistic performance and political action. Our discussion here can be facilitated by recalling Rancière's definition of theatrical spectacle: "All forms of spectacle—drama, dance, performance art, mime and so on—that place bodies in action before an assembled audience." (2008, p. 2) If there is no theater without a spectator, as Rancière would have, perhaps the reverse is also true: any events that "place bodies in action before an assembled audience" might be called theatrical and performative in a broad sense. Performance and theatricality so defined can thus extend to any relation between the staged performance and an assembled spectator, inside or outside the theater, and mediated or unmediated by the camera.

The vibrant media sphere and radical avant-garde experiments provide a rich ground for artists across different disciplines to bring their artistic expertise into cross-pollination. Angura troupes of the time often make appearances in films, with Zero Dimension (Zero Jigen) in Matsumoto Toshio's Funeral Parade of Roses (1968) and the Situation Theater in Oshima Nagisa's Diary of a Shinjuku Thief (1968) being the most prominent examples. Filmmakers appropriate and remediate news events, often juxtaposing them with documentary footage of angura performances. Such a cross-medial phenomenon points to a strange affinity between two forms of spectacle: political protests and theatrical performances. A closer look at the film—another medium anchored by performance—not only offers pivotal insights into Rancière's conception of politics discussed earlier in this paper, but also leads to more questions to ruminate on. The documentary-within-film structure, as I will discuss later, powerfully breaks down borders between fiction and non-fiction, while cultivating an active, self-conscious mode of spectatorship that paves the way for emancipation.

Diary of a Shinjuku Thief opens with Kara running through the street of Shinjuku. A few men are chasing after Kara while shouting "Thief!" Once Kara is caught, he takes off his clothes, revealing a flower tattoo on his belly. At this point, it is revealed that Kara and his pursuers are performing a skit. The camera cuts to a young man in the crowd, who turns out to be the protagonist (played by graphic designer Yokoo Tadanori) of the film. This scene brings together two modes of performance, namely the performance of the Situation Theater actors and the performance of the actor Yokoo Tadanori. As the film progresses, the two levels of performance converge in the site of Kara's Situation Theater, as Yokoo enters the Red Tent to play Yui Shōsetsu, a Japanese rebel who attempts to overthrow Tokugawa shogunate's rule.

Fig. 2 Kara's Appearance in the Beginning of *Diary of a Shinjuku Thief* (1968)

Towards the end of the film, the Situation Theater's performance gives way to a playfully inserted documentary sequence that captures the start of a riot on 29 June 1968. The footage of riot is juxtaposed with a series of intertitles that infuse the film with a sense of global synchronicity.

147

"Washington": April 1968 after the assassination of Martin Luther King the city experienced days of rioting and civil disorder swept the States. "Paris": May 1968 civil unrest, occupations and strikes gripped the city and France. "Brazzaville": August 1968, Massamba-Débat was overthrown in a military coup in Congo. The dramatic nature of this street action further blurs the boundary between fiction and nonfiction, theatricality and actuality, and diegetic and nondiegetic worlds. Seen in this light, the "documentary moment" in Shinjuku is a self-conscious appropriation of journalistic sensibility, a combination of factuality and temporal immediacy. The instance of cinema remediating journalism brings the tension between fiction and non-fiction into play, wherein cinematic artifice comes to expose the constitutive theatricality of journalism itself.

As such, Kara's theatrical performance and Oshima's film form cross-medial webs that encompass not only the two artists and their works, journalistic discourses, but audiences all as inter-related subjects. The instance of making art based on and inspired by, human relations and their social context exemplifies what Nicolas Bourriaud terms "relational aesthetics", which he defines as "a set of artistic practices which take as their theoretical and practical point of departure the whole of human relations and their social context, rather than an independent and private space" (1998, p. 113). Moreover, the self-conscious appropriation of journalistic medium in Shinjuku—the documentary moments of the riot and Kara's performance in particular—opens for new possibilities of spectatorial engagement.

Drawing on Maurice Merleau-Ponty's Phenomenology of Perception, Vivian Sobchack argues that even in the middle of one film, the spectator is capable of switching between different modes of consciousness. In fictional consciousness, the cinematic object is perceived as "not real" or "imaginary", while in documentary consciousness, the viewer is aware that those images do not exist "here" in the virtual world, but exists "elsewhere" in the real world (Sobchack, 1999, pp. 245 − 246). Released in the immediate aftermath of the 1968 student uprisings, struck too close to home to a contemporary audience whose memories about political upheaval were still fresh. Seen in this light, the documentary-within-fiction structure moves the spectator back and forth between documentary and fictional modes of consciousness, assigning her/him a critical position: looking both at and through the screen, dependent upon the image for knowledge but also is aware of what it evokes beyond the realm of fiction.

III. From Privileged Body to the Distribution of the Sensible

As Terry Eagleton tells us, aesthetics is born as a "discourse of the body" in the 18th century (1990, p. 13). Despite the numerous vicissitudes in its long march into the present, bodies remain central to aesthetics as well as an aesthetic understanding of politics. Influenced by Sartre's existentialism, Kara provocatively espouses what he calls "The Theory of the Privileged Body (tokkenteki nikutairon)". The privileged body, in Kara's formulation, is defined as "a figure that crystalized the peculiar (dokutoku) and inherent (koyū) existence of fictional characters, one that draws on the actor's body as source material" (1997, p. 16). Theater attracts audience precisely because the actor's body is both peculiar and inherent. Hence, what is at stake for Kara is not the script, but the raw and expressive body of actors on stage. Kara went on in an interview to articulate the mission of theater as "rediscovering the possibility of human body that has been rectified, concealed, or forgotten by modern institutions" and ultimately "the resurgence of everything suppressed by modernity" (Higuchi, 2011, p. 52).

Freeing the body from the shackle of rationalism allows Kara to unleash its full expressivity without "trapping" it—in the sense of providing a fixed representation that overdetermines the body, and consequently closing the body into definitive categories. In his performances, more often than not, he pushes the body to its extreme—eyes rolling up, limbs inverted, legs bowed and mouths widely open—a state of pure corporeality beyond the regulated movements of the everyday. The body on stage thereby gains a powerful and compelling sense of immediacy that resonates in and through the spectator's body, prompting visceral responses more than as cognitive ones. Here, the focus is on an aesthetic of sensation, where the tends to be given precedence over plot, dialogue and conventional narrative progression, and

149

as such, pre-empts and determines the function assigned to the theater form as a narrative and representational construct, or as the articulation of an ideological discourse.

Kara's emphasis on the actor's body can be better understood within a broader context of post-war biopolitics that was under tremendous transformation. Compared to post-war era, wartime ideology valorizes the spirit over the body; to give one illustrating example, governmental publications of the period contain words such as spiritual construction (seishin kensetsu) and spiritual education (seishin kyoiku), while the body was talked about only so much as it is related to the nation, or in the form of polity (kokutai). However, along with Japan's defeat came the collapse of the intellectual foundation for wartime society, notably the ideology that privileged the spiritual (to use the term favored by Japanese officials) over the corporeal. It can be argued that for Kara, staging the body becomes an attempt to restore individual plurality of nikutai (body) that has been blatantly suppressed by collective singularity of kokutai (national polity). By asserting the centrality of the body in everyday life, Kara's reflection also critiques the Japanese wartime discourses of spiritual construction that led the country into militarization.

More crucially, Kara's conceptualization of the privileged body gestures towards a dissolution of the boundaries between art and life: "The actor, by virtue of his privileged body, is capable of an expedition (ensei) from life to art, as well as an assault (shūrai) by art on life." (Kara, 1997, p. 16) Kara's theater is a conflation wherein spectacle, spectator, and actor are equated and come together in a moment of joint existence. For Kara, there is no difference in nature between the spectator and the spectacle, the seeing and the seen, because what is on the stage and what is gazing at the stage, are ontologically the same thing: a living body. The ontological equivalence between the bodies on and off stage that enables the actor's body to reach the spectator's body and reconfigures itself in the spectator's body/mind. According to Kara, it is precisely the combination of "expedition" and "assault" between art and life that grant his work "political actuality (seiji-teki akuchuaritii)". Envisioning theater not so much as an inferior copy of reality but as a reality in its own right, Kara also differentiates his theater with new drama (shingeki) which sees theater as merely a narrative and representational construct.

Kara's preoccupation with body as a concrete reality enables us to carve out a hidden path between his theory and Rancière's conception of "distribution of the sensible" through their shared concern with body, sensation and affect. Rancière does not explicitly use the term "affect", but he articulates a form of sense perception that emphasizes the politics of seeing, speaking, and hearing. The governing of the senses, I suggest, must also be conceived in terms of bodily affective sensations central to Kara's theory and theatrical practices.

When it comes to Rancière's thoughts on politics, the body and affect is a crucial yet less noted dimension. Rancière's aesthetic understanding of corporeality is essential to his interpretation of intellectual emancipation. As noted earlier in the essay, he defines political activity precisely as "whatever shifts a body from the place assigned to it or changes a place's destination" (1999, p. 30). In several interviews, Rancière hints at how crucial the body is to the aesthetic dimension of emancipation by pointing out that "emancipation does not imply a shift in terms of knowledge, but in terms of the position of bodies" (2009, p. 575). In *The Emancipated Spectators*, too, he defines theatre as "the place where an action is taken to its conclusion by bodies in motion in front of living bodies that are to be mobilized" (p. 3). If politics is, as Rancière would have it, a struggle for visibility, a voice out of noise, and a shifting of body's places and designations, then one must construe Kara's theater as a socially transformative, imaginative, and political engagement which is grounded in the realm of corporeality and has the potential for social critique and collective politics.

Conclusion

Let me conclude by returning to my starting point. As I have illustrated in this paper, many of Rancière's thoughts are highly pertinent to Situation Theater as it does with the operation of politics. They set up an interface through which theater and politics can interact and shed light on each other.

Kara's theatrical performance, viewed in this way, challenges the boundaries that maintain the distribution of what can and cannot be seen, and the commonsense division between the actor and the spectator. It is a double performance, making the point that seeing and experiencing art is also an embodied process of making art. His theater is a political one not so much because it comments on political and social issues, but because it gets the world of its subjects and its operations to be seen. The theoretical underpinning of both Kara's theatrical practices and Rancière's conception of politics, as I have argued, is firmly grounded in the myriad possibilities of the sentient, sensual, and sensible human body, the locus of everyday experience. In a nutshell, the intersection of politics and aesthetics illuminates an alternative angle from which the "newness" of arts in the 1960s can be critically reexamined.

References:

Akihiko, S. (2007). *Kara Jūrō no gekisekai* (Kara Jūrō's World of Theater). Tokyo: Yubunshoin.

Bishop, C. (2012). *Artificial Hells:Participatory Art and the Politics of Spectatorship*. New York: Verso.

Bishop, C. (2005). "Art of the Encounter: Antagonism and Relational Aesthetics." *Circa*, 114, 32-35.

Bourriaud, N. (1998). *Relational Aesthetics*. Dijon: Les presses du réel.

Eagleton, T. (1990). *The Ideology of the Aesthetic*. Malden, MA: Basil Blackwell.

Eckersall, P. (2006). *Theorizing the Angura Space*. Leiden: Brill.

Hallward, P. (2009). "Staging Equality: Rancière's Theatrocracy and the Limits of Anarchic Equality", in *Jacques Rancière: History, Politics, Aesthetics, Gabriel Rockhill and Philip Watts*, eds. Durham: Duke University Press.

Havens, T. R. H. (2006). *Radicals and Realists in the Japanese Nonverbal Arts:The Avant-garde Rejection of Modernism*. Honolulu: University of Hawaii Press.

Higuchi, Y. (2011). *Kara Jūrō-ron* (Theorizing Kara Jūrō). Tokyo: Michitani.

Kara, J. (1997). *Tokkenteki nikutai-ron* (Theory of the Privileged Body). Tokyo: Hakusuisha.

Rancière, J. (1999). *Disagreement: Politics and Philosophy*. Rose Julie, (Trans.) Minneapolis: University of Minnesota Press.

Rancière, J. (2009). *The Emancipated Spectator*. Gregory Elliott (Trans.), London:

Verso.

Rancière, J. (2013). *The Politics of Aesthetics*. Gabriel Rockhill (Ed. & Trans.), London: Bloomsbury.

Sobchack, V. (1999). "Toward a Phenomenology of Non-Fictional Film Experience". In Michael Renov and Jane Gaines (Ed.), *Collecting Visible Evidence*, Minneapolis: University of Minnesota Press, 241—254.

Tomii, R. (2007). "Geijutsu on Their Minds: Memorable words on Anti-Art", in C. Merewether and R. I. Hiro (eds.), *Art, Anti-art, Non-art: Experiments in the Public Sphere in Postwar Japan, 1950—1970*. Los Angeles: Getty Research Institute.

Author:

Zhao Xinyi, Ph. D. candidate in East Asian cinema and media at Columbia University, USA. She is broadly interested in East Asian cinema, Japanese visual culture, and media archaeology.

作者简介：

赵心怡，哥伦比亚大学东亚电影与媒体专业博士研究生，主要研究方向为东亚电影、日本视觉文化和媒体考古学。

Email：xz2468@columbia. edu

书　评　●　●　●　●　●

发现中国听觉叙事美学：读傅修延《听觉叙事研究》

陆正兰

作者：傅修延

书名：听觉叙事研究

出版社：北京大学出版社

出版时间：2021 年

ISBN：978-7-3013-2010-5

　　人类是能讲故事的物种。人类用故事总结经验，学会生存，并将这生存经验，又通过故事的形式一代代传递给后人，由此各种物质文明和精神文明开始累积。

　　讲故事的方式多种多样。用文字语言来讲故事，已经是人类文明较为成熟的时候了，而前期过程相当漫长。科普作家詹姆斯. 格雷克（James Gleick）写过一本《信息简史》（*The Information: A history，a Theory，a Flood*），开篇就从"会说话的非洲鼓"说起。早期非洲部落用鼓传递一些简单的信息：作战时候的进攻或撤退等。虽然只有一部分人知道怎样用鼓声来沟通，但几乎所有的人都能够听懂鼓声的含义，哪怕鼓手的击鼓方式不同，节奏有快有慢，但不妨碍他们表达同样的意思。这一点很有趣，就好像我们能理解同样意思的不同方言。在此书中，他还举了一个让我们很惊奇的例子，说鼓声能传达很复杂的意义：有个人去世了，请大家明天清晨到河边去参加送别仪式。如何证明？有个传教士把仪式记录下来，次日清晨他看到人们果然纷纷从不同的地方向河边聚集。

一只会讲故事的鼓，一种听觉的力量，至今保留在某些没有被现代文明之光照到的原始部落里。这也不难理解，就像中国，作为一个多民族国家，也有一些一直没有自己文字的民族，比如居住在贵州黔东南地区的侗族。"以歌养心"是他们的生活方式，歌告诉人们生存的法则，如何做人，如何做事。一首"侗族大歌"，把不同的声部有机地汇合在一起，就如同一个大家庭和谐地生成，完美地生活。与其说是"侗族大歌"体现了这个民族的特点，不如说这种"听觉叙事"教会了人们如何按照"歌的内容"以"歌的完美形式"生活。

写了这么多，其实想说傅修延教授的这本《听觉叙事研究》太新颖深刻，太能启发思考了。

《听觉叙述研究》是傅修延教授近年出版的一部具有重大原创理论价值的学术著作，作为中国叙事学的领军人物之一，傅修延教授一直致力叙事学，尤其是中国叙事学的研究，为中国的叙述学做出了巨大贡献。他四十多年如一日，孜孜不倦，锲而不舍。这种不断求索的精神，也体现在他的每次学术出场，都带给我们巨大的"学术惊艳"，无论是观点还是研究视角。

傅修延教授是一个致力寻找奥秘的学者，他最早的著作就叫《讲故事的奥秘》。正如他在这本《听觉叙事研究》中所坦露的："笔者多年来致力于探讨中国叙事传统的发生与形成，一直在念兹在兹地思考为什么它会是如我们今天所讲的这种样貌。"（2021，p.298）念兹在兹，必有所得。这本《听觉叙事研究》石破天惊，不仅在于它开创了一个新的叙事领域，还在于它对中国叙事美学的重大发现；它也不仅是作者多年中西叙事学探索道路上的又一次重大突破，也是中国叙事学乃至世界叙事学征程上一个新的里程碑式，它从源头上发现了中西叙事差异的根基。

傅修延教授在书中提出："中西叙事的不同，源于各自的结构观念乃至观念后面的文化，而这归根结底是因为双方在视觉和听觉上各有倚重。"（p.298）这个结论一反以往的中西文化差异表层的比较视野，而是通过人类最基本的感知世界方式，重新认识了中西叙事特征及中国叙事美学。

在书中，傅修延指出了中国文化中的听觉统摄功能，傅修延从繁体字"聽"的造字法，分析了一个字内纳入的耳、目、心三种人体重要器官的意义，继而得出："'听'是一种全方位的感知方式。中国在很长时间内一直保持着听觉社会的诸多特征，相比于'看'，中国人更多用'听'来统摄各种感知，由此产生了中国叙事的中各种差异。"（p.270）全书以中国的汉字源头为基点，以中国传统中的各种叙述文本为实践依据，令人信服地证明了这一创新观点。

中国人以"听"为统摄，用联觉通感的方式整体感知世界，这也是整个中国传统认识论的根基。比如，在绘画中，中国传统美学并不强调对特定线条、形式、运动或自然事物的感知体验，而是强调对整体环境的感知，这种感知连接起人的本性的觉醒。

傅修延讨论借用唐代诗人韦应物的《咏声》的诗句"万物自身听"，把由听觉构建的世界扩展到万事万物，从而让世人警觉人是世界的中心这样的世界观。他精彩地写道："人也是万物之一，人物一词突出人的物性，标明我们的古人早就注意到人与物之间的对立统一。"（p.372）

回想王维的诗《辛夷坞》："木末芙蓉花，山中发红萼。涧户寂无人，纷纷开且落"，韦应物的"野渡无人舟自横"，就如同此书所论述的"无人之听与无文之听"甚至"万物自在听"。这一充满东方魅力的听觉统筹，让一个充满生机的世界流动起来。对此，傅修延教授精妙地概括为"我听故我在"。"讲"与"听"互生互长，看起来似乎"讲"是主动，"听"是被动，实际上，"听"反而是一种主动，这里充满了美妙的东方辩证法。"万物自身听"蕴含了"万物自身讲"，只有"听"最能将一种"待在"变成"显在"。因为你在与不在，我都在，除了心能感受到你存在，眼睛看到更实在。但你听与不听，我都在听，就更彻底，除了心能感受到你存在，耳朵永远不会闭合。

罗兰·巴尔特写过一篇"La Grain de Voix"，有好几种译法，有人翻译成"声音的纹理"，声音似乎由触觉可感，就像"音色"这个词，好像声音有颜色可见，每种声音就如同色彩光谱中的某一条，这正好是人的通感联觉所体验的。这也正是"听"的能动性，把各种通感统筹起来。

佩特也说过，一切艺术都走向音乐。他说的只是艺术各种媒介形式的表意方向，从具象走向抽象。而中国文化则不同，"虚空""见性""澄怀味象""气韵生动"这些美学表述，从来就不是以一种感官能说清楚的。"大象无形，大音希声""万物自身听"，更是西方人难以理解的，而在这本书里，傅修延教授从听觉叙事角度都做出了深刻的分析，非常值得我们一读再读。

孔子有句名言困扰了笔者很久——"兴于诗，立于礼，成于乐。"一般人都这么解释："人的修养开始于学《诗》，自立于学礼，完成于学乐。"为什么一个人的终极修养必须在学乐中练成？音乐是如何帮助一个人变成君子的呢？

按《听觉叙事研究》的思想来理解，"耳""目""心"组成的"聽"字，就是一种声音的听觉实践。学音乐首先需要的就是耳朵的听觉，不仅要听自己的嘴巴发出的声音，听自己手中的乐器发出的声音，还要听到同伴演奏的声音，更要让"听者"有共鸣；不仅必须自己得心应手，找到身体与声音的共鸣，还需要与协奏者协调共鸣，同样也要与听者协调共鸣。这当然是以孔子为代表的贵族阶层的"乐教"理想。在那个时代，普通老百姓没有条件"知乐"，就像《乐记》中所说："知声而不知音者，禽兽是也；知音而不知乐者，众庶是也。唯君子为能知乐。"

如傅修延教授所说，"用文化差异来解释叙事并不新鲜"（p. 298）。这么多年来，大部分叙事学的研究，都是借用西方叙述学的理论框架来理解中国叙事，文明有同有异，如果将对"异"的理解，都归结为"文化差异"这样大而化之的结论，不只是"不新鲜"，也不可能真正追根溯源，就如同发现中国人和外国人都有五官，但并不能真正得出外国人为什么是深眼眶、高鼻梁一个道理。

中国人讲故事多倚重听觉，西方人讲故事多倚重视觉。这个精深的发现，如同撩开的一层面纱，终于让很多解释不清的叙述学问题敞亮澄明。

傅修延教授早年就一直关注音乐文学，对听觉文化有深刻的研究。这本50多万字的著作，旁征博引，对中国叙事文本如数家珍，信手拈来皆是例证，有一种庖丁解牛般的酣畅淋漓。

在这本著作中，傅修延教授提出了听觉叙事中"语音独一性"（p. 104）问题。这个看似落在听觉文化和声音文化甚至语言学交汇处的重要理论点，在他的听觉叙事视角下有了独特的洞见。"语音独一性"听起来很简单，不仅是语音相对文字的独特性，也是每个个体声音的差异性。就如中国人各说各地方言，各人有各人的发音特征，但用文字写下来，这些语音个性就会被抹去，文字让交流毫无障碍。但是每个人都说同样的话，那什么才能让我们真正辨识出"语音独一性"？

傅修延教授举出的例子十分精彩：一个人站在门口敲门，里面人问，"谁啊?"外面人不报名字，而是说"我"，里面的人就能知道是谁了。这个精妙的例子，很好地解释了"语音的唯一性"。

傅修延教授指出，"语音作为一种特殊的能指，其所指不仅指声音通过语言符号所传递的事物概念，同时也指向语言本身的源头"（p. 7）。而这个源头通向一个感性的存在，就好像这个回答："我"，既是声音，也是声音发出的人，还是个抽象的代词。它们是一个整体的存在，只有听觉才能将其统筹起来，感知到它的"唯一性"。回到此著作的开头，傅修延解释这本书为什么叫"听觉叙事研究"，而不是"声音叙事研究"，笔者十分赞同。除了避开"声音"的复杂性，以及容易产生歧义的"比喻用法"（比如，个人、社群甚至国家政治），"语音的唯一性"必须通过"听"才能真正将其"唤醒"，只有通过"听"，才能整体把握，才能感受到。说到底，语音的唯一性，并不是客观地存在于那里，而是接受者的感知。

文明互鉴，理解对方，发现自我。在这本著作中，作者不仅回答了为什么麦克卢汉说中国人是"听觉人"，还回答了为什么不是中国学者而是麦克卢汉指出中国人是"听觉人"。反思中国传统叙事，他从听觉叙事角度，为中国传统一些不被认可的叙述独特性正名。因为这些叙事特征，不只是被西方人误读，连中国人自己也缺少"视觉耽溺的自省意识"（p. 257），例子有鲁迅、胡适、陈寅恪对明清章回小说中的"缀段性"的批评。

正如傅修延指出，听觉叙事展开一个听觉空间，中西方的叙述方式在此存在差异，视角统筹的叙事总是追寻序列的、连续的，而听觉叙事却是开放的、通感的、模糊的、不求序列的。中国式的"缀段性"或许就是中国小说开枝散叶的方法。就如法国当代哲学家德勒兹与心理学家加塔利指出文化也有两种传播模式——"树状模式"与"块茎模式"。"树状模式"有根有源头，可回溯意义的权威源头；而"块茎传播"则相反，可以侧生，随意蔓延，很难回溯源头。既然中国人理解"大音希声"的效应，中国叙述技巧中就蕴含着"尚简""贵无""趋晦""从散"的美学，所以我们有必要"重听经典"，从听觉叙事角度，重新感受中国的叙事美学。

傅修延教授的这本著作，开创了"听觉叙事"这一新学科。一个学科的建立，需要一些概念范畴。在这本《听觉叙事研究》中，他从听觉对象，到听觉主体，再到听觉方式等，都为我们提出了一些重要的理论范畴并做出了精辟的论证。比如与图景对应的"音景"，与观察相对的"聆察"，与"听"相对的"被听"，与形象相对的"声象"。这些概念用作者的话来说都是被当今主宰人类的视觉文化"倒逼"出来的产物，实际上都是一个个值得深研的课题。

例如，此著作中对"听之种种"的精彩分析。听什么固然重要，如何听可能对听觉叙事来说更为重要。此书分析了幻听、灵听与偶听、偷听，因声而听、因听而思和因听而悟。这些不同的"听觉方式"引发的不同的听觉事件，真正蕴含了"讲故事艺术的丰富与微妙"。

傅修延教授的这本《听觉叙事研究》，纵横捭阖，大开大合。他还将很多深刻的学理与日常生活哲理贯通。比如，对于在公共场合中的大声喧哗，他没有随大众一味地谴责，而是从听觉角度来深刻理解中国人之所以然。他的著作中有一节的题目就叫"最大的好客就是倾听"（p. 166），这句在生活中经常听到的处事名言，被他注入了深刻的"倾听"的意义，这样的论述思路从另一个层面，揭示了听觉叙事与中国文化的深层思维结构的相互关联。

傅修延教授写到，讲故事本来是一项诉诸听觉的艺术，从听觉角度重温叙事作品中的相关书写，既是为了抗阻日趋严重的视听失衡，也是对人类叙事"初心"的一种回望。这个"初心"，意味深长，也任重道远。值得展望的是，在傅修延教授的引领下，听觉叙事作为一个研究新方向正冉冉升起，生机盎然。

引用文献：

傅修延（2021）. 听觉叙事研究. 北京：北京大学出版社。

作者简介：

陆正兰，四川大学文学与新闻学院教授，博士生导师，主要从事艺术符号学研究。

Author:

Lu Zhenglan, professor of school of Literature and Journalism, Sichuan University. Her research interest mainly covers art semiotic.

Email: luzhegnlan69@163.com

叙事学中国化的历程、经验与反思：评王瑛《叙事学本土化研究（1979—2015）》

邓心强

作者：王　瑛

书名：叙事学本土化研究(1979—2015)

出版社：北京大学出版社

出版时间：2020 年

ISBN：978-7-3013-1475-3

华南农业大学王瑛教授 2020 年出版《叙事学本土化研究（1979—2015）》，这项厚重的学术著作系国家社科基金后期资助项目的结题成果，也是她反复打磨后奉献给学界的一部精品力作。该著广泛涉猎中西叙事学理论的方法、历程、特征及影响，带领读者在时空穿越中感受中国学者数十年来为建构本土叙事学做出的不懈努力，领略中国学派叙事学的各种支脉，读来酣畅淋漓，受益良多。无论是对这个宏大学术问题本身的深入论析和精辟观点，还是在影响、比较等多维视域中展开中西叙事学的对话与比较，这部著作在问题、观点、方法等方面均给读者多元的启迪。

叙事学在 20 世纪 80 年引入中国后，如一股清新而强劲的理论新风，引起国内文学界不同专业方向学者的浓厚兴趣，并在近年波及、扩散到新闻学、教育学、艺术学等多个学科，相关成果如雨后春笋不断涌现。它在中国发展演进了四十年，长期作为学术前沿和热点，也充分证明它是一门显学。作为一门学术性很强的学问，叙事学对研究者的理论思维和抽象思辨能力提出了较高要求。尤其是探究叙事学本土化之研究，在熟稔西方叙事学理论的基础上，更多地观照其理论的东方旅行和国内学者的各种回应与建构，这既需要在空间跨越中进行理论钩沉，也需要在本土化的各种尝试与既有成果中披沙拣金，进行理论的概括和提示。简言之，这是一项有学术难度的课题。然而王瑛教授多年来孜孜以求，硬是在这块中西结合部的沃土上种植出了庄稼，难能可贵。从框架结构和章节表达来看，作者深入浅出，举重若轻，尽显女性学者的优雅与从容。王瑛教授在学术之路上的执着追求和攀登精神，令人钦佩。

　　这部著作的第一个突出特征是有着强烈的问题意识，敢于直面西方文论中国化立场中具有宽广学术空间的真问题，并展开多维而立体的研究，体现出作者的使命担当，著作也由此具有极高的学术价值。在习近平总书记针对中国文艺发展和哲学社会科学发展发表系列讲话后，学界尤其关注立足国家导向、社会需求、现实问题等来展开创作与研究，从而建构中国本土话语体系。在叙事学引入中国的四十年间，在申丹、乔国强、董乃斌、赵毅衡、唐伟胜、龙迪勇等大批学者的耕耘和探索下，各种国家和省部级课题立项，相关著作出版，各种流派纷纷产生。可见，西方叙事学引入中国后发生了巨大的变化，尤其是经中国学者改造、创新后，触及中国古典叙事传统的挖掘与传承，与中国的文艺现实结合更紧密，并直面中国当下的各种叙事问题。通过研究叙事学的本土化，读者能从中管窥近十年乃至百年来西方文论中国化的漫长历程及中国学者在翻译、引入、借鉴和转化西方文论后的种种理论成就，以及创建中国本土学术流派的种种努力与开拓，也能从这一本土化的立场中，见出我们在吸收和改造西方文论、进行中西诗学对话过程中遇到的种种问题。从这个角度来说，这部著作是近年来西方各式理论中国化探索之一种，聚焦叙事学如何被中国学者创造性转化，如何在中国本土扎根后产生种种新变，并从中获得怎样的成就、规律和特点等，具有强烈的问题意识，有助于思考和解决中西诗学互动中种种复杂的理论问题。叙事学自"文化大革命"后传入中国，在四十年左右的发展演进中，经历了与文体学的融合、审美文化叙事学、比较叙事学、空间叙事学、广义叙事学、跨媒介叙事学等多个复杂阶段。① 王瑛把握历时的脉络，在细致的学术史梳理中展现出较强的理论洞察力和分析力，全书采用问题而非历时演进和学人学案的方式建构章节，六章标题依次是"叙事学本土化及其动力元""构建叙事诗学新方向""方法论创新""中国传统叙事理论钩沉""现代汉语叙事的实践与经验""中国叙事学的初步构想"，打破了将叙事学本土化按时代发展排序和以代表性学者立案的单一框架，挑选出问题来形成专题，在每个问题域中深入论析。由此可见，作者对中国叙事学四十年发展极为熟悉，具有较强的理论驾驭力。诚如蒋述卓所言，作者紧密围绕四大问题来推进和研究：叙事学本土化的内

---

　　① 见王瑛《叙事学本土化研究（1979—2015）》（北京大学出版社 2020 年版）第二章。

涵界定及展开方式，本土化后的特色与经验，涌现出的问题及其解决方案，对当代文艺批评实践和学科建设之意义。"这种充满探险式的学术研究使该书能够将历史的梳理和专题探讨很好地结合起来，呈现出一幅清晰的叙事学在中国本土化进程的学术版图。"（王瑛，2020，序）不仅如此，作者在多个章节中也以问题来带动论述，体现出鲜明的问题意识。如第四章第三节曰："建构中国叙事学要从哪里开始？中国叙事学从哪里起源，又是如何生成的？叙事传统生成以后，又是什么力量推动其向前演进？是什么原因导致叙事传统经由了这样一种发展途径？要建构中国叙事学，我们必然会如此叩问。"（p.146）催生问题是学术敏锐性的标志，也是实现学术目标的首要前提，类似以问题来带动具体论析的方式，几乎贯穿全书每一章。

第二个突出特征是开阔的学术视野与细致的理论分析。在厘清和展现叙事学本土化过程中，分析中国学者的创造与变化，这是一个横跨中西的学术课题，"辨析差异是吸纳西方理论最基本的工作"（p.111），"本土化的最基本含义，就是要化去西方之异质，融源自西方的理论为中国的理论，使叙事学成为中国当代文论有机整体的一部分"（pp.10—11）。基于此，作者凭借丰厚的学术积淀，一方面在比较的视野中分析叙事学传入中国后基于本土语境和传统而形成的特色，另一方面描绘和勾勒学者们在不同叙事领域的多维开拓和突出成就。作者认为"辨异是构建独特的、具有民族特色风姿的叙事理论的前提"（p.115），"差异也是中国叙事学存在的理由和根基，既有文化差异，又有国别差异，民族差异，更能刺激中国叙事学找到新的生长点，不同于西方叙事学的新的研究领域、新的叙事规律、新的学科范畴、新的概念……——挖掘整理开拓出来"（p.17）。书中很多章节便围绕这些方面展开，呈现出宽广的学术视野。勾勒申丹、赵毅衡、龙迪勇等近十名学者所形成的本土叙事学类型是本书的研究对象，作者在第二、三章中分别从模式与方法维度就这些具体而有特色的叙事学类型（支脉）的发展历程、方法特色、学术创新等进行了细致的论析。如王瑛所指出："一方面我们要充分重视我国古典叙事诗学的传统经验，另一方面中国现代小说叙事经验也应引起更为广泛的重视。"（p.220），于是，第四章中她聚焦"古典"，探究傅修延、赵艳秋、王平、董乃斌等学者对传统叙事思想的挖掘，跟随着这些学者在古典的时空中穿越，结合大量古代作品来分析和评价他们的叙事学研究路数和成就。随后，第五章转换视角论析"现代汉语叙事的实践和经验"，结合典型案例分析了现代小说、先锋小说的叙事性。这些章节和文字可谓涵盖古今中外，王瑛以开阔的学术视野和细致的笔调，在多个维度中展现近十年叙事学本土化的理论谱系和学术版图，完成了一幅五彩斑斓的叙事学画卷的修饰与描绘。由于有长期缜密而深入的思考，在具体论述中，王瑛教授果敢论断，针对某些问题大胆发表有理有据的看法，充分显示出自己的创见。如针对龙迪勇空间叙事学的提出，她认为"显然，空间不能代替视角，在寻求其诗学地位的同时，它必须承认时间的合法性和强大功能，没有时间，空间一无是处"（p.47）。在她看来，只有回到文本和叙事，空间才能真正登堂入室。"我们的学者是能够在西方学者和前人所忽略的空隙之处，提出并构型一种新的诗学理论、开拓新的学科方向的。""我们需要的是独立思考和敢于担当建构具有民族传统特色诗学理论的勇气。"（p.51）王瑛看到了中国学者在这方面的努力，在多章中充分肯定其成就，给予读者和学界极大的希望；她也是在朝着积极促进中国本土叙事学理论建构的方向努力，作为一名学者面对诸多叙事学支脉，从中做出理论总结。作者指出后经典叙事学生机勃勃，"比它的前身视野要更广阔，胸怀更宽广，思虑更繁复"（p.93）。针对近四十年本土化中存在的突出问题，她认为"我国的叙事学研究中，方法论创新已经滞后于理论的建构，这将大大不利于叙事学本土化进程"（p.118）。她还认为，正确处理中国和西方的关系，不仅是西方文论本土化要关注的问题，"更进一步地说，是我国的叙事学研究的创造性问题，这不仅是一个学理上的讨论和认识，更需要在具体的研究实践中体现和贯穿"（pp.119-220）。类似论断表明作者敢于独立思考，发表自己的创见。

第三个特征是创建本土叙事学流派的强烈意识及宝贵的学术反思精神。西方叙事学的中国旅行只是一个开端，其本土化的过程与结果才是应关注的重点，从全书来看，历时和线性地梳理中国学者接受和转化叙事学理论、运用此理论来研究中国文学并非重点，著作采用提取问题和设置专题的方式展开论析，有着强烈的建构中国本土叙事学的逻辑趋势和叙述导向，作者在全书多处对此有明确的表达。"中西叙事理论之异，可能会成为我国叙事学研究的出发点和理论生长点"（p.15），她认为异域理论必有一个内化的过程，"只有与本土融合在一起，西方的理论才会真正与东方气质相契合，才能成为本土理论"（p.25）。建构具有本土特色的叙事学或文艺理论，既是众多学者的追求，也是作者理论钩沉和总结的重点。王瑛在论述中格外重视本土问题的解决和理论的建构，"我们发现，即使以西方叙事学为研究阵地，中国的问题也始终是最根本的问题，也就是说，对西方的重视最终还是要落实到解决中国自身的问题"（p.20）。她认为四十年来中国各分支、各流派的叙事学研究，看似各自为政、经验散乱，但总体看来确是一个整体，共同勾画出叙事学本土化的进程轨迹。这也深得龙迪勇教授的肯定，"王瑛所从事的这项研究，并不是西方叙事学的理论旅行问题，而是立足于广袤的华夏大地和深厚的中国叙事传统之上的理论创新问题"（序言，p.4）。而这种创新的落脚点便在本土化叙事学的理论建构上，从某种意义上说，这也是当前建构文化自信的重要组成部分。

此外，作者在梳理和分析申丹、傅修延等学者的叙事学研究时，格外关注其本土化创新，区分不同于西方叙事学理论的独到运用，她将本土化意识和历史意识作为叙事学本土"理论自觉意识"的两大体现。在总结赵毅衡广义叙事学研究的历程与心声后，她认为"只要克服了思维惰性，中国学者完全可以开辟自觉的一片新的疆域"（p.62），尤其要反思自身的思维方式。此书从根本上说是对学术史和学者的研究和思考，作者站在一定的学术高度评析国内叙事学各家各派的成就、特征、价值和影响，给予其合理的定位，在重视和呼吁创建中国本土叙事学的同时，体现出强烈的反思精神。这种反思集中体现在三个维度：一是某一流派叙事学面向和解决中国问题之情况；二是所探索的空间、所采用的方法是否具有独到成就，是否能将中国学派叙事学的建构向前推进一步；三是中国本土学界的回应与跟进是否理想。在评析谭君强的叙事学研究成就后，作者针对国内基于学术外的因素而使开拓者"孤军奋战"式的后续研究难以推进的现状，指出："这些方向能否成为叙事学新的学科分支，能否在中国的土壤生根发芽，长成参天大树？到目前为止，除了提出者本人外，应和着似乎寥寥。"（p.90）"这种浪费是致命的，或直接扼杀许多有价值的思想。学术界相互之间的互动——商榷，研讨，甚至是崇拜和礼节意义上的喝彩，都是前行中孤独者的温暖和动力。"（p.218）作者既表现出浓郁的人文关怀，也在忧虑中提出反思，在理性中发出呼吁：中国本土学派叙事学的创建，需要更多同行重视、勉励，加强互动和联系，携手前行。

第四个突出特征是多种学术方法的综合运用，在解决学术问题上具有明显的成效。在绪论中，王瑛教授首先交代"本书采用的研究方法是细读法、历史研究、整体考察与个案研究相结合和比较研究法"。这四种研究方法是合适并得法的，相互融合，有助于探索叙事学的本土化。在盘点和梳理国内不同阶段借鉴、转化叙事学进而逐渐本土化方面，作者采用了历史研究法，充分结合中国文艺语境予描述这一历史进程，将其置于历史发展的线索中去，进而把握脉络和梳理线索。这是作者全方位把握四十年来国内叙事学研究各种支脉、派别、人物和著作的基本前提。鉴于叙事学研究成果良莠不齐，作者"择其典型，立足个案，整体观照"，她打破线性描述本土化历史的写法，将问题和专题融入整体考察中去，这在第一章、第三章中表现尤为鲜明。而将具体学人、支脉、派别移入个案研究中去，则形成了该书的第二、第四章，并且它们是在问题的统率下以横向专题的形式构成框架，这比单纯地学人学案研究更具学理性，也更突显逻辑性。这种搭建章节和展开论述的方法是成功的，有助于对叙事学本土化的深层学理问题进行多维度挖掘和探究。和文学文本从语言、结构、文体等方面进行细读的方式不同，王瑛将赵毅衡、申丹、傅修延等学者的学术著作当作文本来细读，在不断的回溯中捕捉作者的研究缘由、研究方法、研究构想及其蕴含的满腔热血和深厚情感。王瑛对学者主要代表作的研读是非常认真和精细的，尽管研读工作量繁复而浩大，却为她的评析和论断打下了坚实的基础。细读学术论著应当是对学术史展开研究的必要步骤，面对庞大的工作量，作者含英咀华、去粗取精，在与数十位学者展开对话和探讨的过程中，真正读出了自己的心得和体会。这才使这项国家社科项目成果通过专家们的层层评审。而中西比较法亦贯穿始终，她"在保持自身立场、立足自身传统的同时，在研究中也始终保持比较的视野。其实，这也是王瑛在研究中所坚持的"（序言，p. 6）。这种方法在著作中被反复运用并一以贯之。一方面，选题的性质决定了中西比较势在必行，在立足于本土基础上着眼于中西比较，是此书的突出特色。如龙迪勇所言，"比较的主要内容则以异为主，即力图勾勒出我国叙事学研究之有别于西方叙事学研究的独特性，从而描绘出我国叙事学研究的独特风貌"（序言二，p. 4），尽管作者并没有对等地去比较中西叙事学的相似和不同。"本土化"这一关键词决定了作者的重心在比较中国学界吸收、运用叙事学理论从事研究方面，究竟有哪些新质和成就。如第二章中，"我们会发现赵毅衡与热奈特之间的继承和发展关系，也可以看见二者的区别"（p. 60）。在结语中，作者指出中国叙事学是高浓度的文化叙事，"它不同于西方形式主义分析，它具有'道'与'技'的结构性思维；不同于西方的线性时间逻辑，它的时间观念具有整体感和生命感"（p. 213），在比较中突显、强化中国本土叙事学之独特与不同。另一方面，作者还将比较法运用于对各支脉的论述之中，从中管窥每一种叙事学流派的特色所在，由此，读者便能清晰看到它们在叙事学本土化过程中所发挥的作用。

第五个特色是学术语言顺畅、优美，读来生动活泼，富有诗性魅力。如上所论，叙事学是学术性很强的一门学问，它的本土化又涉及诸多学者、论著的解读和评析，按通行的学术语言，有可能写得比较思辨和理性。而这部著作以顺畅易读的语言来行文，有时不乏文采优美的句子，淡化了谈论纯粹理论问题而带来的客观与板滞，增添了几分诗意和趣味。王瑛同时擅长创作，曾出版过诗集，有着女性学者丰富的感性元素，其对语言的熟练运用在学术批评著作中表现得格外鲜明，增添了几分活泼，读来仿佛一次愉快的旅行：如"小说家像个高明的调酒师，把古代与现代放入了同一个酒盅。……这个几乎家喻户晓、正气凛然的暴力英雄带上了嬉皮士的某些特征"（p. 167）；如"人们已经认识到这一道围墙无论多么高峻，都不能挡住它向外伸展的枝条，罗兰·巴特的叙事之思率先在围墙之外盛开了嫣红的花朵"（p. 186）；再如"研读傅修延的这部著作，是一场充满惊喜的发现之旅：一个博雅、激情、睿智的作者，以中国叙事学为核心，谈古道今，叙事说理，不仅伦理通透，而且内蕴激情"（p. 215）。凡此佳句妙语，信手拈来，将文学的诗意融入理性的评析之中，部分地稀释了理论书籍的晦涩，无怪乎蒋述卓先生在序中由衷称赞"能遇上这么易读的学术著作，也是可遇不可求的事情"。在述学文体普遍以冷静理性风格取胜的当下，这种表述及文风无异于一股清新的风，值得后学传承和借鉴。

引用文献：
王瑛（2020）. 叙事学本土化研究（1979—2015）. 北京：北京大学出版社.

作者简介：
邓心强，文学博士，中国矿业大学人文学院副教授，硕士生导师，主要从事阐释学、文体学研究。
Author:
Deng Xinqiang, Ph. D. , associate professor of School of Humanities, China University of Mining and Technology. His research interests mainly cover hermeneutics and stylistics.
Email：csdxq@163. com.

致　谢

　　本书在编辑过程中，得到了四川大学中央高校基本科研业务费期刊资助项目与四川大学外国语学院的支持，特此感谢！

著作权使用声明